UNINVITED

BOOKS BY EMILY SHINER

EMILY SHINER

UNINVITED

bookouture

Published by Bookouture in 2025

An imprint of Storyfire Ltd.
Carmelite House
50 Victoria Embankment
London EC4Y 0DZ

www.bookouture.com

The authorised representative in the EEA is Hachette Ireland
8 Castlecourt Centre
Dublin 15 D15 XTP3
Ireland
(email: info@hbgi.ie)

ISBN: 978-1-80550-089-6
eBook ISBN: 978-1-80550-088-9

For incredible teachers, who are some of the best people in the world.
More specifically, for Julie Funderburk, Charles Reed, and Genell Gamblin.

PROLOGUE

I feel the police officer's gaze lock on me as I sit down in a straight-backed chair.

Even though I know it's crazy, it feels like the room keeps wobbling back and forth.

I'm terrified.

I shift position, my knees pressed together, unwilling to look at either person sitting next to me.

There's three of us.

There's supposed to be four.

Across the room, three uniformed officers talk to someone in a suit. I'm assuming she's a detective, judging by the confident way she walked in here and took over. The gun on her hip terrifies me, but not nearly as much as the handcuffs I see poking out from her belt.

What if this doesn't work?

All of us had high hopes for this trip. Sure, we all wanted different things out of it, but everything's changed since we all got into that taxi together. I glance up at the officer standing guard, but he hasn't looked away from the three of us.

None of us speak.

It would be nice to have someone hold my hand and tell me that everything is going to be okay, but I know that's never going to happen. Too much has happened for anyone to be willing to lie to me to make me feel better.

But here's what will happen:

They're going to separate us into different rooms. I'm not sure how many conference rooms this place has, but I'm sure there are enough to keep us all apart.

Then they're going to interview us. They'll look for any holes in our stories and wait for one of us to crack. I bet there will be a good cop/bad cop routine they play into. Someone will offer each of us water; someone else will yell.

Everything we do, everything we say... it will all be analyzed.

Judged.

Picked apart.

My leg starts to bounce when I think about that. The two people sitting next to me aren't trustworthy. They're rash. Abrasive.

And willing to throw anyone under the bus if it means they walk away from the wreckage in one piece.

But, then again, so am I.

ONE

AIMEE

Friday

South Florida is hot. Sticky. It's also a far cry from somewhere like Cancun, which is where I thought my fiancé might bring me as an apology trip after I found out he'd cheated on me.

But the cheating is neither here nor there, not when I'm already counting down the days before I slip this ring from my finger, hand it to the guy at the pawn shop, and walk out a thousand dollars richer.

A thousand dollars? Is that being too optimistic? I glance down at my ring. Maybe only a few hundred dollars richer, if I'm lucky. I don't want to call Dale a cheapskate, but he didn't spring for an international trip for his apology tour, and I know we both have our passports, so he obviously was keen to save a few bucks.

Is it even a real diamond?

I bring it closer to my face to peer at it. It's sparkly, sure, but that doesn't mean anything. Moissanite is sparkly. Cubic zirconia is sparkly. I never questioned it until now, but just because it's sparkly doesn't mean it's a real diamond. On a whim, I pull my phone out and text my best friend, Laurel.

Do you think my ring is a real diamond?

Her response is immediate.

LOL. No.

I sigh and tuck my phone back in my pocket. It might not be real, but she didn't have to laugh that hard about it.

A few hundred or a thousand, it doesn't matter. I just want it gone. I want the memories of it gone. I want to forget about how terrible it felt to see the man I loved—the man who promised to love me forever—with someone else. He betrayed me and broke the trust I had in him, and that's not something he can ever get back.

Even if I only get fifty bucks for it, I'm sure a lot of people would be thrilled to stand in line to call me a gold digger after agreeing to come on this trip because I already know I'm going to break off the engagement.

Let them judge. They're not the ones who saw the woman their fiancé cheated on them with spread out on the dining room table like a buffet. They're not the ones who had their hearts absolutely ripped out and crushed.

I think, given the circumstances, I get to do whatever I want with not only this ring, but also with our failed relationship, and I choose to put them both firmly in my rearview mirror. As I stand here waiting on him to get our luggage, in fact, my three best friends are in the apartment Dale and I share, grabbing all of my things and moving me out. Who cares that I'll be couch-surfing for a week or so until I get my own place?

All that matters is being away from Dale. I'm taking the TV, but he can have the dining room table since he probably has such fond memories of it.

The memory of walking in on them twists my stomach and makes me tear up, but I slap a smile on my face as Dale hurries up to me, one suitcase in each hand. They have wheels, and he could have easily just pulled them across the floor, but that's Dale for you.

He loves showing off. He's a CrossFit junkie, which used to be something about him I thought was kinda cute. That is, until he became obsessed with the workouts of the day as well as a certain CrossFit bunny.

That's the dining-room-table girl, for anyone following along at home.

"Got 'em," he says, hoisting the luggage so his muscles are on full display.

Before I can respond, he bends down and kisses me, not really seeming to notice that the kiss I give him is half-hearted at best. Do you know how hard it is to kiss the man who broke your heart?

"You would think this was an international airport, as busy as the baggage claim was. Man, I'm so glad we didn't fly somewhere any bigger than Miami."

"Oh, totally," I say sarcastically as I reach for my suitcase. He shifts position and steps back, holding it away from me so I can't take it from him. My hand falls back to my side. "I'd hate to be greeted with a fruity drink and a lei when we disembarked."

He chuckles. "You're so funny, Aimes. Always keeping me on my toes. Why don't we go wait outside and I'll get us an Uber?"

"That's a plan," I tell him, forcing a smile to my face again. When I agreed to this trip, I pictured white-sand beaches. Little umbrellas in my drinks. Tan pool boys in itty-bitty Speedos.

Would I have agreed to come if I'd known we were only going as far south as Miami?

Maybe I would have thought longer and harder about making the trip. But I wanted to put the screws to Dale, really wanted to make him hurt where it matters the most to him: his wallet. That and this three-day trip is the perfect time for my girls to get me moved out of his apartment. No way would they be able to get it done if we'd stayed in town. I'm a nurse at the local hospital, so I'm away at work all hours of the day, but Dale works from home.

This trip to Miami was the best shot at me getting out cleanly.

He leads the way through automatic doors that spit us out under an awning. It's hot, almost steamy out here, and I pluck my pink T-shirt from my chest. The air in planes and airports is so recycled, so dry and clean that it's almost clinical, and this is the opposite. I suddenly feel like I'm swimming.

That, of course, makes me think of the non-existent pool boy of my dreams, and I have to fight to keep from scowling.

Someone honks. Another person flips them off. I turn to Dale, waiting for him to call an Uber, like he offered. Normally, I'd take control. Take care of business. But I want him to do the work right now.

"Oh, geez." He's tapping away at his phone. "Man, this is a shame."

"What?" I scoot closer to him, angling myself so I can see his screen.

He tilts it to the side so I can't make out what he's looking at.

"We're gonna be waiting a long time for an Uber."

"How long?"

"Close to an hour." He clicks off his phone. "But I'm sure we can find a taxi." He makes a big show of looking around, his chin tilted up, frowning a little, even going so far as to block the non-problematic sun from his eyes.

We're standing in the shade of an awning, and he looks ridiculous.

"Cool. Cool, cool," I mutter, turning and doing the same. As soon as I do, however, my heart sinks. The traffic here is insane. To our right is a place for Uber pickup, and the people there are jammed together like sardines. To our left is the taxi pickup, and we'd have to fight through a few dozen people to make it to the front of the line.

"We could wait inside," I say, touching his arm to get his attention. "There's AC, and chairs, and—"

"Dale!"

The sound of someone calling my fiancé's name makes me drop my hand from his arm and whip around.

I know that voice.

"Dale! You need a lift?"

There. At the closest taxi. There's a guy half in the door, half out, waving at us like he couldn't be happier to see us. He's staring right at Dale, who jerks with recognition and waves back.

"Mitch! We'll be right there!" He grabs our suitcases and grins at me. "This is perfect! We can go with Mitch and not have to worry about getting our own ride! Come on!"

"Mitch?" I ask, but Dale is already pushing through the crowd. I follow, muttering apologies and wincing as he almost takes out a little old lady with my suitcase.

It isn't until we reach the taxi that I remember who Mitch is. A CrossFit buddy, of course. Also, a fantasy football buddy. The Venn diagram of those people in Dale's life is almost a circle. We've met once or twice, and he's always been overly nice.

"You hop in the front," Dale tells me. He gestures with his chin, then carries the suitcases to the open trunk. Without any good reason not to, I slide into the front seat.

I hear the trunk slam shut just as I'm clicking my seatbelt.

The driver is playing '90s rap, and I take a deep breath to calm myself before turning around to thank Mitch for the ride.

Dale hops into the back just as I turn around. I have a huge smile plastered on my face to thank Mitch, but it slides off as soon as I see who's sitting between him and my fiancé.

The woman Dale slept with. The woman he doesn't realize I recognize on sight. She's beautiful, with a huge smile and stunning hair. She's the type of girl any woman would be afraid of taking their man, and the knowledge that she was able to do just that stabs through me. My mind races as I think about what to do. How to handle this. Even though I agreed to come on this trip for a very specific reason, I decide in this moment to change plans.

It's no longer enough for me to waltz out of Dale's life. I've daydreamed about him crying in his bed, missing me, but that's no longer enough. I want to get back at Dale for what he did to me. He can't hurt me like he did and expect me to walk away, quietly licking my wounds. He's going to cry, alright, but I want to see it happen.

And her? Why is she here? There has to be a reason. Once I find out what it is, I'm going to make them pay for everything they did to me.

TWO

HANNAH

Even though traveling usually wears me out, right now I feel jazzed up, like I stuck my finger in an electric socket.

I saw the regret written all over Dale's face when he got in the taxi with Mitch and saw me sitting there.

But by then it was too late.

I'd grinned at him. Reached out to lightly trace his knee. Now I lean back, a smile playing on my lips, while I listen to him hiss words at Mitch.

"I didn't know you were going to be in Miami," he says.

It's obvious what he's doing. Speaking just loud enough that Aimee will be able to hear him from her spot in the front seat. He wants her to know that he didn't plan this, that he had nothing to do with Mitch and me showing up unannounced and uninvited. I know what this trip means to him. It was supposed to be an apology for cheating on her.

Not that they'll get a lot of time to reconnect with Mitch and me here.

"It was kinda spur of the moment." Mitch has a toothpick stuck between his lips. He rolls it from one side of his mouth to the other before plucking it out and stabbing it through the air at Dale. "But you were going on and on about how much fun you and Aimee were going to have that I thought Hannah and I should check it out. There was this amazing deal for a last-minute booking, and we snagged it. I couldn't pass it up, could I?"

Dale has never been good at hiding his emotions. He frowns, and his cheeks flush. It makes me giddy, to see how concerned he is. I have no idea whether or not he'll believe Mitch's lie, but it doesn't matter. We're here.

"I guess not," Dale manages. He clears his throat, and I speak up.

"Mitch made it sound like a fun trip. No way was I going to miss out." I snap my gum at him. He'll never guess the real reason I'm here. Not until it's too late.

He closes his eyes and swallows hard. When he speaks again, it's to Mitch. "What hotel are you two staying in?"

"The Sunrise Hotel on the beach. It's smaller, private." He waggles his eyebrows. "Sound familiar?"

Dale looks like he's going to throw up. I grin and lean forward to get a better look at the expression on his face. When he glances at Aimee, I follow his gaze.

Aimee is sitting perfectly still, her posture stiff, but I can see the way the tips of her ears are turning red. She might act like she's not paying attention, but she's hearing everything that's being said.

"You booked the same hotel we did?" Dale leans across me to speak to Mitch, and I exhale just a bit so he can smell my peppermint gum.

While he waits for Mitch to respond, he glances up at me.

I wink.

Dale looks like a deer in headlights as he tears his gaze away from me and looks again at Mitch.

"Hey, it could be fun," he begins, but Dale cuts him off.

"Fun? No. This," he says, gesturing from him, to Mitch, to

me, "is not going to be fun. I'm here to be with Aimee. Not you guys. I need this time." He lowers his voice, like that's going to be enough to ensure Aimee doesn't hear him. "You know that."

Mitch stares at him. Then, before I realize what he's about to do, he leans forward, bracing himself on the back of the driver's seat for leverage.

"Aimee. Hey. You don't mind that Hannah and I are here too, do you? It's just that hearing Dale talk so much about how amazing your trip was going to be made me jealous. I want sand and sun, you know? I deserve it."

Aimee barely turns to look at him. From here, I see the tight set of her jaw. I can't see the expression on her face, but I don't have to see her eyes to know that she's probably glaring at Mitch.

"You deserve it?" she asks.

Dale sinks down in his seat.

"Sure do," Mitch boasts. "What, Dale hasn't told you how hard I work? Neurosurgery is no joke."

"He sure has." She pauses, and I feel giddy, like I'm on a rollercoaster, and we're at the top, about to barrel down towards the ground. "I was hoping for some alone time with Dale, but you two seem like such a lovely couple. I'm sure you'll have your thing to do, and Dale and I will have our own."

Wait. What?

A lovely couple? Did I hear her correctly? If I could see her face, I'd be able to look for a tell, proof that she was lying, that she doesn't really think Mitch and I are a couple. Didn't she see my face that one time at her apartment?

Maybe she didn't.

It all happened so fast.

I'd been there, and Dale had... been there obviously. Then Aimee came home early from her shift at the hospital because she didn't feel good.

There was screaming. Tears. Mostly from her, but I put on a good show before yanking on my shirt and jeans and bolting.

Maybe Aimee has no idea who I am.

This could be interesting.

If she really thinks that Mitch and I are a couple, that will make this weekend that much more enjoyable.

"We're not—" Mitch begins, but Dale cuts him off.

"Not going to hang out with us every meal, I know. And I appreciate it." He reaches forward and lightly touches Aimee's shoulder, but she doesn't turn to look at him. "Aimee and I want a lot of quiet time alone, but maybe the four of us can go on a double date like we were talking about."

Mitch stares at him. His eyes are wide like he doesn't even speak English, but before Dale has to try to lead him further along into the lie, I save the day.

Hey, what can I say? I'm just that kind of person.

"That sounds perfect," I say. As I speak, I reach over and put my hand on Mitch's thigh. "I love double dating. Don't you, sweetie?"

Aimee is still turned, watching what's playing out in the backseat. Mitch glances at her, then at me, then plasters the fakest smile I've ever seen on his face.

"Love it so much. This weekend is going to be one to remember."

Dale visibly relaxes. He buys it, probably because he's desperate for it to be true, for me to not be a problem that will come between him and Aimee.

That was easy.

He convinced Aimee to stay with him, and I have no doubt he's not going to want to lose her now. I remember how distraught he was after she caught us at his place, crying and carrying on like his life was over.

No. I know what it's like to have someone actually ruin your life.

Sighing, I lean back in my seat and turn to stare out the window. Florida zips past us as the driver presses down on the gas.

When Aimee found Dale with me, she threatened to leave him right then and there. I wasn't there for what happened next, but I can imagine it as perfectly as if I were watching a movie.

Dale got down on his knees, I guarantee it. He begged and cried and pleaded with her to stay, until he finally wore her down and she agreed. I bet you anything he told her it was a one-time thing.

That was a lie.

He probably told her he wouldn't ever do it again.

I'm going to make sure that was a lie as well. A woman like her? Who's lying about the horrible thing she did in her past?

Yeah, she deserves what I've got planned for her.

THREE

AIMEE

Our hotel room is right on the ocean, the waves so loud I can barely hear Dale inside.

He's unpacking his suitcase, carefully putting his clothes in the dresser while I stand on the deck, a glass of wine in my hand, the hot sun already burning my shoulders. From here I can look straight down to the pool and the cabana. Further out is the ocean, smooth sand stretching out to crashing waves.

I have to admit it... this place is gorgeous. Our room is huge, with bright-white linens and blankets. The sliding door moves silently on its track, and the balcony out here boasts a bistro table with chairs. The fresh flowers on the table smell amazing, and I catch their scent in every breeze.

In short: it's heaven. The staff look like they strolled out of a magazine; the thick carpet in the halls feels like walking on a cloud. If this were any other trip, I'd be in heaven.

But my heart aches. Tears burn my eyes, and I close them to keep from crying. It's hard enough hiding my hurt from Dale, but now I have to hide it from Hannah and Mitch as well?

My stomach twists. This was supposed to be a simple trip for me. Get in, get out, *move out*. But now I want more.

I want Dale to suffer the way I have.

And yeah, it was almost impossible holding my tongue in the taxi on the way over here, but I have to keep reminding myself that I'm not here for a wonderful weekend away with Dale, no matter what he might think. I'm just here so my girls can get me moved out of the apartment. Avoiding the huge blowout that would occur if he caught me in the middle of leaving him is worth coming here for a few days. But man, it's gonna suck harder than I thought it would.

And now it means I have to put up with Mitch and Hannah for a few days. Hannah was going to avoid my ire, but showing up here like she did wasn't an accident, I'm sure of it. No way would the woman sleeping with my fiancé accidentally book the same hotel as us on the same weekend.

She's here on purpose. I don't know if she wants to rub in the fact that she slept with Dale or try to get him back, but her beach trip isn't innocent. It can't be. I don't care that she brought her current boyfriend with her on the trip—no way do I think she'd stay loyal to him if given the chance to cheat again. I'm not sure what role Mitch has in all of this, but I do know one thing: Hannah deserves to suffer just as much as Dale does. My plan keeps changing, keeps evolving, but that's okay.

At first, I just wanted out of the relationship. Then to punish Dale.

But Hannah? She doesn't deserve to walk away from what she did to me without suffering a little. She blew up my life and left me gutted.

They're both in my crosshairs now.

I can accept the fact that I'll be miserable for a long weekend. I can do pretty much anything for a few days, as evidenced by the fact that I didn't murder Dale the moment I found him screwing around.

That terrible memory is interrupted by a kiss on the nape of my neck. Dale loops his arm around my waist and pulls me close to him. It takes me a minute to relax and for my skin to stop crawling, but I force myself to soften against him.

"Enjoying the view?"

"It's gorgeous," I admit. I don't know if there's a storm coming or something, but huge waves crash against the sand. I can smell the brine of the sea and already feel the salt in the air working its magic in my hair. I swear, it doesn't matter what products I use, my hair always looks its best when we're at the beach.

"I hoped you'd like it. I really wanted this to be a fresh start for us."

He kisses me on the temple, and I know he's going to try for one on the lips, so I lift my glass and take another sip to stop him.

"And I'm sorry about Mitch and Hannah."

"It's fine." I try to sound nonchalant, like I really don't care about them being here, because I shouldn't. It doesn't matter who's on this trip; it's not going to change the outcome, but it still hurts.

"We don't have to spend any time with them if you don't want to. Okay? I have no problem telling Mitch to get lost."

"Thanks." I take another sip while I think. I was shocked to see Hannah in the car with us. Then came anger. Outrage even. But now that we're unpacked and I'm watching people run around on the sand and drinking a glass or two of wine... well, let's just say maybe things aren't as bad as I thought they were at first.

I mean, why not use this to my advantage? I don't really care to reconnect with Dale. This trip isn't about our future; it's about securing mine. And if Mitch and Hannah really want to spend time with Dale, why not exploit that?

I want to punish her for what she did to me. It'll be tricky, especially with Dale watching my every move, but it could be worth it. I'm already mentally cataloging what I have planned for Dale to see how I can punish Hannah as well.

"You know," I say, turning to face him and carefully leaning against the railing, "I don't see a reason to avoid spending time with them."

"You don't?"

"Gosh, no. You and Mitch are such good CrossFit buddies. And I have to say it: Hannah looks like she throws tires around with the best of them. I bet she's there a lot too, isn't she?"

He swallows hard. "She is."

"Yeah, I thought maybe. No, as much as I'd love alone time with you all weekend, I don't think pushing them away is the right idea. It's much better if you get to spend time with them. Can you imagine going back to the gym next week when we get back and them feeling like we ignored them?" The thought of spending time with everyone horrifies me, but I'm not a masochist—I have a plan. The more time I spend with Dale and Hannah, the more opportunities I'll have to punish them both.

I just have to make him think this is a good idea. If he digs in his heels, I won't have a choice but to go along with what he wants.

He clears his throat. "The box."

"The what?" I know what they call their gym; I just like pushing his buttons, and I think the name is stupid. *The box,* like they're in some military movie or something.

"It's not a gym. For CrossFit, it's called a—You know what? It doesn't matter. You're so kind, Aimes. I don't know anyone else who would be willing to let another couple crash their romantic vacation."

"See, but I'm not like anyone else," I tell him, smiling my sweetest smile. He blinks when I reach out and boop him on the nose. "You're always saying that, so don't forget it."

"How could I?" This time, when he does move in for a kiss, I'm not fast enough to get out of the way. "So what do you say about having a group dinner tonight then? That way we can spend some time with them, finish out the day, then have a fresh start by ourselves tomorrow?"

I stare down at the beach before answering. Of course I'm going to say yes, especially after I just decided that this trip will be a lot more fun if I punish both Dale and Hannah for what they did to me.

But I still have to sell it. I have to make him think I want to only be with him.

"Please, Aimee. I know this isn't what the two of us signed up for, but it would mean a lot if you were cool with them coming along with us. I promise you—I'll make it up to you later." He winks at me.

"Okay, sure. I think that could be a lot of fun. But then maybe nightcaps in our room? Alone?"

"Heck yeah. Let me text Mitch." His arm drops from around my waist, then he pulls his phone from his pocket and starts tapping on it. A moment later, he grins at me. "They're in! This is going to be great. Thank you."

"Of course." I give him another of my megawatt smiles, the kind he told me made him fall in love with me, then down the rest of my drink. If I'm going to make it through this evening in one piece, I'm going to need a lot more alcohol.

"Let me refill that for you." He snatches it from my hand and hurries back into the room. I watch him go, watch as the wind coming off the ocean blows the curtains in after him.

I hear him humming to himself as he pours my wine and graciously accept it when he hands it out to me.

"To us," he tells me, tapping my wine with his own glass.

"To the trip," I respond, taking a sip. It's good. I love an oaky Chardonnay, and I hold it in my mouth before swallowing. The entire time, I'm watching Dale.

Right now, he's happier than I've seen him in a while. Even when he booked this trip, even when I told him I'd come with him to Florida, he still didn't look as excited as he does about the prospect of hanging out with Mitch.

And Hannah.

I can't forget Hannah, with her perfectly whitened teeth, her blue eyes, her enviable tan. She's all-American: not the woman next door, but a centerfold. The two of them deserve everything they've got coming, and although I'm going to have to think on my feet to punish them, I'm ready for the games to begin.

FOUR

Then

I look at myself in the mirror and swear, then turn to show my sister my outfit.

"It should be a crime to look this good," I tell her, spinning slowly to give her the full effect. My heart hammers with nerves and excitement. Tonight has been a long time coming, and it's crazy to me that it's actually, finally here.

"Josh is going to go feral," she agrees. She takes a long drink of water from her bottle. "Tonight's the night, right?"

At least I think it's water. Steph's always in trouble for one thing or another, and most recently it was for dipping into Mom and Dad's alcohol. I could get close enough to smell what she's drinking, but I know that would only piss her off.

"Tonight's the night." Goosebumps break out all over my arms, and I rub my hands up and down them to warm back up. It's not chilly in Steph's bedroom, but the excitement of the night and what I'm planning has me nervous and goosebumpy.

"Well, I expect a full blow-by-blow. No details left behind. I want to know everything."

"Everything?" I cock an eyebrow at her. "You sure about that?"

"Oh, please. You really think you're going to do something that I haven't, like, a thousand times?" She sighs and makes a rude gesture with her hands. "I can give you pointers, if you want. Tips. Tricks. Josh won't know what hit—"

"You're being gross."

"No, I'm not!" she says. "I'm being fun, which is exactly what you're going to be later. No reason why you shouldn't get some enjoyment from all of my expertise. In fact—"

She's interrupted by the sound of our bedroom door squeaking open. Both of us whip around. I'm fully expecting one of our parents to peek in, wanting to make sure that we're appropriately dressed to leave the house or giving us another last-minute lecture about staying safe at a party with boys.

But it's not Mom or Dad.

The girl looking around the door at us is thirteen, nosy as sin, and a pain in the butt.

"You know you're not supposed to be listening in on our conversations," Steph says, rolling her eyes and flapping her hands at the door. When the door opened, she tucked her bottle by her side but now takes another long drink of it.

That pretty much confirms it. Vodka.

"I want to go with you." Our sister stands there, staring at both of us. She definitely doesn't look cool enough to go to a party with us. Her hoodie is huge, her sneakers are dirty, and her hair hangs in lank threads around her face.

Steph barks out a laugh. "Not a chance. Especially not if you're going to look like that."

"I could change." She pouts, pushing her lower lip out at the two of us. I think she believes it makes her look older, but really it makes her look like a baby.

"I don't care what you want," I tell her. "No way are you coming." I eyeball her. "First of all, you're not old enough. And

Mom and Dad would never let you come to a high school party."

She stares at me with wide eyes and then looks at Steph. When neither of us speaks again, she nods solemnly and closes the door.

Steph groans.

I groan too, flopping down on the bed.

"She's such a pain in the butt," Steph says.

"I know," I tell her. "Can you imagine if she came? All she'd do is ruin the night. She'd make it so nobody wants to dance with us. They'd see her with us and think that we were boring babysitters. It sucks."

"I know," Steph agrees. "Good thing she's lame and not invited because she's the perfect spy."

I nod. "Boring enough that she'll blend in at the party and not nearly cool enough for people to not care that we brought her. Mom and Dad won't make us take her, will they?"

"Not a chance." She takes another sip of her drink.

"Take it easy on that," I say, gesturing at her bottle. "We still have to walk downstairs and get past Mom and Dad. If they so much as suspect that you had something to drink, they'll lock you up and throw away the key."

She doesn't respond, but she does cap her bottle and tuck it under her pillow.

"I'm going to miss this," she says. Her back is to me, and she doesn't turn around as she speaks.

My heart squeezes. College is right around the corner, but only for one of us. Steph didn't have a chance at getting accepted anywhere. It's going to be the first time we're apart, and I hate the thought.

"I'll come home all the time to see you," I offer, but from the way she flinches, I know my words cause more harm than good. "You could still—"

"Still what? Stop goofing off at school and get accepted

somewhere? Maybe next year after I've held down a job and can prove that I'm not a total screw-up." She turns to face me, her eyes shining with tears. "But the damage is done. You know that as well as I do. I blew it, and I hate myself for it. All I wanted was to escape this house, this town, this life, but in escaping the way I did, I lost every chance at really getting out of here."

I don't answer because she's right. She can't leave, and it's not because of anyone else but her.

Outside, the sky is getting dark. It's a much later party than we've gone to in the past, and I'm shocked that our parents are allowing us to go. They're probably only agreeing to it because it's so close to the end of the school year. Graduation is right around the corner, and after that, college. Well, for me.

Tonight is a final hurrah, if you will. I know I'm putting a lot of importance on the night. Butterflies in my stomach confirm my excitement. Swallowing hard, I glance at my watch and mentally do the math on how long it will take to get to the party.

You never want to be too early. Being first is the kiss of death for an event, but if we're too late, then people will have drained most of the keg, and we'll be left with warm beer.

Steph must realize what I'm thinking because she stands up and stretches. Her outfit perfectly matches mine. We don't often match when we go out, but it's sometimes fun to keep people on their toes, and tonight seemed like one final night to enjoy how similar we are.

Except for her septum piercing. That's something I definitely don't want.

"Does it still hurt?" I ask, gesturing at her nose.

"Unbelievably." Steph grins. "But I think you did it right. *Finally*. I'm pretty sure this time it's going to stay in."

"Here's hoping, although you can't get mad at me if it rejects again. I'm not a piercer, and I told you that before you begged me for my help," I say, then grab my car keys from the bed. "Shall we?"

Steph nods and grins, then flips her piercing up so we can get past our parents without them seeing it. "Tonight's gonna be a night to remember," she tells me.

Butterflies flutter in my stomach. "In all the best ways."

FIVE

HANNAH

Dale, like most men, is an idiot.

He told me one time what he thought was the difference between Aimee and me.

Aimee is safe. She's a soft blanket wrapped around your shoulders at the end of a long day. She's a cup of tea, a cozy book, a movie you've seen a hundred times and can quote in your sleep.

But you? You're the opposite. You're leather, not worn flannel. You're spitfire and vigor, not welcoming and inviting. If Aimee is taking a nap on a rainy afternoon, you are bungee jumping.

And then, in the same breath, he told me that I'm not the type of woman you settle down with, that I'm too much, too abrasive, too confident, too strong. So basically, I'm the kind of woman you want to go to bed with, the kind you show off to your friends... but not to your grandmother.

It gutted me, if I'm being honest. I'll bounce back, sure, but no woman wants to be told that she's only good for one thing. No woman wants to be an embarrassment at the family picnic.

Mitch knows that Dale and I hooked up. Even if I hadn't told him, I know Dale would have. They're close, the kind of buddies who not only spot each other during a workout, but spot each other during an affair.

But Mitch will keep quiet. I know him. He'll play along with the idea that he and I are together, not because he's worried about Aimee's feelings, but because he owes me.

Right now, though, I push all of those thoughts to the side and concentrate on the moment. Mitch and I are already in the restaurant waiting on the not-so-happy couple to arrive.

It's hopping, which is what I'd expect in a bar on a Friday night. We were able to secure space in the back room, which only has three tables, so at least we have a little privacy. Still, pop music is being piped in through the old speakers that hang on the walls, and we can hear the laughter from the crowd in the main room.

Before I can worry too much about whether or not this is the right place for us to meet up, Dale and Aimee come in. She's leading the way, her chin held high, her eyes flicking around the room until they land on the two of us.

She's wearing tight jeans and a dark top. Her dark hair is swept up into a high ponytail, and she has on more makeup than usual, which really makes her brown eyes look deep and mysterious. Is she trying to look nice for Dale? Or trying to look better than me?

Dale went all out and is dressed to the nines. I can only imagine how long it took him to get his hair into the perfect style. It looks messy and unintentional, but those styles always take the longest. He's tan and fit and showing off his physique in a shirt I bought him. Funny that he'd bring it on his vacation with Aimee. I wonder if she knows where he got it?

The two of them approach, and I watch as I slowly grab the huge margarita in front of me. I've already had about half of it, and I lock eyes with Dale while I take another sip.

He has to fight to drag his gaze away from me and look at Mitch. "This is a much better place to hang out than in the main room," he says. "Good call." He reaches to pull out a chair for Aimee, but she's already settled in, right across from me.

I can't help but grin at her.

She's bold. Bolder than Dale made her out to be. Of course, there's always the possibility that she doesn't know the truth of who I really am, and in that case, she's just being friendly. Bonding. Trying to make the best of the situation.

Which one is it? I wonder. Does she know the truth and she's hiding it? Because that would make this weekend so much more interesting.

Dale looks at her, then at me, then back to Aimee. He's like an open book, and I can see it written all over his face that he's wondering what he was thinking coming to dinner with both of us.

Because really, I could blow it all up right here, right now, by telling Aimee the truth. And wouldn't it be satisfying to see the look on her face as she realized that I slept with her fiancé? She'd leave him. She'd have to in order to save face, even if she already knew or suspected. No woman wants to be made out to be an idiot.

"Aimee," Dale says, grabbing the back of her chair and pulling on it a bit, "why don't you sit across from Mitch? You'll be closer to the window, and I know how much you love to people-watch while you eat."

"Don't be silly." She waves her hand at him over her shoulder without looking away from me. "If Hannah and I are going to be spending so much time together, then why not get to know her better? You know me—I'm a girl's girl."

"That's what Dale says about you," I tell her. I lean forward and touch Aimee on the hand. That'll get a rise out of Dale, even if he thinks he's being cool with this.

"He tells you that?" Aimee sounds pleased.

Oh, you poor thing.

"Oh yeah, he talks about you all the time at the box." I pull my hand back and take a sip of my margarita. "You'd think he didn't have a life outside of you, the way he's always bringing you up."

Dale sits down, but his eyes don't leave my face. He's worried about what I might say, and he should be. I'm so focused on Aimee that I'm only vaguely aware of Mitch flagging down a waiter and ordering a round of shots.

"What kind of things does he say?" Aimee still sounds pleased. Her cheeks are pink, and she tucks some stray hair behind her ear.

"Oh, he's always saying how smart and funny you are. How he can't keep a secret from you because you always ferret it out. He was worried you'd catch on to his proposal, in fact, but we kept it secret!" I grin at her to really drive my words home.

"You knew about my proposal?" Aimee's still smiling, but there's a bite to her words.

I see Dale stiffen. When the waiter appears, he grabs a shot glass and tips it back without paying attention to what it is.

"I helped him plan it, silly." I laugh, pressing my hand to my chest. "He didn't tell you?"

"I had no idea." Aimee turns to Dale, then looks at Mitch. "Did you know about it too?"

"I didn't." Mitch has a chip halfway to his mouth and stuffs it in before speaking around the bite. "I've always thought Dale was quiet about personal stuff. Why didn't you tell me about your proposal, man? I would have helped you."

"Oh, he didn't need help." I scoot closer to Mitch so it's clear I'm involved in the conversation. Aimee's gaze snaps to my hand when I rest it on Mitch's arm. "I handled it. It would be silly to loop even more people in when we were trying so hard to keep it a secret, don't you think?"

Even though my words are for the table, I keep my eyes on

Dale to see how he's going to respond. This is a dare. I'm laying down the gauntlet to see how far he's willing to go. How long does he want to keep this charade up with Aimee?

He clears his throat and shifts his arm away from me, so my hand falls from it. "Anyway," he says, "it's in the past, and it all worked out in the end. Aimee said yes."

"Thanks to my help," I remind him. They've been dating for five years and engaged for six months, and while she might think her life is perfect right now, I'm dead set on revenge and have had something in the works for a decade. I'm nothing if not patient.

And the best part? My revenge has been so long in coming that there's no way she'll catch on before it's too late.

"Right." The word is clipped, and he doesn't look at me.

There are only three shots left since Dale already downed one. He grabs two of them and hands one to Aimee, then downs the other. Mitch moves quickly, picking up the final one while I watch.

Fine. That's totally fine. I love drinking as much as the next person, but I have absolutely no problem sitting this round out if it means I'm in control of the situation. I feel like a puppet master, and everyone here is on strings.

Mitch and Dale take the shots like champs, but Aimee cringes, grabbing the water in front of her and chugging it. I watch as Dale pulls his phone from his pocket and taps on it while she's distracted.

My phone buzzes just a moment later.

Stop it. Now.

I'm discreet while I check my phone. The last thing I want is for Aimee to figure out my plan on the first night here. What would be the fun in that?

But I don't want Dale to think this weekend is going to be easy, and that's why I text back just one thing.

A kissy-face emoji.

SIX

AIMEE

If my fiancé's going to cheat on me, I'd prefer he do it with someone less... gorgeous.

I'm sorry, but knowing that the woman Dale cheated on me with could be on the cover of *Sports Illustrated* has been a bit of a hit to my confidence. She's me but turned up to ten.

We both have long, thick hair, but hers is a honey blonde that looks like she gets it done every other week, while I stretch my salon appointments to once a quarter. And while I'm pretty handy with mascara, she knows how to do a full face without looking like a clown.

And don't even get me started on her clothes. Dale takes me shopping, which isn't why I love him but is nice. Hannah, though, has to have a personal stylist. Even in shorts and a tank top, she looks worlds better than I ever will.

It's demoralizing. I thought I was enough for Dale. I wholeheartedly believed that he and I could get through anything, but I wasn't enough. I never was, and having Hannah here only serves to drive that point home.

Although, to be fair, if I looked like that, I'd probably sleep with whoever I wanted to as well.

But did it have to be *my* future husband?

I'm standing in the oversized bathroom, my bare feet cool on the smooth travertine tile, examining myself in the wall-to-wall over-the-sink mirror. I mean, I'm not terrible. I'm not as tall as her, or as thin, or as tan, but my teeth are good, and I'm strong.

Great. I'm basically one Quarter Horse.

There's a knock on the door, but Dale doesn't wait for me to acknowledge him. He sweeps into the bathroom, already stripping out of his shirt to hop in the shower.

"Whoa," he tells me, stopping with the shirt halfway up his neck. "You're looking good."

"I'm in underwear older than most middle schoolers, and I forgot eye makeup remover," I tell him. "So if you like feral racoons, then yes. I look good."

He laughs and shucks the rest of his clothes before leaning in to turn the shower back on. "I've always loved your sense of humor, Aimes. It's one of my favorite things about you."

Oh, I'm a funny Quarter Horse.

"Well, I love how kind you are to everyone," I tell him, pulling on a bathrobe and cinching it tight so he gets the hint. Whatever he might hope is going to happen is definitely not happening. "You've always been a collector when it comes to people."

"It's just who I am." He blows me a kiss and hops in the shower. I watch as he closes the sliding door behind him and steps under the spray, then leave the bathroom, closing the door behind me.

The bedroom itself isn't huge, but the bathroom and balcony more than make up for it. I grab a bottle of water from the mini fridge and eyeball the beds.

Two queen-size beds. He would have preferred a single king, but since I made the reservation, I went with what would make me happier. Dale will obviously expect us to share one, but he runs hot when he's been drinking a lot. If I get into bed first and spread out, he might get the hint.

I've just pulled back the comforter when there's a knock on the door.

Surely not.

But when I hurry to the door and look through the peephole, there's nobody there.

Another knock, and this time I hear someone call my name.

I take a step back from the door and look around the room, trying to reason out what's going on. There are two beds with matching bedside tables. A dresser where Dale has already stashed his clothes. Mini fridge. TV mounted on the wall. And... another door?

I hadn't even noticed it there when we arrived earlier, but now I walk over to it and take a deep breath. I throw the door lock and carefully swing it open.

"I knew you'd let me in!" Hannah crows triumphantly as she pushes her way past me into the room. "Where's Dale?"

"Shower," I say, then stare at her. "What are you doing? How did you get into that other room?"

"We're connected," she says, gesturing between the two of us. "Or our rooms are! We were on the second floor, but I swear, we could hear everyone clomping around up here, so I asked to be moved and told them your room number, and they put us next to each other so we could open up our rooms! Isn't that cool?"

She either doesn't notice my distinct lack of enthusiasm or honestly doesn't care.

"I—" I begin, but she cuts me off.

"So Mitch and I thought—"

"No, Mitch didn't think anything," he interrupts from behind her. He walks into our room with a six-pack and looks around. He keeps his hair longer than most guys his age, but it works on him. He has just a bit of curl in it, and the blond streaks in it really show off his tan. When his shirt sleeve pulls up a bit, I can see the hint of a tattoo on his arm. "Where's Dale?"

"He's in the shower," Hannah tells him. "Okay, I was thinking we could leave the doors unlocked, then if anyone needs the others, it's easy to get through. What do you think?"

"I..." I say, then pause as I frantically race for some way to tell her that I'd rather chew off my own hand than share a room with her.

"I'm not so sure." That's Dale, out of the bathroom before I can get rid of these two. He wears a towel slung low around his waist and is running his hand through his hair as he speaks.

"Oh, come on," Hannah tells him, sticking out her lower lip in an impressive pout. "It'll be like we're in college or something!"

"I'm not really keen on sharing a room with anyone but Dale," I begin, but before I can continue my argument, she cuts me off.

"Don't be so boring. Or is that your default?"

Bitch. I take a deep breath as my mind races. On one hand, I don't want her anywhere near me. On the other, if I'm going to get revenge, having her closer will make it easier. I don't like it, but it might be the best option. "Fine. But if you show up when I'm showering, I'm locking you out."

"Really?" Hannah squeals and jumps up and down. "This is so much fun. What a great vacation!" She turns to me and grabs my hands. "Maybe you're not as boring as I thought!"

"Wonderful," I deadpan. "I can't see how this could go wrong."

My insides are in turmoil. Much like the hideous modern art hanging above each bed, I feel like I'm swirling, like I can't get my thoughts and feelings to slow down.

Yes, I'm going to dump Dale as soon as we get home from this trip. And yes, I want to punish her for ruining my relationship, although if it were that easy to ruin, maybe it was going to happen eventually.

But I'm not going to let myself think like that. She and Dale broke my trust. She ruined what I had. She made me out to be a fool, and both she and Dale are acting like I don't have a clue that they were sleeping together.

It's infuriating that they think I'm so stupid.

Having her close should be a good thing. Dale and I haven't been together since I caught him and Hannah. Her being one door away gives them all the time in the world to reach out to each other, to maybe slip off together so I don't have to deal with him.

But at the same time, the thought of this woman having unfettered access to our sleeping quarters and to me burns me up. Not that I have a choice. However they got that room, they're there now.

And you know what? That's fine. I was okay with punishing Dale by walking out of his life, but that's no longer enough. I no longer want to settle for him crying when I leave. I want to rip his heart out. Ruin him. I want him to feel the pain I felt when he cheated on me.

And as for Hannah? Well, I'm thinking on my feet, but I have an idea or two for her as well.

SEVEN

HANNAH

Saturday

Aimee wanted to kill me last night when I popped through our door into her room. Anyone paying attention would have seen it written all over her face, but I pretended I didn't notice the murderous rage in her eyes. The more I can keep an eye on her, the better my plan will go. She walked away without being punished after what she did as a teenager, and while I know we're supposed to let the court of law dispense justice, it failed in this case.

But I'm not going to.

I'm sure she and Dale want to have some alone time today, but I'm going to do everything in my power to keep that from happening.

Sure, it had been an early morning for me so I could get to the café down the street and pick up breakfast for everyone, but I know it's going to be worth it to shake Dale up a little and insert myself in their relationship.

He's not going to be able to get rid of me, no matter how

hard he tries, and once I separate her from him, she won't have anyone to protect her.

I'm going to ruin every good thing the two of them have going together.

What I don't think he'll ever understand is that it's not about taking him from Aimee; it's about punishing her for what she did. She may think her past is in the past, but I'm here to remind her that you can't run from what you've done. I mean, honestly? After all the years of stalking her, of trying to get close to her, of waiting until the right time to strike? There's no way she's getting away from me now.

"You ready?" Mitch appears behind me, his voice cutting through my thoughts. He's holding the coffees I grabbed at the café, and I have the bag of baked goods. "Cause I am if you are."

"So ready," I tell him, then turn to the door that separates our two rooms. We both have to have our doors unlocked to use this little passage. It also means that Aimee could lock us out at any time. I fully expect that to happen at some point this weekend, but not yet.

She has no idea what's coming her way.

Without further ado, I knock on the door, then open it and push through. As soon as I walk into Dale and Aimee's room, their main door to the hall slams shut, and I turn to look.

Aimee. It had to be her. Dale isn't the kind of guy to get up and at it in the morning unless he's on his way to the box.

"Yoo-hoo!" I call, wiggling my fingers at Dale. He's sitting on one bed, but it definitely looks like both of the beds were slept in. Did he and Aimee not sleep together last night?

Was it because he was thinking of me, wishing I were in bed with him? If so, that will make this even easier.

I hurry over to the empty bed and settle in. Let Aimee come back into the room and see me sitting right where she was just sleeping. Replacing her once again. Gosh, I'd love to see her face if she catches me here.

"I went downstairs to the café and got us all some break-fast!" I chirp, grateful I'm not hungover, then put three bags of food on the bed next to me. Who cares if there's a little grease on her sheets? "Muffins and bagels with cream cheese, of course, and lots of coffee."

At that moment, Mitch walks into the room carrying four paper cups of coffee. "Lattes for us, a cap for you, and we didn't know what to get Aimee, so we got her drip coffee." His voice is apologetic. "No cream, no sugar."

"She seems like a plain kind of gal," I add as I unwrap a bagel and hand it to Dale. "Where did she pop out to, by the way?"

"Gym." His voice is flat. He takes the bagel from me and then takes a bite, chewing mechanically.

"Oh, the gym. Good for her, working out even on vacation."

Behind him, Mitch rolls his eyes, but Dale doesn't respond. He keeps eating, only pausing to take a cup from Mitch so he can wash it all down.

"Crap, that's hot!" His face is red as he takes the to-go cup away from his lips. "What is that, a molten cappuccino?"

"I'm sorry." I wrinkle my nose, the muffin in my hand currently forgotten. "I asked them to make everything extra hot so it wouldn't get cold on the way back."

"Well it didn't, and now I burned my mouth. I need some water," he says, throwing back the covers.

"I'll get you some water! Sit still." I shove Aimee's to-go cup into Mitch's hand, then hurry to the bathroom.

Crap. I really didn't mean to burn him. Out of anyone, I wouldn't have minded giving Aimee a scalding, but this really was an accident. Still, I can use it to my advantage.

In the bathroom, I pause to orient myself, then call to Dale. "They always have these glasses right here by the sink, isn't that nice? And did you see the little packets of flavoring you can add if you want? They're on the mini fridge."

"I saw them," he says.

I take my time grabbing a glass and lifting off its paper lid. That's the sign that you're in a nicer hotel—the glasses have little paper hats, so no roaches fall in them. When I run the tap, it takes a minute for the water to cool down.

I put my finger under the stream to check the temperature, then fill the glass up.

But after I turn off the water, I put the glass on the counter and take a deep breath.

What I'm doing? It's... well, not *dangerous*, per se, but definitely stupid. There's an element of danger to it, not to me personally, but that I might screw up and not have another chance to do what I want.

Still, it's worth it. Psychological warfare. That's what I saw it called on some documentary I watched last week. It's a great way to keep people off-balance until you finally get what you want from them.

"Psychological warfare," I whisper to myself. "You got this, Hannah."

I reach into my pocket and finger what I have stashed there. I'm absolutely determined to get what I want out of this weekend, but that doesn't mean I can't have some fun.

Sow some chaos.

If I'm going to really punish Aimee for what she did before this weekend is over, I have to do more than just take her fiancé. It's a good thing she's totally clueless, or I'd be worried she'd figure out what I'm up to.

But no. Aimee is sweet. Dependable. Remember: according to Dale, she's everything you'd want to marry, but that doesn't mean she's smart.

And what she did in the past? What she got away with? Luck. It was all luck and good timing on her part.

But that's the thing about luck, isn't it?

It runs out.

EIGHT

Then

Eighteen and free: free like the wind blowing through the car window, free like a wild animal, which is how I feel right now, my heart pounding along with the bass, my twin screaming lyrics in the passenger seat, my Jeep whipping around the mountain curves like it was made to take them.

"Turn's coming up!" Steph reaches out and turns the music down so I can hear her over the drum solo. "Bet you can spray a ton of gravel if you don't slow down too much."

I can't help but grin because that's Steph. Impulsive. Wild. I'll miss her at college, just like I'm going to miss Josh.

He and I have been together for over a year now, and I think I'm finally ready. He's the one. I know he is. I'll do anything for him, and I made it clear that I would finally be with him before I left for college.

The clock's ticking. One month and I'm out of here. So is he, but since we'll be going to different colleges, I want to make sure we have a reason to stick together. I want to make sure he isn't going to move into a coed dorm and decide there's someone else for him.

The turn appears, and I slow way down so I don't flip my Jeep on the loose gravel. I want to do what Steph suggested— tear up it, announce our arrival by honking and screaming out the windows, but I don't want to flip.

Out here in the country, there are plenty of houses without anyone else around, and that's the case here. Josh told me one time that his parents live on twenty acres, complete with a pond, a barn, and a huge garden. It's a great place, but one I don't want for myself.

I want to live in a city. I want to feel the energy of the people around me. I want music and dancing and laughter, not crowing and mucking out stalls.

We park next to a lifted pickup truck and both slam our doors when we're out. My denim skirt keeps riding up, and I grab the bottom and yank it back down into position. After half an hour doing my makeup, I know I look great, but I still take time to reapply a bit of gloss.

Steph loops her arm through mine. "Best night ever?"

"That's the plan." We walk towards the house. The front door is flung open, inviting, but the real party is out back. Although there are only a dozen or so cars here, by the time the party really gets going, there will be three or four times that many.

Nobody wants to miss a party at Josh's. His parents travel a lot for work, or pleasure, or whatever, and always leave him plenty of cash for food.

And alcohol. I don't know where he gets it, but someone is always happy to run to the ABC store for Josh as long as it means they get to come to his party.

It's chilly out tonight, and I'm already looking forward to getting something to drink. That and dancing will warm me up.

In my mind, I can feel the heat on my skin, the sweat beading on my forehead.

I want to remember every single detail about tonight. I want to collect my memories and keep them forever. Everything hinges on tonight going the way I want it to. Everything will change after this.

"You okay?" Steph is one step ahead of me and turns back to look at me. "You stopped walking."

"I'm just taking it all in," I tell her, and she laughs.

Steph's laughs aren't small. She throws her head back, the sound rolling out of her. Some people turn to look and see who's making so much noise, but they're all smiling. She's not a great student. She's not top of the class. But she's popular because she's fun and knows how to party.

"You want to soak in it, and I want to *live it*. Come on—I'm not waiting out here on the driveway while everyone else has a great time."

She yanks me forward. I take a deep breath, let go of the worries I have, and lean into the excitement. I know she's said before that she wishes she were more like me, but I've often wanted to be more like her.

As soon as we step in through the front door, we walk into a wall of sound. It's all around us, thumping and throbbing, and I feel my body start to move before I have a chance to think about what I'm doing.

I love dancing.

I love parties.

I love feeling alive.

Steph disappears, leaving me to dance by myself, but she's back a moment later, pressing a red Solo cup into my hand. I take it gratefully, not even caring that the beer is a bit warm.

It's still wet, and I'm going to be sweating my butt off. I'll have to hydrate later, but right now I want to drink.

I want to find Josh. Celebrate what the two of us have. It's special, you know? A lot of high school couples think that their love is the one that will make it, that they're the only ones to have ever really known love, but what he and I have is real.

It's never-ending, and the best way for me to prove that to him is to show him just how much he means to me.

I chug the beer, then set the cup down on a table next to a few other empties. You know, as often as Josh throws parties, you'd think he'd have figured out by now that he needs to have trash cans throughout the house.

That's okay. I'll come back in the morning and help him pick up. Tonight is going to be perfect, and I'm not going to worry about a little mess.

Nothing can ruin my evening.

NINE

AIMEE

By the time I leave the hotel gym, I'm much more confident about how I can get revenge on both Dale and Hannah.

It's no longer enough to just leave him; I want to make him suffer. Is this mostly because Hannah showed up, flaunting her little body around like she's God's gift to mankind?

Yeah, absolutely that's part of it.

But it's also because he apparently looped her in on his proposal. And because he didn't have the balls to kick her out of our room last night. He's infuriating and doesn't deserve to just be dumped.

He deserves to hurt the way I do.

I want him stressed. I want him worried.

And what about hurting him physically? That I'm not sure about.

But what about Hannah? No way is she off the hook for what she did, but my plan this morning is all about Dale. Then I really need to figure out what to do about her. No way do I think she came here by accident. And no way do I believe she's got anyone's best interests in mind beside her own.

My idea is circling around and around in my head, and I smile to myself as I think about how upset Dale will be once I put my plan into action. Finding the right person to help me with my cause was easy, and it was luck.

If I hadn't seen her, I probably never would have come up with the plan, but sometimes things just work out.

The thought puts a spring in my step.

I stop outside our room and carefully press my ear up against the door. It's silly to try to listen in like this, but I want to know if Hannah and Mitch are in there with Dale. Or maybe they've all gone to breakfast or to sightsee, and I can take a long, hot shower by myself.

Just when I think the coast is clear, I hear laughter.

Dale.

It's a terrible thing—to go from loving someone so fiercely that you want to be with them for the rest of your life, to scowling when you hear their laugh, but that's what's happened to me.

I hate that he and Hannah have turned me into this person. That they've stolen what Dale and I had together. And yes, I know it's wrong to want to see him suffer for what he did to me, but I can't help myself.

Sometimes people just need to be punished.

That thought is unbidden, and I shove it away as quickly as possible. If anyone were to ever find out the truth of what I did, of what I've kept hidden for over a decade, then nobody would look kindly on me wanting to take revenge on Dale, would they?

Because what I did is far worse than cheating on the person you claim to love.

A cold sweat breaks out on my brow. I stab my keycard at the door and miss once, twice, then on the third time, the door swings open before I even have a chance to insert the card.

It's Dale. His face is flushed. *Has he been drinking?* But

before I can ask him, he screams my name and pulls me into a hug.

"Aimee!" He's spinning me around now, out in the hall, my body crushed so hard to his that I couldn't pull away from him if I tried. "When were you going to tell me?"

"Tell you?" I ask, but he's not listening. He's putting me back on the ground, his hand gentle on my lower back, then leading me into the hotel room. "Dale, what's going on?"

"You didn't tell us the great news!" That's Hannah, and before I can stop her, she launches herself at me. Her arms loop around the back of my neck, and she pulls me to her, just as hard as Dale did. "You're going to be an incredible mom!"

"A mom?" Now I do try to get away from her, and I push back, my hands on her shoulders. "A *mom*? What in the world are you talking about?"

"Congrats, Aimee." Mitch steps forward and gives me an awkward side hug. His hand barely brushes me, like he's too nervous to touch me, but his eyes sweep up and down my body, a tight smile on his face. "Dale's so excited."

"You're going to have to stop and explain what's going on." I hold up my hands and take a step back from the three of them. "Because honestly... it feels like you guys have all lost your minds. I have no idea what you're—"

Dale interrupts me by holding up a small white stick. "This was in the bathroom trash. Two pink lines. That's positive, right?"

"It is," I say slowly, my mind on overdrive as I try to sort through what's going on.

Hannah gasps. Her hands fly to cover her mouth. When she's sure we're all looking at her, she lowers them slowly so she can speak. "What about the baby? We were all drinking so much last night. Is it going to be okay?"

"Oh no." Dale turns to me and grabs my hands. "How far

along are you? Should we call a doctor? Hannah's right—something could happen to the baby if you keep drinking like this."

"There is no baby!" I yank my hands back from Dale and shout the words with my whole chest. "Listen to me! No way am I pregnant!"

Yeah, it's been stressful recently, but I have been taking my birth control. Even without checking, I do know one thing.

That test isn't mine.

"Okay, then whose test is it?" Hannah crosses her arms and stares at each of us in turn. "Because this is not a funny joke."

"Yeah, Aimes, how would the test have gotten in our bathroom if you didn't take it?" Dale looks perplexed.

I can't believe this. I stare at him, then at Hannah, then look back at him.

"I don't know, Dale," I say, keeping my tone as even as possible. "But out of the four of us, only two of us are able to have babies."

He stills. I watch as the smile fades from his face. He's a lot faster on the uptake than I thought he would be. It can be hard for him sometimes to put two and two together, but the math is adding up really quickly for him right now.

"You're pregnant?" That's Mitch, and his mouth drops open as he turns to look at Hannah.

She stiffens and shakes her head. "No way! It's not me."

Mitch stares at her. "Then who?"

"Who found the test?" I ask. "Who actually went into the bathroom and found it there?"

"Hannah did," Dale says. His voice is strangled, and I don't blame him. He just went from thinking his fiancée was pregnant, to thinking his fling was pregnant, to finding out neither are claiming the positive test.

Poor guy looks like he's about to have a stroke.

"You found it?" I stare at her. When she nods, I continue.

"Like... you found it in the bathroom, or you *found* it because you planted it there?"

"Aimee." That's Dale, and he sounds acceptably irritated with me. "Don't."

"I found it in your bathroom," Hannah tells me. Her eyes are locked on mine like prolonged eye contact is going to be enough to make me believe her. "Why would I plant it in your bathroom? And how would I even get it in there?"

"You have pockets," I counter. "And as for why—"

"You think I stuck someone's pee stick in my pocket and hid it in your trash can?"

"Not someone's." I take a deep breath. "Yours. I don't know what game you're playing, but I want you out of here."

"Holy crap. I'm not leaving until you see that I didn't bring a freaking pee stick in here." She throws her hands in the air and walks over to the room phone. Before I can move, she picks up the receiver and mashes a button.

"What are you doing?" That's Mitch, and he crosses the room to her. When he reaches for her, she bats him away.

I raise an eyebrow and look pointedly at Dale. Why isn't he doing something? He should help me kick them out of here, not stand around while she keeps up whatever charade she's doing. "Dale. Get them out of here."

He hurries to my side and leans down to whisper in my ear. "I don't know what's going on! I can't just—"

"You can," I tell him. "Get them out."

He holds his hands up like he's fending me off. "Hannah has a strange sense of humor! If she's behind this, she probably thought it was funny."

"If?" The word drips with anger. "If? She's definitely behind this. Besides, positive pregnancy tests are not funny. They're serious." I want to continue ripping into him, but Hannah interrupts me, speaking loud enough for her voice to fill the room.

"Hello, room service? Do you have pregnancy tests for sale that you can charge to my room?" A pause, then she gives them my room number and hangs up. When she speaks again, she's staring right at me. "I've bought two pregnancy tests, and you and I are taking them."

"Great. I can't wait to prove that I'm not pregnant."

"Me either." Her eyes flick to Dale, then back to me. "One of us is lying, Aimee. Let's see who it is."

TEN

HANNAH

If looks could kill, I'd be dead.

Aimee came out of the bathroom triumphant, a negative pregnancy test in her hand, and the first thing out of my mouth was, "How do we know you didn't dip it in a glass of water? How do we know you really peed on it?"

After that, she offered for me to smell it.

I'll admit it: things fell apart from there. I think it's fair to say that neither of us were at our best.

But that's what I want, isn't it? I want her off-balance and unsure of herself. The pregnancy test was a stupid little trick just to distract her, to make her unsure of what's going on. Buying it on Facebook was a brilliant move and thirty bucks well spent. It's just one of a few tricks I have up my sleeve for her, and I'm confident I can play it off as just that: a trick. A practical joke between friends. The more I can keep her on her toes, the more likely it is that I'll get what I want out of this weekend.

And that's the thing about me: I never fail.

I've been working towards this for years now. I've taken my

time, done my research. I've considered how this could go from every single angle.

I followed her for the longest time, but I never got close enough to her for her to recognize me or pick me out of a crowd. She didn't make it easy. Aimee likes to keep her private life private, so it was tricky to find a good in.

But she made her first mistake in her early twenties, and that was joining an online grief group. Like all good grief groups, there was a vetting process to ensure they only let in the people who really deserved to be in there, but it was easy enough to join. I didn't even have to lie on my application.

And, once I was in, I was able to create my own username. To hide behind the anonymity of an online presence. But Aimee was still careful.

She mostly kept her mouth shut about what happened when she was younger. But she let a few things slip, and those little bits of information were more than enough for me to find out more about her. I slowly drew closer to her, and she didn't have a clue I was lurking in the shadows.

And it's finally time she pays for what she took from me.

Instead of insinuating myself in Aimee's life, I worked my way into Dale's. I don't love working out, but I don't mind the way I look now that I lift weights and throw tires around four times a week. And, sure, I probably could have run into Dale another way. Like at the bar. Or the grocery store. But Aimee was always with him, a shadow hovering right there, ruining all of my plans, so I knew I had to think outside the box. Or, rather, inside.

Ha. Get it?

So I joined CrossFit and started working out. But my goal wasn't to sleep with Dale right away. No way did I want this to be a one-off. I needed it to be something more.

I became his friend. Mitch vouched for me, which was helpful, because it allowed me to get my foot in the door even more. Slowly, I became part of Dale's everyday routine.

When he mentioned he wanted to go shopping for a ring, I volunteered to help. And man, you should have seen the relief on his face. He was so screwed, so useless, and then I came along and fixed everything.

Little by little, I got my hooks in him. I became indispensable. Dale never realized how much he was relying on me until he was calling and texting late at night, opening up to me, telling me all of his little secrets.

Affairs can happen one of two ways. They can be explosive, happening because of chance, a wild night that doesn't result in anything but a hangover and some regret. Or they happen because you take time to build a foundation, to create a relationship. I created a need and then filled it, and Dale didn't have much of a choice. He wanted me. He *needed* me. And I let him have me.

But Dale isn't the endgame. I know Aimee thinks he's so hot and incredible and walks on water, but he's not the real prize here. I need her to admit what she did. To finally take some responsibility. She's been living a lie for years, and it isn't fair.

I refuse to do anything if I'm not going to be the one in control, which is why I researched this hotel. I encouraged Dale to bring Aimee here, even going so far as to tell him what an amazing place it is. I told him it was a great way for them to patch up their relationship. Gosh, can you imagine if he'd flown out of the country with her?

I know how the good ole U-S-of-A operates, I know how to get away with things, and I wasn't about to take a risk with another country's laws.

Now, though, something eats at me. I've taken so many steps to ensure I'm the one in control, that Dale, Aimee, and Mitch are just along for the ride. Nothing has been left to chance.

Which is why I'm a little concerned about what just happened.

Dale and Aimee are on the beach together. Fine. That's fine. They need to take a little walk and try to figure out what just happened with the pregnancy tests.

I don't want to just take Aimee down. I want to drive her crazy. Push her to the edge. Then, when she can't take any more, I want to ruin her. Take everything from her like she did to me.

Kill her.

Anything I can do to throw her for a loop is exciting. I feel buzzed. Energy courses through me, and I shiver at the sensation.

When was the last time I was this excited about something? Maybe when I was coming up with this plan in the first place. I was over the moon when I realized that all of my hard work was going to come to fruition. Every interaction with Dale, every time I slept with him, hoping Aimee would interrupt us, every single thing I did with him has been carefully planned out for almost a year and designed to bring me to this moment in time.

And that's why I'm so confused.

Because the way I saw Mitch look at Aimee? Yeah, that was definitely not part of the plan.

ELEVEN

AIMEE

I don't know what the heck Hannah was doing with the freaking pregnancy tests, but I wanted to kill her. And Dale, so excited about the thought that he might have knocked me up, like that would actually be something to be happy about.

No, thank you. If he had accidentally gotten me pregnant, that would be the worst thing in the world. I can't imagine having a child with a cheater. And what if I had a baby, and he and Hannah stayed together? Would I really have to share custody with that homewrecker?

Can you imagine? Just the thought makes me sick. How quickly your future can change based on someone else's actions. I thought I had my life mapped out, and I was happy with what it looked like.

And now nothing is how I thought.

Dale and I are on the beach, but we're not walking hand in hand like I'm sure he imagined when he suggested the trip. I'm five paces in front of him, stalking more than walking, my arms swinging stiffly at my sides. I don't want him near me right now, and the angrier I come across, the more likely it is that he'll leave me alone.

Besides, in just a moment he's going to get his first real shock of the trip.

We walk past a little boy building a sandcastle. His shoulders are pink from the sun, but he's laughing as he pats the sand into place. For a moment, I consider kicking out and knocking the entire thing to the ground, but then I shake my head to clear it.

That's not who I am. I've always wanted to be a mom, even though that's not something I'll admit to many people. Seeing the positive pregnancy test hit me hard because that's something I wanted with Dale, and now I'll never have it with him.

Dale knows I want children, and the two of us have talked about when to start trying. I was hoping to get pregnant as quickly after our wedding as possible, and he was on board. The fact that I was hoping to hold a positive pregnancy test in my hands in under a year, and instead I had to hold Hannah's little joke, tears me up.

And sure, our little group decided to put the pregnancy test debacle behind us, but I haven't forgotten what Hannah did, and I certainly haven't forgiven her. How can someone be so cruel? Sure, she slept with my fiancé, but she also tormented me with the pregnancy test, even if she doesn't know how bad it hurt.

"Aimes, wait!" Dale speedwalks to catch up with me.

When he reaches for my hand, I make sure to swing it closer to my body to prevent him from taking it.

"Hey, are you okay?"

I don't answer for five steps. What kind of a stupid question is that? But then I turn on him, my heel digging into the sand, and stab a finger into his chest as I speak each word. "Am. I. Okay?"

To my surprise, he doesn't take a step back.

"This trip was supposed to be about us, Dale. It's one thing for you to have an affair. I hate it, but we're moving on. But it's another entirely for you... for Hannah to accuse me of being pregnant."

"She got overzealous," he says. "And I wouldn't use the word *accuse*. She was trying to be funny, to lighten the mood. She knows this trip is important to us."

This time, when he reaches out to take my hand, I let him.

The desire to yank it back is so strong it's almost overwhelming, but I manage to fight the urge.

"And she just happened to have a positive pregnancy test with her? You think that was an accident? Because that seems really well planned out to me."

"We all agreed that it must have been left in the bathroom from the last guest. You can't keep harboring anger towards her about it when you agreed with us." He sounds whiny, and I frown.

"You honestly don't think she brought it with her?"

"No, I think she found it in the trash and tried to play a practical joke that the rest of us thought was funny. You know, she was right. You need to relax."

I need to what?

Instead of killing him, I try something else. "What does she know about this trip being important to us?"

His eyes dart to the side. "Um, just that I was excited about it. That's all."

"So she doesn't know about your affair? Just like she knew about your proposal?"

"No." Sweat beads across his forehead. I'd bet a million dollars that he wants to wipe it away right now but is too worried to do that because he knows it'll make him look guilty.

"I just don't know about this," I say with a sigh.

"About us?"

I eyeball him. "About this trip. With Hannah and Mitch. You don't think it's weird that they'd want to hang around all the time?"

"We're just good friends. You said it yourself—that we should spend time together, so things aren't uncomfortable when we're all back at the box."

He's whining. I hate whining, and of course he'd parrot my words back to me in a desperate attempt to get out of the corner he's backed into.

"I did say that, and I stand by it. But I meant a few meals out together. Maybe meeting up after you and I spend the day together. I didn't mean sharing a room and being attached at the freaking hip. I didn't mean her accusing me of being pregnant."

She's messing with me. She has to be. Sleeping with my fiancé and breaking up our relationship obviously wasn't enough for her. But what else does she want from me? Is it Dale? Does she really want him that badly?

Because she can have him when this is all over.

"We don't share a room," he argues, but before he can say anything else, a little girl runs up and inserts herself between us. She stares up at Dale, her long blonde hair wet against her neck.

Perfect timing.

"What's your name?" Her voice is sweet.

"Dale," he tells her. "Now go find your mom."

"Dale!" She gasps and jumps up and down. "You look like my dad. And you have the same name!"

"That's cool." He glances around us, making a show of looking for her parents. "Hey, where is your dad? You should go find him."

"I don't know." She's still staring at him. "Mom said he never called her after she got pregnant with me. We're from Vermont! Where are you from?"

Blood drains from Dale's face. His eyebrows crash together, and I feel his hand tighten on mine. He's glancing at the girl and looking at me, but I know what he's really doing: cataloguing how they look the same, how they look different. Are there more similarities or differences? They have the same light hair, the same blue eyes. Dale's skin is a bit paler, but the girl could be tan from spending a few days in the sun.

Is he thinking about all of the women he's cheated with? I wonder if he has a mental Rolodex he's flipping through, trying to remember someone who could be this girl's mother. And, knowing Dale, he's worried about what other people are thinking as they walk by. Would someone who doesn't know any better think that the three of us are a family?

"How old are you?" I ask the little girl.

"Free." The girl holds up three fingers, and Dale sucks in a breath.

Dale and I have been together five years.

I pull my hand from Dale's and cross my arms.

"Hey, what's your mom's name?" he asks the girl.

Instead of responding, she claps her hands against her cheeks and squeals.

"I know!" The girl holds up one finger, triumphant. "I'll go get her! Then you can see her again!"

Again.

The word lands like a bomb between the two of us. Dale reaches out for the girl like he's going to stop her from spinning away and racing off to find her mother, but his fingers swipe empty air and hang there for a moment before he shoves his hand into his pocket. A breeze kicks up, and I shiver.

"Aimee, I promise you, I've never seen that girl before in my life." He was whining before, but now he's pleading.

I shake my head. "Dale, I thought this trip was about us. First Hannah and Mitch come along, and now this? You wanted to go on vacation with me to prove to me that you're serious about us, but that's not what's happening. This is the last straw."

"I know I screwed up, but I swear to you, the woman I slept with was a one-time thing."

"Yeah? And it was only one woman? You didn't cheat with more than one person?"

"Of course not." Dale has a tell when he's lying, and I look for it, not surprised to see one eye squint a little bit closed. He's lying through his teeth, trying to salvage whatever might be left of our relationship. He looks like he's going to puke.

He turns to face me, his hand reaching towards me like he needs my support, but I take a step back. It won't kill him to feel like his world is falling apart for a bit for a change.

"Aimes, there's no way that's my daughter," he says, but I know him well enough to know what he's thinking.

Is there really no chance she's my daughter?

And that's exactly what I wanted him to think. To worry about.

He might think this morning was bad, but judging by who's walking towards us, it's about to get a lot worse.

TWELVE
HANNAH

Even though I know Aimee isn't in her room, my heart still thuds in my chest as I push through the door and walk into her space.

Mitch is right behind me, crowding me, and while I wish he would go away so I could be in here on my own, I don't have any way of getting rid of him. He's just as interested as I am in getting into their hotel room, although I'm not really sure what the driving force for him is.

Still, I wanted him to come on this trip with me. He's here now, and there isn't anything I can do to get rid of him. Whatever I find, we're going to find together, and I have to accept that.

"What are you doing?" He's standing too close to me, and I shift to the side, moving around Aimee's bed to her suitcase. This is where the good stuff is going to be. If there's anything in here that I can use against her or to throw her for a loop, it'll be in her personal space.

"Just looking," I tell him as I flip open her suitcase. It's a mess, and I frown, wrinkling my nose as I look at the tangle of clothing. "I want to get to know her better."

Being this close to Aimee after all these years is intoxicating. Sure, I've been in Aimee's space before, but it's not like Dale left me alone long enough to go digging through her things. We were only at their place long enough for... you know. I think he would have noticed if I'd snuck off to look through her side of the closet, no matter how much I would have loved to get to do just that.

I have no doubt that Mitch probably thinks this is weird, but I'm not going to let him ruin this for me. It's my time to dig through her things, and he can't stop me. He can annoy me by being in my space while I do it, but I'm not backing down now.

Without thinking about what I'm doing, I grab the top shirt in her suitcase and press it to my face, really breathing her in.

"You're being weird," Mitch remarks, but I ignore him.

Of course he doesn't get what I'm going through. He's not the one who has made Aimee his entire life, and while there are some people who would tell me that I need to relax, or give it up, or find a new hobby, I can't.

She has been my obsession for so long that I don't think I can ever give her up. Even when this is over, I know I'll wake up thinking about her. She fills every one of my thoughts. She's the driving force for everything I do.

My life will be different without her in it. Mitch knows that. He's been with me this entire time, but it's one thing to know that something is important to another person and another entirely to understand it. Rationally, he gets it. Emotionally, I'm on my own here.

I drop her shirt back in place and eyeball the rest of her things. How long do I have? The thought of her walking in on me as I look through her belongings almost makes me laugh, but I stifle the sound.

My hands are shaking as I dig into her clothing. She had on a cover-up when she left the hotel with Dale, so I'm not sure what bikini she has on, but I'm sure she carefully chose it to drive Dale nuts.

"How long are you going to be in here?" Mitch's question interrupts my thoughts, and I fight back my annoyance before turning and looking at him. "I want to get outside and—"

"Then go. I'll be out in a minute."

He's sitting on the end of Aimee's bed, and a flash of frustration shoots through me. She'll notice that someone was sitting there and rumpled up the cover from when she made it. I have to remember to smooth it back out before leaving her room.

Mitch sighs and stands up. He gives me a hard look before leaving me alone in the room.

Finally.

I turn back to Aimee's suitcase and sift through it, then walk into their bathroom. Her hairbrush is on the counter, and I pick it up and run it through my hair. Some of my lighter strands snag and are left behind, standing out against her darker ones.

If she notices that, she'll freak out.

Satisfied, I put the brush back down on the counter. Her makeup bag is open, and I dip my hand in. After digging around a moment, I find her lip gloss and I pull it out. It's a lighter pink than I normally wear, but I slick it on my lips anyway, then lean forward to admire myself in the mirror.

The color washes me out, but I leave it, then step into the shower. It's a mirror image of ours, with white tile and three showerheads so you can get clean from all angles. I consider taking a quick shower for the fun of it, but instead grab her shampoo and tip it out down the drain. Her conditioner follows, then her expensive face wash.

It's not like she's going to need any of this when I'm through with her.

Back in her room, I ignore Dale's things, then reach under Aimee's pillow for any journal she might have stashed. There's nothing, so—

A door slams.

I jump and whip around, my stomach flipping as my eyes find their door. It's closed, and nobody is in here with me.

"Mitch?" My voice sounds small as I call him, then hurry through the connecting door to our room. It had been a moment of brilliance to go to the front desk and complain about loud upstairs guests so we could move rooms. Of course, a little flirting went a long way to ensure we ended up right where I wanted to be.

I did my best to perfectly plan out this trip, but without knowing their room number, I hadn't been able to snag their neighboring room. Lucky for me, the adjourning room was still empty last night, and I was able to get it.

There's no response from Mitch, but when I walk into our room, I quickly decide what I must have heard: him leaving the room and slamming the main door shut.

Fine, that's fine. It gives me time to change for the beach. I do so quickly, grinning to myself as I don the bikini I bought especially for this trip. It had taken me a while to find it, which is what happens when you're looking for something specific. I'd gotten lucky that it arrived just a few days before we left for the trip, and that was only because I sprang for expedited shipping.

No way did I want to come here without having it. Mitch had rolled his eyes when I told him what I was doing, but that's a man for you. There are a lot of things they don't really understand, no matter how much they might claim to.

But back to the bikini. It fits like a dream, and I hurry into the bathroom to check myself in the mirror.

Stunning—10/10. No notes.

I grin to myself, then my hand hovers over the counter as I look for the sunscreen. No way am I going out into the hot Florida sun without protection, but it isn't here. I look in my toiletries case, but no dice. It's also not in Mitch's...

Which means he probably still has it in his suitcase. I

vaguely remember that now, asking him to be the one to pack it because my case was getting so full.

Rolling my eyes, I walk to his bed and flip open his suitcase. There's the sunscreen, and I grab it, already turning away from his suitcase when my eyes land on something interesting.

What in the world does he want with Aimee's phone?

THIRTEEN

AIMEE

The only thing that matters right now is keeping Dale's eyes on me while the woman approaches us from behind him.

"Are you sure that's not your kid?" My voice is tight.

"No way." He shakes his head. "Not a chance. I promise you." His voice catches.

Tears well in my eyes. "I want to believe you," I whisper, then take another step back. And another. "I *trusted* you! But then you brought me here with Hannah, who thought it would be funny to make it seem like I'm pregnant, and now this?"

"I didn't—"

Whatever he's about to say is cut off by the approaching woman.

"Dale? Is it really you? Cora said she saw you, but I didn't think that was possible. I mean, what are the chances?"

The woman I've been keeping an eye on has finally reached us. She's gorgeous, with thick dark hair flowing around her high cheekbones, full lips, and a bikini body that would make a Victoria's Secret model envious.

In short: she's exactly his type.

He turns to her, and even though I'm only looking at his

profile now, I see the way his jaw drops open. A flush creeps up his neck to his cheeks. "Who are you?"

"Margot," she tells him with a squeal. Then, before either of us can predict what she's going to do, she launches herself at him and wraps her arms tight around him. "It's so good to see you! I tried calling you a few years ago, you know, but you never picked up! How wild is this? To run into you here, in Florida of all places! They say it's a small world, but I never really thought it was *this* small."

"Yeah, but—"

She cuts him off. "You hear stories about people running into acquaintances while on vacation in Japan, or Costa Rica! I guess it is more likely to run into you here, if you think about it. No way did I think it was really you over here, but life is weird, isn't it? Let me buy you a drink, and we can catch up on everything. I have so much to tell you, and I want to hear all about what you've been up to."

Dale takes a step back, his hands out from his body like he's afraid to touch the woman hugging him. When he glances at me, the flush is gone from his cheeks. He's pale and looks even sicker than he did when the little girl approached him. "I don't know—"

"I know you don't know her." The woman drops her arms, and, like magic, the little girl appears at her side. She wraps her arms around her mom's waist and grins up at my fiancé. "But you finally get to meet her. This is Cora. Your daughter."

"No." His hands are up now like he's going to be able to fend off what she's saying. "No. I don't know you, and I don't have a kid."

The girl starts to cry, and the mom leans down and picks her up. When Cora is firmly nestled on her hip, Margot turns back to Dale. "You," she hisses, stabbing her finger at him, "are a terrible father, you know that. One night and then what? You left me in the lurch. Did you change your number after we were together so I couldn't reach you? Unbelievable. I wasn't even going to ask you for child support. I just wanted you to know you had a daughter. Then I see you here, which is crazy, like kismet, and you act like you don't know me?"

"Lady, listen. I don't know who you think I am, but I promise you, I've never seen you before in my life. You've got to stop whatever charade this is." He turns to me. "Aimee, I promise you. I don't know these two people."

"Oh, is that how it's going to be? Screw you, Dale." The woman reaches out and shoves him in the shoulder. "You didn't have any problem sweet-talking me into bed with you, but now you refuse to man up and admit that you screwed up? Typical man." She leans forward and spits in the sand at his feet.

He's simmering with rage now. His hands are clenched into fists. His jaw is tight, and I can see a muscle tick. When he speaks, his words are so filled with venom that I actually take a step back to clear myself of their interaction.

"You are crazy. If you come near me one more time, I promise you I'll call the cops. I'll—"

"We met at the Flying Snail," she says, cutting him off. "You love their hot wings with extra ranch. I was nursing my heart after a breakup, and you bought me a few shots. You really don't remember?"

The Flying Snail is Dale's favorite dive bar, one I loathe because the only vegetable they serve there is wilted celery as a sad little side for your wings. I have a personal belief it's the same three pieces they keep putting on everyone's plate because nobody ever eats it.

For once in his life, Dale is stunned into silence. Then: "The Flying Snail," he repeats slowly.

Margot nods. "Yep. It was luck that we met there, and luck that we met again here." Her eyes cut to me. "You told me you had a girlfriend but that the two of you were on a break. Her decision. That's what you said."

Dale groans and runs his hand through his hair. "I didn't... Aimee, I didn't." He turns to me and reaches for my hand, but I jerk it away. "I swear to you, I made a mistake just recently, but it was a one-time thing. I promise you—this isn't what it looks like. She's lying, and—"

"Is she?" My heart is pounding in my chest. I've never been one for confrontation, and this makes me feel really uncomfortable. "Really? She's lying? Because she knows your favorite place to go on cheat day. And her daughter..." I gesture at the girl on her hip. When I speak again, my voice is high and tight. "She looks like you."

"I promise you: I didn't sleep with this woman." He points at Margot, whose face has fallen. "Please trust me."

"I—"

But Margot cuts me off.

"So, what? You want me to just leave? This is insane, Dale." She pauses, giving him room to answer, but he doesn't say a word. Her eyes flick between the two of us, and I see her decide to end this. "You know what? Fine. We'll go. But I'm hiring someone to find you. I'm getting a paternity test. You might think this is over, but it's just beginning."

With that, she storms off. Cora wiggles out of her mom's grasp and runs ahead. Even though I can tell Dale wants to say something to me, I can't tear my eyes away from the two of them. They march back towards the hotel, and I feel the knot in my stomach loosen a bit.

Finally, I turn to him. "You want to explain that?"

"There's nothing to explain. I'm serious, Aimee, I've never seen that woman before in my life."

"Sure, but you and I both know how wasted you get on cheat day. You take an Uber every time you go to the Flying Snail. Do you think you'd even remember her?"

"I promise you I would." He tilts his head back and exhales hard. "I know I've screwed up, but that woman isn't one of my mistakes. Besides, how weird would it be to run into someone from home while we're here? That doesn't happen in real life!"

"Yes, it does." I stare at him, and he shakes his head.

"Not this time."

"But she knew you." My voice trembles.

"I don't know her."

"I don't know, Dale. I don't know what to believe right now."

"Believe me. I screwed up once, but I'm telling you the truth now. Believe that I love you more than anything and that I'd do whatever you wanted to prove to you how much you mean to me. You're everything, Aimee, and we've turned a corner together. Some crazy woman on the beach isn't going to—"

I throw my hand up between us to cut him off. "Just stop. I can't listen to this right now. And don't follow me. I need time."

"She's not my daughter!" he calls after me, but I refuse to turn back around and discuss this with him.

I'm already running across the beach, really pumping my legs and arms. The hotel grows in front of me, and I dodge around another sandcastle, then avoid a family setting up an army of beach towels.

Dale is going to be a wreck after this. He's going to question every single time he slept with someone during our relationship. I have no doubt this will eat at him like a worm.

And I love it.

Only once do I glance back to make sure he's not following me, and I'm relieved to see that he isn't. In fact, he's still standing right where I left him. Even from this distance, I can see that his fists are clenched tight at his sides.

He's going to do everything he can to find that woman and her little girl.

I have to find them first.

FOURTEEN

Then

"Hottie at two o'clock," Steph whispers in my ear, and I whip around, a smile already on my face. It's Josh—it has to be Josh—because Steph knows me well enough to know that there isn't anyone else I want to see tonight.

But it's not my boyfriend.

The man—because that's what he is, a man at a high school party—is staring at me, his dark eyes expressionless, making it impossible for me to hazard a guess at what he's thinking. If he would smile, or smirk, or do anything other than stare, I probably wouldn't be feeling this terrible tight ball in my stomach.

"Who is he?" I whisper back.

But all I get in response is a shrug.

"I don't know, but you're taken. I'm not." As confident as she has always been, Steph flips her ponytail back and saunters over to the man. It's only when she's a few feet away from him that I see any expression cross his face.

He licks his lips. A small smile curls one side of his mouth.

"Steph," I call, but then I stop. Who am I to tell her not to hook up with the strange hottie? Sure, he's an unknown, but that doesn't mean he's a bad guy. And besides, Steph has always appreciated a little danger. If I worry too much about her, I won't have time to enjoy myself.

"You know you're only allowed to look at me like that." Josh is beside me, whispering in my ear. I jump, not because I think I'm doing anything wrong, but because he wasn't there and then suddenly he was.

"Hey, you." I turn from Steph and loop my arms around his neck. The kiss he gives me is sloppy, but I don't comment on how much he must have already had to drink.

We're both almost grown-up. If he wants to pre-game before a party, that's fine. But I do wish he had let me know. I would have come over to get started with him.

Although Steph had already started, hadn't she? She would have been thrilled for me to join her.

I turn and look over my shoulder for her.

"You looking for a new boyfriend?" Josh says, and I turn back in time to see him stick his lower lip out, feigning hurt feelings.

"Nope." I grin at him. "Even if I were, you're the only cute guy here."

"Cute?" He takes a step back as he claps both hands over his heart. "You wound me. *Cute*. Is that what you're going to say when you go to college? That you have a boyfriend at another school and he's *cute*?"

"Oh, get over yourself." I kiss him again. He tastes like whiskey and cigarettes, and I fight to keep from frowning. Josh knows that I hate it when he smokes, but I don't want to get into a fight with him right now.

This night is going to be perfect. Steph is happy, even though that guy does give me the creeps, which means I can focus on Josh.

"Hey, why don't we go out back? Some of the team started a

bonfire. There are marshmallows, and I thought we could roast some."

"Sounds perfect." I snuggle up against him as we walk through the house. People move out of the way for him to pass, which is what happens when you're the best quarterback the school has seen in decades. I might not be anyone but a nerd, but with Josh, I'm someone, and I'm important.

It's intoxicating.

"Here," he tells me as he grabs two full Solo cups from the counter and presses them into my hands. "Hang on to mine for a minute, okay? I have to talk to her." He jerks his chin past me, and I turn to look at who he's talking about, even though I'm already sure I know who it's going to be.

Jess Hart. Cheerleading captain. Perfect 36-24-36 measurements. She's blonde, gorgeous, and head over heels for my boyfriend.

Good thing he's not a cheater. Do I love the fact that he's leaving my side to go talk to her? No, I don't, but I'm not so paranoid that I feel the need to argue with him or tell him to stay with me. Josh is a great guy, and even though he might have cheated on girlfriends in the past, he's never done it to me.

So instead of worrying, I lean against the kitchen counter and have a drink of my beer. Around me, people dance, they drink, they laugh. A few kids from class wave at me, and I wave back, but really I'm just killing time until Josh finishes talking with Jess.

Knowing him, he's telling her to back off. Again. He's telling her that there's no chance he'll ever be with her, not when I'm alive.

Someone puts on a Beastie Boys song, and I start to dance without thinking about it. By the end of the song, Josh still isn't back, so I down his cup and toss both empties into the kitchen trash.

The house has an open floorplan, and I can see straight into the living room from here. There's Steph, dancing in the corner with tall, dark, and creepy. I frown and consider going over there to break up whatever is happening between the two of them, but first I want to find Josh. He is...

Not here.

I frown. Surely I missed him. He was right there talking with Jess, and there's no way he would have wandered off with her, especially not when he knows how I feel about her.

"Great party, huh?" A girl I have chemistry with sidles up next to me. Monica? Miranda?

"Sure is," I say, accepting the shot she hands me. We shoot our drinks, and she laughs, brushing her hair out of her face.

"Where's your boytoy? You two are never apart. I swear, it's like you're literally attached at the hip."

"He's talking to someone," I say. Her words are innocent, or at least I think they are, but I still bristle at them. Then again... are she and Jess friends? Is she a cheerleader?

Maybe they're working together to keep me away from Josh.

Sweat breaks out on my brow, and I wipe it away without thinking.

"Hot?" she asks with a smile.

"Excuse me," I tell her, then push past her. Before, I casually glanced around looking for Josh, but now my head is on a swivel as I try to find him. He should be right here, but then where in the world is he?

I'm about to head upstairs, about to face my fears that he's doing something stupid, when someone screams my name.

And, at the same time, I feel a hand close on my arm.

FIFTEEN

HANNAH

I sink down onto Mitch's bed, Aimee's phone in my hands. It's locked, but I still turn it over and over as I consider what's going on.

Mitch had to have taken it from her bed when I was distracted with her suitcase. It's why he sat on her bed, why he left their room before I was done poking around. He's sneaky, Mitch is, and part of me is impressed, but I don't like that he's going off-book like this.

Because now I'm in a bit of a mess. Do I get rid of her phone? Do I keep it? No way am I going to hand it over to her and tell her that Mitch took it from her, but I sincerely doubt that he has good intentions for taking it.

He's supposed to follow my plan, not make up ones of his own. I don't like the fact that he's doing whatever he wants without running it by me. It pisses me off actually. I came on this trip for a single purpose: to punish Aimee for what she did years ago, and I don't want to have to work against Mitch to achieve my goal.

No way can I trust Aimee. Or Dale. And now to think that I might not be able to trust Mitch? It gives me a headache.

I tap on her phone to wake it up. The lock screen is a selfie of her and Dale, and they look... happy. Really happy. I stare at her face, at how bright it looks, at the ring on her hand. She's resting it on Dale's chest like she's trying to show off her bling.

Scoffing, I toss it onto the bed next to me and fall back beside it. I'm still and might not look like I'm doing anything, but my mind is racing as I try to sort through what I should do next.

Part of me wants to confront Mitch, but the other part of me doesn't want to give him an opportunity to lie to me, which is what I'm afraid will happen. If I tell him I found her phone, he'll get mad at me for snooping through his things, even though I was only looking for sunscreen.

And there's no way I can get into her phone.

I grab it and verify that it's locked, then drop it back on the bed. No, the best thing for me to do is get rid of it. I don't want her to have it, and I don't like the fact that Mitch seems to want it so badly.

"You can't lie here all day," I mutter to myself. "You have to keep her on her toes before you end this."

Exhaling hard, I sit up, then redo my hair, brushing it up and away from my face.

In the bathroom, I wipe her ugly lip gloss from my mouth and apply some darker red lipstick. Only when I'm satisfied with the way I look do I sashay to the bed and grab her phone.

Instead of heading straight outside, I take the elevator to the top floor. The ride is smooth, the piped-in music somehow not terrible, and even more importantly—I'm alone. On the top floor, I head straight for a trash can, then pause.

Halfway down the hall is a cleaning cart. The worker must be cleaning out the empty rooms here, and I fully intend to use this to my benefit.

The phone doesn't make a sound when I drop it in the trash

attached to the cart, then I hurry back to the elevator and head downstairs.

On the way, I take a deep breath, then plaster a smile on my face when I exit the elevator. Next on my to-do list?

Find Aimee.

She's going to lose it when she sees what I'm wearing.

SIXTEEN

AIMEE

The little girl is standing right where I told her to wait for me, her hand already out, a grin on her face. Her mother stands next to her, her cheeks flushed with excitement.

"Pay up," the girl says, and I nod, already digging into my pocket for some cash.

It was luck finding her on my way back to the room from the gym, and even better luck that she took direction as well as she did. No way would I have trusted a real three-year-old to talk to Dale the way she did, but at six, she was perfect. How fortuitous that she's a little shrimp of a thing.

"Fifty bucks," I tell her, putting the money in her hand. "And two hundred for you." I give the last of my cash to her mom. "You guys were awesome. Seriously, thank you. His head is spinning! But now you have to stay away from him, okay? Don't talk to him again."

"We won't, don't you worry. And good luck with that guy— he sounds like a jerk." The mom lightly touches my shoulder as she and her daughter pass me.

The little girl turns and yells over her shoulder. "Thanks!"

I sigh, tighten my ponytail, then head up to our room. I'm

really hoping for some time alone to come up with my next way to torture Dale, and I'm crossing my fingers that Mitch and Hannah will be making themselves scarce for a bit.

Sure enough, after I've rapped on our connecting door and had no response, I feel myself relax. Some alone time is just what the doctor ordered, and I crack open a bottle of Chardonnay from the mini fridge and pour some into a Styrofoam cup.

Normally, I don't endorse drinking so early, but things aren't normal right now, and I just want to make it through the day as best I can. So a little day drinking isn't such a bad idea.

I take the first sip, then the next thing I know, the glass is empty. I'm a little woozy from skipping breakfast thanks to the great pregnancy test debacle, but I pour another glass anyway.

It's my vacation too. I want to enjoy it as much as possible.

I'm standing on the balcony watching people play on the sand, halfway through my second glass, when it hits me. Hannah and Mitch aren't home. There's nothing keeping me from looking through their side of the room.

Warmth flows through me. Whether it's from the alcohol or the idea, I'm not entirely sure, but I quickly down the rest of my wine, put my cup on the bedside table, and boldly walk through the connecting door.

The room is a mirror image of ours. The first thing I notice is that they're not sharing a bed, which is strange. Are they on the outs like Dale and I are? I think about how touchy-feely they were in the cab on the way over here yesterday. Hannah seems smitten with Mitch, but something feels off.

I ignore the bed that is clearly Mitch's. The boxers and Axe deodorant on the coverlet are a dead giveaway. Instead, I walk over to Hannah's and sit down on the edge of it. It smells like her. Just the act of entering her space, of touching where she sleeps, engulfs me in her scent.

Frowning, I stand up. My eyes flick to her suitcase, and I

walk to it, but then I hurry back to the hall door and hook the chain so nobody can get in while I'm in here.

The last thing I need is for either of them to return, try to get into the room, and see me digging through their things. I'm not even sure what I'm looking for, not sure what evidence on them I want to find, but I'm sure I'll know it when I see it.

In the bathroom I open her toiletries bag. After a careful inspection, during which I discover the kind of toothpaste she uses (Burt's Bees), her deodorant (Native), and her perfume (Firebird Snowdrift), I decide there isn't anything interesting here and prepare to dig deeper.

It's time to dig into her suitcase, and the first thing I find is her stash of lingerie. I feel dirty sifting through it all, so I close my eyes and plunge my hand deeper into the suitcase, to see what else there might be in here.

My fingers close on a slim, hard volume, and I yank it free, excitement bubbling up in me. It's a journal. I recognize the feel of faux leather, the thickness of the volume, the little ribbon used to mark your place.

I settle back on the floor and flip it to the ribbon marker. No, I'm not interested in reading about how she feels about Dale, but I feel like there's something more to her. Something... not evil, maybe, but darker. For a woman to cheat with an engaged man, then follow him to another state on a trip, there has to be more to her than meets the eye.

"What in the world?" I stare at the words on the page, then flip backwards. Again. And again.

There isn't a single thing about *Dale* specifically, but the notebook is full of love poems. Terrible love poems. Like, Live-Journal-era angst.

"'Being with you here, when you're not supposed to be mine, makes me feel alive.'" I roll my eyes and have to fight the urge to rip out the page. It's clear to me, because I know what's really going on here, that these are about Dale. Does she really feel that way about him? I know they had an affair, but has she really fallen that hard?

I don't know which is worse—the thought of the affair being only physical or the two of them connecting on a deeper level. But which is it? Is it simply her wanting him or something darker, something deeper that has driven her to sleeping with my fiancé?

I toss the journal to the side and dig back under her lace thongs.

Unlike me, she packed neatly, everything perfectly folded and carefully placed in her suitcase. The smart thing to do would be to lift things out in layers, like I'm conducting an archeological dig, but I'm too impatient for that. Besides, the damage is done. I can't turn back now.

My fingers brush jeans. A belt. Something crocheted, like a sweater or bathing suit cover-up. It isn't until I'm about to pull my hand out of the suitcase that I feel a small case.

A jewelry box.

Triumphant, I yank it out and open the lid before giving myself time to think about whether or not I want to know what's inside.

My breath catches in my throat when I see what it is.

It's a necklace. Made from a fine gold chain with a single pearl hanging in the middle, it's absolutely stunning. It is, in fact, the sort of thing you'd have custom-made for your fiancée on your fifth anniversary.

I know that because I'm wearing a matching one.

Anger rushes through me, hot and insistent, and I yank the pearl necklace out without thinking about what I'm doing. The self-control I exhibited when faced with her terrible poetry is gone, and the fine chain breaks before I can stop myself. Without thinking, I shove it in the pocket of my jeans, then snap the box shut and throw it across the room.

It smacks the wall and falls behind an armchair. I'm

breathing hard, my vision blurry with rage, when I hear someone at the door.

There are footsteps, then the soft slide of a keycard in the lock. It whirs, clicks happily, and they try to open it. But the door slams against the security chain.

I freeze.

"What in the world?" It's Hannah, and I can hear the frustration in every word. "Did you do something with the chain, Mitch?"

"How would I have done that? Let me push."

The chain grinds into the corner of the door. Like a spell has broken, I come to life and grab Hannah's journal. As I shove it back into her suitcase, I look around the room for the jewelry box. No way can I put the broken necklace in there, but I could at least put the box back...

"We'll have to see if Aimee or Dale are in. Maybe housekeeping did something to the door." That's Mitch. Always calm. Always thinking things through.

"Oh yeah? You think they hooked the chain before the left our room? I think—"

Whatever she was going to say is cut off by the door closing.

Crap. Screw the box.

Maybe they won't see it where it fell behind the chair, or maybe I can come back later and get it before she notices it's gone. I hop to my feet. As quietly as possible, I race through the door into our room. Someone is already banging on the door and calling our names, but before I open it, I pause, mess up my hair, try to look sleepy.

"Sorry, sorry! I was napping," I lie as I open the door. "You guys okay?"

The pearl presses into my leg. It feels huge, like Hannah could look down and see it there, could easily recognize it for what it is, even through the fabric of my shorts.

"Napping? So early in the morning? I'd swear you're

hungover or pregnant, Aimee." Hannah grins, like that's going to offset what she's saying. "Which one is it?"

"Hungover," I grit out.

She throws me a wink. Her eyes are blue, bright blue, sparkling blue, like the ocean.

Just once I'd like to see her look at me with respect.

No. Not with respect.

I'd like to see hurt fill those gorgeous blue eyes.

SEVENTEEN

HANNAH

"Well, hungover is better than pregnant. Especially in your case."

"In my case? What does that mean?"

I blink at her. "You know what I'm saying," I tell her, but she doesn't respond, so I continue. "With Dale not always being faithful."

It's a gamble, and I'm hoping she doesn't call me out on being the person her fiancé wasn't *faithful* with, but I don't think she will. She doesn't have the guts.

"He would be if—" Her voice breaks off as she actually sees me for the first time. Her eyes flick up and down me, and her cheeks grow red. "What are you wearing?"

"What?" I glance down like I'm just now seeing the clothing on my body. "A bikini," I tell her, then flash her a smile.

Behind me, Mitch shifts uncomfortably, but he hasn't said anything yet, and I'm not interested in giving him a moment to speak. Whatever his opinion might be, he can keep it to himself.

"Yeah, but it's—" Her words fail her. She looks like she could scream, she's so mad. I fight back a smile and act surprised when I speak.

"Oh my gosh, we have the same bikini!" My hands fly to my mouth as if I'm surprised, but I'm really trying to hide the fact that I'm laughing. "Can you believe it?"

"No. I can't." Her words are ice. "In fact, it seems so far-fetched that I'd say it wasn't an accident."

Nope, it totally wasn't. I'd gotten lucky when she posted a selfie of her in her new bikini on Instagram. What was I supposed to do? Ignore the fact that she'd just given me a wonderful way to mess with her? Yeah, I don't think so. No way was I about to let that opportunity pass me by, even though it took me forever to find the stupid bikini since it was apparently from some small brand and only a few were made. I overpaid for the stupid thing, but you know what? It was worth it.

"I guess we both have great taste," I tell her. I'm still grinning at her, but she isn't smiling. Her face is stone, and her eyes are sharp. If looks could kill, I'd be dead. "Makes you wonder what other things you and I both like, doesn't it?"

A shadow crosses her face, but she doesn't respond. I want to keep pushing her and goad her into doing something stupid, but Mitch clears his throat.

"Do you think you'll head outside now, Aimee?" He sounds innocent. No, *eager*.

Frustration stabs through me. Whose side is he on, anyway? I don't like that he's trying to make nice with her, even if he thinks doing so can make my life easier. Mitch already went off-book by taking her cell phone and putting it in his luggage, and I'd love to know what's going through his mind right now.

"Yeah, a walk to clear my head might be nice," she tells him, and he starts nodding. He's next to me now, almost pushing me out of the way in his eagerness to be close to her.

"I could go with—"

"You may not," I tell him, then grab his arm and squeeze to try to draw his attention away from her. "I need to talk to you."

The three of us fall silent, then Aimee speaks.

"It's fine; I can go by myself." She steps forward, forcing the two of us back, then makes to pull her door closed behind her, but I kick my foot out and catch it.

"Our door is locked, remember? We'll have to go through yours."

She stares at me. Glances at Mitch. Swallows hard.

"Yeah, of course. You two do that and I'll catch you later," she says, holding the door open for the two of us.

It's obvious that Mitch wants to go with her, but I take his hand and yank him into her bedroom. We hurry through the door into our room, and I turn on him.

"You can't follow her around like a little lost puppy," I tell him. "What, do you really think she's ever going to like you?"

"I'm not a little lost puppy."

"You're acting like it."

"Yeah, well, at least I didn't spend my money on that." He flaps his hand at me.

"My bikini?" I feel my eyebrows crash together. "What's wrong with it?"

"You're wearing it to stress her out."

I shrug. "And?"

"It's immature."

"Oh, I didn't know I was supposed to be the epitome of a grown-up. I'll do better in the future."

"Your sarcasm is grating. Come on, Hannah. Do better."

I stare at him. The actual audacity of him telling me to *do better* is almost enough to make me scream and pull out my hair.

Instead of continuing our little fight, I take a deep breath. "You're right."

"I am?" He sounds shocked.

"Yep. I need to do better. And I will. Feel free to chase after Aimee; I'll be outside in a bit." I force myself to smile at him, but inside I'm seething.

He grins at me and runs his hand through his hair. "Okay,

great. I'll go check on her and see you outside." He turns and lets himself out of the room. I stare after him until the door slams, then exhale hard.

I don't like not knowing what's going through his mind. He's supposed to be on my side, but he's not acting like it right now. It's scary, the thought that he might go off on his own. It tells me that I need to hurry up with my plan.

I'm halfway to the door when I stop and turn to look around the room. Something caught my eye, something—

I hurry to the chair and drop to my knees. There, behind it, up against the wall. A small box, one I know really well.

I feel like I'm going to throw up. I don't want to reach out and take it, don't want to allow myself to think about why or how this box ended up where it is, but I don't have a choice.

Right as I grab it, my phone rings. I glance down to see Dale's name lighting up the screen.

EIGHTEEN

AIMEE

My heart pounds as I race towards the elevator. For a moment, I consider going outside and finding Dale, but I want to be alone right now. Besides, do I really want to be the one to pick up the pieces for him after he fell apart thanks to Margot's confrontation?

No, I do not.

He deserved that little scare, and his reaction spoke volumes about the man I was planning on marrying.

I had no idea how difficult it would be to be here, but I don't trust anyone. I don't trust Dale and Hannah because they were having an affair. I don't like the way Mitch was looking at me when Hannah and I were talking just now... like he knows me?

Or like he wants to?

I can't wrap my mind around anything, and the worst part? How bad it hurts. I knew it was going to be emotionally draining to come here with Dale after how bad he hurt me, but I had no idea I would be in this much pain. It'll all be worth it in the end, when I'm free of him. Just a little while longer here with him while my friends move me out, then I'm free.

Tears streak down my cheeks as I enter the elevator and mash the button for the top floor. A place this nice? I bet there's a balcony up there, and I fully intend on having some time to myself without any interruptions.

As the elevator ascends, I reach into my pocket and pull out the necklace I just stole from Hannah.

As I first thought, it's a twin of the one Dale gave me. Just looking at the perfect pearl and thinking about Dale buying not one but two necklaces makes me feel like I'm going to throw up.

How dare he?

How dare he tell me that he loves me then crush my heart like this? It's not only the worst betrayal I've ever felt, but the most pain I've ever been in. Leaning to the side, I brace myself on the elevator wall. My mind races, and I question if I'm doing the right thing, but I'm sure I am.

The elevator stops, the doors open, and I step into the hall before letting myself out onto the balcony. From here, you get a great view of the area around the hotel. It's bustling, with lots of little shops and bars for people to visit. A bit further out is the ocean, the water so bright and sparkling that it looks fake.

More tears race down my cheeks, and I let out a sob as I reach out and grab the railing. It's smooth and warm under my hands, and I grip it as tightly as possible as I force myself to take deep breaths.

Someone clears their throat.

I whip around, fear creating a hollow space in my stomach. The last thing I want is for the person out here to be Dale, and I'm relieved when I see that the man is a stranger.

"I'm sorry, I don't want to interrupt you, but I thought it was weird to sit here in silence while you were crying." He gives me a small smile, which I force myself to return.

He's older, probably in his fifties, and looks gentle. His hair is thinning, his middle soft. No, I'm not attracted to him, but he gives off strong dad energy, and I feel myself relax a bit.

"You're fine. I shouldn't have used this balcony as my own personal place to cry."

He has a bottle of water in his hand and takes a sip before speaking. "That's what my daughter does when her heart is broken. Please tell me some jerk didn't break your heart."

Great. There go the tears again, just because this guy was nice to me. I wipe them away on the back of my hand and nod. "Yeah, but it's okay. We're going to work through it."

"Hmm." He stands and moves slowly towards the door to go back inside. "Well, I'll leave you to it, but let me give you the same advice I've given my daughter."

I stand perfectly still, waiting.

"You can do better." He throws me a wink, then, just as quickly, steps back inside the building.

I don't move for a long time as I think about what he just said to me. *You can do better.* That's the kind of thing one of my friends would have said if I were able to get in touch with them, and it feels like a sign.

I'm no longer crying as I rush back into the building and hit the button for the elevator. It's taking way too long, so I use the stairwell to go back to our floor.

You can do better.

Yes, I can.

Relief washes over me when I step into my room and nobody else is around. Just to ensure it stays that way, I lock the door that leads to Hannah and Mitch's room, then walk into the bathroom. Keeping it locked the entire time we're here is a good idea, but I know Dale will have an opinion on that.

Cold water is bracing but makes me feel more alive. I put on a bit of makeup to hide the fact that I was crying, then grab my hairbrush to redo my ponytail.

But before I can run it through my hair, I see what's in it, and I freeze, an impossible rage boiling up inside me.

There's only one person with long blonde hair who would have the audacity to use my hairbrush.

Hannah.

NINETEEN

HANNAH

I know Aimee was in our room. She was digging around. A nosy little rat. And the worst part?

She found something.

And she took it, but I'll get it back.

Right now, though, the necklace she stole isn't that important. Dale called me, and I met him outside. She must have really pissed him off for him to reach out to me like this because now I lean against him. He hesitates for a moment, but then wraps his arms around me, pulling me closer to breathe in my scent.

Peppermint. I always wear it or chew peppermint gum when we're together. I've Pavlov-dogged him into thinking about me when he smells it.

"I think Aimee went through my things," I tells him, and he stiffens.

"What? What do you mean?"

"Just that. I think she was in my suitcase." When I pull back to look at him, his hand drops to my waist. "Mitch and I went out for a walk, and when we came back, my suitcase wasn't right." My bottom lip sticks out.

"It wasn't right?" He laughs, and I frown, taking a step away from him. His hands fall from my waist, but he doesn't reach for me. "I'm sorry, Hannah, but I've been to your apartment. Your entire place tends to be a bit messy. How would you even know—?"

"The security chain was engaged. How would someone have locked the door like that unless they were in our room?"

"One of you had to do it, then you left through our room. Simple. It's the most obvious explanation if you think about it."

I hate it when he does this. Acts like I'm stupid. No, Dale, the most obvious explanation is that Aimee was in our room.

She's more dangerous than I thought, and that's a concern. Not that I can't handle her. I'll just be a bit more careful. She can't know who I am, can she?

"Yeah, but we didn't," I say. "Don't try to gaslight me."

"I'm not gaslighting you. I promise." He takes a deep breath like he needs to calm down, then throws me an easy smile. "It's just that I think you're jumping to conclusions about Aimee being in your room."

"Because?" I cock an eyebrow at him.

He sighs. "Because you're envious? I know it has to be because you don't like her."

Envious? "It's not that I don't like her. It's that I like *you.*" He swallows hard but doesn't respond, so I continue. "My necklace is missing."

His eyebrows crash together. "Necklace?"

"The one you gave me."

"The pearl necklace?"

"That's the one."

"Why did you bring that here? Are you crazy?"

Am *I* crazy? I'm not the one who gave the girl I was screwing on the side the same necklace I gave my fiancée. If anyone's at fault here, it's Dale.

"I love that necklace. You know that."

"You can't wear it in front of Aimee." He exhales hard and puts his hands on the back of his head as he closes his eyes. "What in the world would you say to her if she noticed you had it on?"

"Well, I guess we don't have to worry about that now, do we? Since it's gone."

"Gone?"

"Did you not listen to me? It's gone. Missing. *Taken*. No longer where I left it." I raise my hands out to the side, then drop them down on my thighs with a smack. "Shall I continue?"

"No." He turns away from me and groans. "Are you sure you didn't misplace it?"

I force myself to laugh. "I'm pretty dang sure, yeah."

"So you think Aimee has it?"

"That would be my guess. Unless you think someone from the staff here dug through my suitcase, went through my lingerie, then took the necklace. Shall I go to the front desk and file a formal complaint?"

"No." He whips around and stares at me. "No. We're not bringing more attention to this, do you understand me? You shouldn't have brought it in the first place. That's on you."

"You shouldn't have given me the same necklace you gave your fiancée," I fire back. "You had to know that something like this would happen." I pause, thinking. "Does she know about us?"

"Not a chance." He sounds confident, and I have to fight to keep from laughing. One hundred percent, Aimee knows that I'm the woman Dale was sleeping with. But if Dale doesn't know that she knows...

"You're sure? You really think she's that clueless?"

"Yeah, she has no idea. The one time she caught us, you were gone so fast she didn't see your face."

Yes, she did. I know she's not as harmless as he thinks she is. Heck, I wouldn't have stalked her as long as I have if she were harmless, if she hadn't already hurt people. "Okay, as long as you think so. But I still think she was the one in my room sneaking around and stealing my necklace."

He bends over, grabbing his thighs and taking a deep breath. I have to fight to keep from rolling my eyes in case he looks up at me.

Dramatic much? If I didn't know any better, I'd think she was playing a game with me, much like I'm playing a game with her. Most women in her shoes would curl into themselves. But not Aimee. She's strong—I have to admit that. I don't like her, and I'm certainly not letting her walk away from what she did in one piece, but I can admit that she's strong. It's why she's survived as long as she has, why she's gotten away with what she's done.

Not only is she strong, she's driven. She's capable. A survivor. But no matter how lucky she's been up until now, she's going to get what's coming to her.

Even after all these years. She took the one thing that mattered most from me. And now I'm doing the same to her.

I have nothing to be afraid of. I'm not the one who—

Dale moans but still won't look at me. I have to fix this, stroke his ego, get the plan back on track.

"I'm sorry," I purr, grabbing him by the shoulders and straightening him up so I can wrap my arms around his waist. "You're right. This is on me. I was stupid bringing it, but I seriously thought the two of us might be the real deal."

"Hannah, I love Aimee."

"I know you think that, but look at you. You can't let go of me right now. You want me, Dale." I lift my face to his, sure he can feel my breath on his lips.

"I can't keep doing this to Aimee." He takes a deep breath like he's drawing strength from the air and steps back. "What we had was wonderful, but—"

"What we have is better than what you and Aimee had." It's

cruel and a low blow, but I'm hurt right now. I'm not used to being turned down, and I'm certainly not used to my plans unraveling.

I shouldn't have brought the necklace, I know that, but the opportunity to wear it in front of Aimee was too good to pass up. Telling Dale after I discovered it was missing was a mistake, but I was just so fired up.

But I can fix this. Watch me.

"Dale, please." I grab his hand and give it a squeeze. When he looks at me, I bite my lower lip. "I want you. Be with me. Not Aimee. You can make that happen."

He's staring at me, and I'm sure that I've won, that he's going to lean down and kiss me and everything will be back on track, but before he can do that, he looks past me.

His eyes widen.

He yanks his hand from mine.

There's only one person in the world whose appearance could make him have that reaction.

Aimee.

TWENTY

AIMEE

I'm not angry that Hannah and Dale are still clearly interested in each other. What enrages me is how bold the two of them are, acting like they're on a private vacation on a private island without anyone around to see them holding hands and staring into each other's eyes.

It's the blatant disrespect that really pisses me off, especially after just finding the necklace in Hannah's suitcase and her hair in my hairbrush. It's disgusting, but hiding under my anger is hurt. Hurt that Dale would not only cheat on me, but that he'd give Hannah something he'd given me, something I believed was a sign of his love for me.

It makes me wonder how much of our relationship was real. Was he always planning something like this? Did he know how painful it would be for me to see that she has the same necklace as he gave me? I don't want to think he'd be that cruel, but this is more painful than I could have imagined.

They both deserve what's coming to them.

Dale's eyes grow wide as he clocks me approaching them, and he jerks his hand back from Hannah's like he's been burned. She pauses, then slowly turns, her eyes lighting up when she sees me.

She's enjoying this.

That thought tears through me like a hurricane, and I grip my hands into fists as I approach them. All the things I want to say to the two of them are swirling through my head, making it difficult for me to think straight.

Do I tell them I know about the affair? Do I throw the ring Dale gave me into the ocean? Should I show them the necklace I took from Hannah's suitcase? I could fling it into her face. Scream at them. Tell them that I know the truth, that it's over between Dale and me, that she can have him.

I'm tempted to do all of these things, and, for a moment, I allow myself to imagine just how incredible it would feel to blow it all up. This whole trip would come to a screeching halt, and I'd go back home to be with my friends. I could put this behind me.

It's temping, it really is, and I imagine walking away from this, but then I remember the pain he put me through. I remember the punch to the gut when I found him and Hannah together. How I swore years ago that I wouldn't let people walk all over me. Dale deserves what's coming to him.

So, yes, there's a part of me that wants to walk away, but is that really the best way to handle things when I've been working on this plan to get a clean break from Dale for so long? I hesitate.

Too long.

Thanks to my hesitation, I don't get the opportunity to do any of those things. Hannah walks away from Dale, hurrying towards me, almost like she wants to talk to me without him there to hear what she has to say.

I stiffen, taking in the sway of her hips, the cocky set to her lips. She invades my personal space, her perfectly manicured nails closing gently around my upper arm, then leans forward, breathing words into my ear.

"I know what you did."

Five words. Who would think that five words could make your life fall apart?

I pull back from her, or I try to, but it's like I'm caught in molasses and there's no good way for me to get away from her. The harder I try to pull away from her, the harder her nails dig into my flesh.

I can't run. I have to confront her.

"I don't know what you're talking about." My voice is loud. Steady. I'm proud of myself that it doesn't shake. Yes, I'm nervous, and I feel like I'm about to come out of my skin, but she doesn't have to know that. I make and hold eye contact with her, daring her to be the one to look away first.

But she doesn't.

"When you were younger," she tells me. "You thought you could hide from it, but I know the truth."

"What?" The ground seems to drop away from me. A moment ago, I'd wanted nothing more than for her to let me go, but now I'm relying on her grip to stay upright. I feel my knees start to give out, and my vision begins to darken.

I'm going to pass out. No way does she know the truth. She's making things up just to mess with me. Right?

I don't even realize I'm reaching for her until I feel my hand close on her shoulder. I need her to ground me, to keep me from falling apart completely, but before I can really catch my breath and center myself, she lets go of my arm and steps back.

That's enough for gravity to take hold and finish what it started.

My knees give out, and I sink to the sand. I'm vaguely aware of the feeling of it pressing into my bare knees, but none of that really registers. I fall forward, catching myself on the palms of my hands.

"Aimee!" That's Dale. Of course it's Dale. Whatever sick game he's playing here with Hannah, he still has to keep up the pretense that things are fine between the two of us, that we're working things out, that he chooses me.

It would almost be easier if he'd walk away now, but instead he drops to his knees next to me and pulls me to him. I breathe in his cologne and close my eyes, fighting against passing out.

"Call 911!" He's obviously saying it to Hannah, and she must not respond because he repeats himself.

"I'm fine," I try to say, but my brain feels fuzzy.

There's a hand on my back, and I feel Hannah sit down next to me. I don't like that—I don't like her that close to me. She knows things about me that nobody else does.

How is that? It's impossible, or it should be, but what she said is terrifying.

No way does she know.

"Aimee's okay," she says, rubbing my back. "I think the heat got to her. There's no reason to call 911, is there, Aimee? No reason to call 911. Not when you're going to be just fine."

No reason to call 911. Not when you're going to be just fine.

I know those words.

"Please," I whisper.

"Please?" That's Hannah again. Her voice usually sounds light and airy, but now there's a dark undertone to it, a shadow I can't ignore, just like the one that's been stalking me for over a decade. "Please—is that what you said?"

Is that what you said?

She's not talking about me. She's talking about someone else. I know she is, no matter how this might appear. And no matter how careful and kind and attentive she might seem right now, I know the truth.

She's talking in code. Her words are only for me, even though Dale has now dropped to his knees next to us.

"I'm sorry," I whisper. Dale can hear me, but my words are only for her.

"Sorry? You didn't do anything wrong, Aimes." Dale hugs me tighter. "You have nothing to apologize for, okay?"

Oh, but he's wrong. I do have something to apologize for. Something terrible.

And Hannah thinks she knows what I've done.

TWENTY-ONE

Then

I whip around, my heart hammering hard. Everyone I'm friends with knows I hate being grabbed. If you want my attention, call my name. Tap my shoulder. Send a freaking smoke signal. But do not, under the risk of me yelling at you or trying to break off your fingers, grab my arm.

But the person standing behind me, a huge grin on her face, isn't a friend. That explains why she felt like she could put her hands on me.

"Hey, girl. You having fun?" Jess grins at me. She recently got a Monroe piercing, and the bit of metal flashes in the light when she smiles.

"It's a great party," I tell her. "Josh does an amazing job and is always so good about inviting people who we normally wouldn't want to hang out with."

She ignores my barb. "I know—he's just the sweetest. When he called me freaking out because he needed help getting set up for the party, I just had to come by. I mean, who wouldn't want to help him out?"

I stare at her. *No. Way.* The logical part of my brain is telling me that she's messing with me, that she just wants to see me upset. But then there's a little voice in the back of my head that notices how she stares at him during class and how he didn't look too upset when he was talking to her earlier.

Do I really think that Josh would cheat on me? Not a chance. He loves me. I know how much I mean to him, and I know that he wouldn't do anything to jeopardize our relationship.

Right?

And he was so happy when he saw me. He walked right up to me and kissed me.

Or did I kiss him?

My head feels like it's swimming, and I give it a little shake to try to clear the thoughts, but the beer, the loud music, and the way Jess is staring at me like she knows some huge joke that I'm not a part of is making it difficult for me to think straight.

"He didn't call you to come early to help," I tell her, and I feel confident about what I'm saying. No way would he do that. Not when we—

"Got me there," she says with a laugh, and I feel myself relax.

See? My mind was running away with me, but nothing bad happened between Josh and Jess. She's just a jerk and wanted to make me worry, but the only worry I have is how to get away from her as quickly as possible because I really do hate her, and—

"He didn't call. I just showed up. You should have seen his face—he was so surprised!" She's grinning at me, but the expression on her face is anything but friendly. She looks evil, with sharp teeth, her eyes narrowing as she stares at me.

"He wouldn't have let you stay to help." I try to sound more confident than I feel, but truth be told, it feels like the ground is shifting under me. I'm off-balance, and Josh is usually the thing that makes me feel more in control. How am I supposed to feel in control, though, if this is true?

"Oh, he let me stay." She leans forward and wrinkles her nose at me. "Trust me, he wasn't totally on board at first, but I managed to get him to change his tune. Guys are all the same, aren't they?"

I force myself to take a deep breath. What I want to do is scream in her face, or grab her perfect ponytail and yank it as hard as I can, but instead I concentrate on taking a second deep breath, then a third, and trying to think.

No way would Josh cheat on me. Jess is acting like the two of them hooked up, but there's not a chance, right? I let my gaze wander down her body. I mean, sure, she's gorgeous. Tanned and blonde, with legs for days, and I'm shorter than most sophomores at school.

But Josh is a good guy. He wouldn't.

"No," I whisper, then because my mind fails me and I can't think of anything else to say to her, I turn and look for Steph. She'll help me get my head on straight. She'll make sure I don't believe any of Jess's lies. And, most importantly, she'll make me feel less alone while I find Josh so I can talk to him.

There's a crush of bodies filling the living room. I turn slowly, doing my best to look through people so I can hopefully find my sister, but she's not anywhere.

It's steamy in here, much hotter than it was when we first arrived, just... what? Half an hour ago? Time has a funny way of feeling warped when you're at a party. How long was I dancing?

"You looking for Steph?" When Jess speaks, she does in a little sing-song voice that makes me grit my teeth. "She was over there in the corner talking to Connor—didn't you see her?"

"Who?" I don't want to give Jess the time of day, but I have to know where Steph is, and if she has any information, then I'll have to suck it up and talk to her. "Who in the world is Connor?"

"My brother."

My eyes flick to her, and I watch as she rolls her eyes. Her thoughts are written across her face as clear as day.

She's enjoying this.

"You don't have a brother," I tell her, and she just laughs.

"Well, obviously, I do. But he doesn't live here, which is why you don't know who he is. That and you're not that cool, no matter what you've managed to convince Josh. Connor is home visiting for the weekend."

"From college? He must be super cool if he thinks that going to a high school party is a good time."

"Not college. He just got out of prison and is here for the weekend before he moves out of town. He's not that much older than us and just wanted a good time."

My lips don't want to form the word. "Prison?"

This guy was in prison, and Steph was over there talking to him, looking for all the world like she was having the time of her life. I have no idea who he really is or what he might want with her, and now I don't even know where they went, and—

"Don't you worry about a thing. I know my brother, and Connor will take care of Steph. Trust me."

Yeah, not a chance. I don't trust Jess, and I certainly don't and will never trust her brother. She keeps talking, but I ignore her as I look around the room, desperation growing in me.

She has to be here.

The front door opens with a slam, and Connor walks through. He's wearing a tight white T-shirt, and I can see every muscle bunch and twist as he makes his way over to where I'm standing with Jess.

Just being this close to him makes the hair on my arms stand up. I avert my eyes when he smiles at me and look to the front door.

Where is my sister?

"Hey, sis." Connor smacks Jess on the shoulder, and she grins at me. Slowly, he turns to look at me, and I drag my eyes away from the still-open front door.

No Steph.

"What's your name?" he asks me.

My back stiffens. This guy gives me the creeps, but I'm not going to let the fact that he's staring at me like he can see through my clothes stop me from finding Steph.

"Where's Steph?" I ask in response, and he frowns.

"Steph?" He shakes his head. "I don't know a Steph. Who are you talking about?"

Sweat pricks my palms. I stare at him, trying to wrap my mind around what he just said, what I saw, what that might mean for my twin.

"Oh, she thinks she saw you talking to her sister, but this party is so busy, it's impossible to know." Jess puts her hand on Connor's arm. "Come with me—I want to introduce you to some people who actually matter."

For a moment, his eyes don't leave mine. Even as he turns to follow his sister, he keeps them locked on me. I want to shrink away from him, but I stiffen and stand up even straighter as I stare back at him.

Finally, he turns away, and it feels like a huge weight has been lifted from my shoulders. I exhale hard and spin back around, desperate now to find Steph.

She was with him—I know she was. Even Jess admitted that they were together.

I have to find my sister.

TWENTY-TWO

AIMEE

I can't find my cell phone.

We're back in our room, but no matter where I look, it's gone.

Is it panic over what I think Hannah knows that's making it difficult for me to find it? I've dug through everything I brought, even looked through Dale's stuff. And although my hands keep shaking when I think about my run-in with Hannah, I don't think it's stress that's keeping me from finding my phone.

I think Hannah took it. And in doing so, she cut me off from my friends and made it harder for me to get out of here.

She knows everything. Or at least she thinks she does.

I turn to sit down on my bed while I think things through, but my eyes snag on the coverlet.

It's rumpled like someone was sitting there. The fabric is messed up, but just a bit, just so you'd only recognize something was wrong if you were really looking.

Hannah. It had to be her. And yes, I know it's wrong of me to get upset about her being in my space when I was poking around in hers, but I'm not just upset.

I'm scared.

I'd been so cocky before we came on this trip. I'd felt in control, but what she said to me makes me realize that I'm not. Not only am I not in control, but she is.

I have to get out of here. Screw sticking it to the two of them. Screw the huge middle finger I was going to wave at Dale after we got home. All my big plans of revenge sound so petty now.

I need to call an Uber or a taxi or something. Beg or hitchhike my way to the airport. If I can find my phone, I can call for a ride and get out of here. No matter what, though, I'm not spending another night under the same roof as Hannah.

But my phone is missing, and that makes leaving a bit more complicated. I wonder where she has it stashed.

Yes, I was poking around in her room and belongings, but that was for survival. Her being in my space and digging through my things is a threat.

I stand in the middle of our hotel room, my hands on my hips, and survey the space. As nice as this hotel is, the rooms aren't huge, and there's not any secret spot where my phone could be hiding. I've already checked between the cushions in the loveseat and looked under the furniture. I didn't put it in the in-room safe when we arrived, which is something Dale always tells me to do, and now I'm regretting it.

"You don't really need your phone right now, if you think about it." Dale comes up behind me and wraps his arms around me. "You can always use mine if you have to call or text anyone."

I stiffen and force myself to relax. His hands on me no longer feel nice, even though I want to lean into him for comfort. His touch is an assault that I have to prepare myself for. Part of me wants to curl into him, to have his arms band around me for support, but I can't do that. I won't *let* myself do that, not when he hurt me as badly as he did. The pain I'm in right now threatens to tear me open if I allow myself to need him.

I haven't told him I want to leave. As much as I'd love someone's help in getting out of here, I think the best option right now is just to go. Wait until he's distracted, wait until I'm not with the group, and bail.

Because I know Dale, and he hates it when things don't go according to plan. He'll be upset if I try to leave, and I kinda wonder if he'd try to stop me.

And then there's Hannah.

She knows. I have no idea how, not when my secret has been hidden for so long, not when even the police couldn't figure out what happened, but she knows, and she could tell everyone. Ruin my entire life. I'd lose my job. Everything.

I need to get away from her. No, it won't solve the issue completely, but it will allow me some room to think. I need space to clear my head, to come up with a plan of action, to decide how to handle her.

Because she's no longer just the woman sleeping with my fiancé.

She's now a direct threat to me.

Maybe this is my punishment—not just for what I did when I was younger, but for coming on this trip, being willing to pretend like things with Dale are fine so I can rip the rug out from under him later. Am I petty? Maybe I am.

Should I have let it all go and not come on this trip? Probably. But I wanted to shock him, to see him hurt a little like he hurt me.

But maybe, by doing that, I brought this on myself. I'm being punished. I know I haven't always been the best person in the world, but I really don't think that I deserve this. The reason I became a nurse? It's not because I have an affinity for taking vitals and long shifts at the hospital. I did it to atone for what I did, to turn my life around. Nursing was never my dream, but it was the only way for me to better myself and make up for what happened.

I may be a better person than I was when I was younger, but that won't protect me now, not if Hannah is after me. I have to get out of Miami. I have to put some space between me and Hannah so I can think things through.

But until then, I have to learn more about her. Isn't that the advice—to know your enemy? The more information I have on her, the better off I might be. The better I'll be able to handle everything being thrown my way.

"You're right, as always," I tell him. "I don't need my phone. I'm fine."

Not. I'm not fine. I'm terrified.

We fall silent for a moment, then he clears his throat. "Hey, about that woman on the beach... I promise you, Aimee, I've never seen her before in my life. I don't know why she thought acting like we had a child together was a good idea, but she's crazy."

I pause for a moment. "Dale, she knew your name. And the bar you love."

"I know." He runs his hand through his hair. "Maybe she's a stalker? Or I'm going to be on some terrible YouTube prank show. But I promise you, I messed up once. But no more than that."

Liar. Instead of accusing him of that, however, I force myself to turn in his arms and smile up at him, although I can't make myself kiss him. That's going too far right now, and I don't want this conversation to continue. He must be feeling really guilty about Margot to bring it back up again. I should be glad my plan got to him, but I can't celebrate that right now. "Thank you. I know you screwed up, but I'm still glad you chose me."

He beams at me. Flattery will get you everywhere with Dale.

"That's my girl. What do you say we head down to the

pool? I know you wanted to get fruity drinks and work on your tan, and now's a perfect time to do that."

I nod. My smile is still in place, but it feels brittle. "Sounds wonderful. And you're right—that's the plan."

I walk to my suitcase and pull out a second bikini. I'd brought the first one I had on because it makes me look amazing, and I wanted Dale to think about how good I looked after I'd dumped him. Now, though, a revenge bikini feels silly, especially if it's the same as the one Hannah has on.

How did she do that? It hits me. I posted a picture on Instagram. She must have seen it and decided to buy the exact same bikini. My stomach drops.

We change quickly, and he takes my hand in his after we leave our room. "Mai tai?"

"Mai tai," I confirm.

As we walk, I think about how to handle what's coming next. Then, before I can help myself, the words are spilling out of me. "Hey, tell me more about Hannah. She pulled that little stunt with the pregnancy test, so I know she thinks she has a sense of humor, but tell me more. Was she voted class clown in senior superlatives? What is she really like?" I pause, weighing my next words. "And why were you two hugging?"

Did he stutter step? Just for a minute, his cool-guy façade dropped, and I felt fear race through him. Just as quickly, though, he composes himself.

"The hugging? No big deal. She goes through these times when she gets kinda depressed, and hugs help. But otherwise, yeah, she's pretty funny. And she works out all the time. She moved here from North Carolina a few years ago."

I'm from North Carolina.

Fear grows in me.

You know, I hoped for a moment that she was bluffing, that she had no idea what happened in my past, but that was wishful thinking.

"Where in North Carolina?"

"Near Asheville." He gives my hand a squeeze while we wait for the elevator. "Why? You planning a trip?"

"No, but if she's from near Asheville, and I'm from near Asheville, maybe the two of us ran into each other at some point in our lives."

"Hmm. Maybe."

"Do you know where she went to high school?"

He laughs. "No, Aimee, I don't. Why the sudden intense interest in Hannah? You got a crush or something?"

"No." I force myself to laugh in response. "Just want to get to know your friends better."

"You're sweet."

There's an edge to his words, a clear sign that he's finished with this conversation. Rather than pushing him more, which will only frustrate him, I drop it.

The elevator dings, and we step inside. We're both silent, and while I can't read Dale's mind, I have a pretty good idea what he's probably thinking.

He's worried I'm going to find out the truth about the two of them sleeping together. He's beating himself up for letting me catch the two of them hugging. He's afraid that she'll say something, or I'll ask the right question, and someone will let it slip.

Like Mitch.

Mitch.

I'd dismissed him when we first met, but maybe I should pay more attention to him. He's obviously close to Hannah, and he might be willing to tell me more about her. Besides, I've seen the way he smiles at me, how he looks at me. He seems like he likes me, like he would be on my side if I needed help. But without knowing for sure, I have to be careful. Keep my guard up.

I can't discount the fact that Hannah seems to know what I did when I was back in North Carolina. If she's from there, chances are good she put two and two together. What I can't figure out is why she didn't go to the police with her information, and why the police weren't the ones to figure it out.

What's so special about Hannah that she'd be the one to suss out my secret?

And what are the chances that she knows what I did, and she's not in my life by accident?

TWENTY-THREE

HANNAH

The only thing better than lying out in the sun on this gorgeous day is being next to Dale knowing that he's probably dying trying to decide how to keep me away from Aimee.

Of course I wasn't going to put my towel anywhere but right by the happy couple. And it wasn't like I was going to stretch out beside Aimee. Dale, on the other hand?

Fair game.

The smell of sunscreen and tanning oil hits me, and I take another sip of my drink as I try to think through what I know to be true.

Aimee took my pearl necklace. The more I think about it, the more I'm convinced she did that as retribution for the pregnancy test stunt. But that's fine—I'll take the licking and keep on ticking. She might think she has the upper hand, but that doesn't bother me.

Things are set into motion here.

I'm still in control, even though I did show a bit of my hand when I let her know that I'm onto her. It was stupid, but I couldn't help myself. I hate her. I've hated her for years. When the opportunity to tell her that I'm onto her presented itself, I couldn't pass it up.

And yes, I tried to clue Dale in to the fact that Aimee stealing my necklace is a dead giveaway that she knows about our affair, but he couldn't wrap his mind around it. He thinks he's so smart. That he can have his cake and eat it too. He's always in charge at work and thinks that control bleeds over into his personal life. You know what? Maybe it does for some people, but not him. Not in this situation. I recognized the threat right away.

Well, let him be oblivious for a little while longer. That's fine.

I turn to look at Dale. As relaxed as most people are here by the pool, he sure looks wound tight. What the man needs is a massage to help him chill out.

He has his drink balanced on his abs, and condensation pools on his skin around it. Even though there's a nice breeze right now, he's sweating hard. I watch as he reaches up to wipe his forehead, then when he puts his hand back down on the towel, I reach out and take it.

His eyes fly open. Slowly, like that will prevent what's happening from continuing, he turns to look at me. Gosh, he really is hot.

Would I have started our affair if he hadn't been as gorgeous as he is? Yeah, of course I would have. But it was my luck that he's pushing six feet, that his thick blond hair makes him look like a surfer, that he has blue eyes that almost match mine.

And don't get me started on his muscles.

I squeeze his hand, slowly sliding my fingers between his. When we make eye contact, I lift my other hand to my mouth, put a finger over my lips, shush him, then wink.

He turns bright red and looks away from me.

Ahh, he's checking to see if Aimee has noticed. Ever the gentleman, Dale. She isn't turned towards us, but the oversized sunglasses she has on makes it tricky to tell exactly what she's looking at.

I watch the slow rise and fall of her chest, and it hits me—I think she's asleep.

Dale must have the same thought because he slowly turns back to me. Carefully, he tugs his hand away from mine, but I tighten my grip. To really drive the point home, I shake my head and give him a little smile.

"Hannah," he whispers, barely moving his mouth as he does. "Let go."

"No." I whisper the word back, but it feels loud, like it's going to be enough to get Aimee's attention and clue her in to what's going on right next to her. "I miss being close to you."

He yanks my hand harder, but I still don't let go.

On the other side of Aimee, I see Mitch walking towards us. Dale is probably afraid of him saying something, but I'm not.

I may not have Mitch completely under control, but no way would he cross me. He has his secrets too.

"Hannah, now." Dale jerks his hand away from mine. This time, he manages to free his fingers from my grip, but he pulls too hard and smacks his right hand into his drink. The cup is slippery and pops out of his grip.

I don't have to watch it to know what's going to happen.

"Oh, come on!" Aimee yells and sits up.

Slowly, Dale turns and looks, confirming what I already knew to be true.

She's soaked. His drink landed on her stomach and splashed all over her. She sits up, disgusted, and raises her sunglasses to look at him. Her eyes flick from Dale to me, then back to him.

"I'm sorry," he says. "I must have fallen asleep, and I jerked in my sleep. I didn't mean to."

"Right. Of course you didn't." She stands and uses her hands to wipe some of the drink from her stomach. She flicks it away from her, not noticing when it splashes onto him. "This is disgusting."

It's not all that bad, but she's already on edge, and it's clear that Dale just wants to smooth things over with her. I keep quiet, my eyes wide as I soak it all in.

"Let me get napkins," Dale offers, but she shakes her head.

"I'm going to go for a dip," Aimee announces. She runs her hands across her head as she speaks, as if she's smoothing down flyaways, then glances at the packed pool and frowns. "Just... clean this up, will you? I don't want to come back to a sticky mess."

"I can do that," he says, at the same time I pipe up.

"Don't you worry about a thing, Aimee. I'll help Dale."

Aimee's eyes are blocked by her sunglasses, but I can imagine the look she's giving her fiancé. Instead of replying, however, she turns and stalks towards the ocean, bypassing the pool. I watch her go for a moment, but then put my hand on Dale's arm to get his attention.

"I'm so sorry about that," I say. "It was an accident."

"An accident?" His voice rises, and he stops himself. When he speaks again, his voice is lower, his words quieter. Meant only for me. "You wouldn't let go of my hand. What did you think was going to happen?"

I grin. "I don't know, but it was kinda funny. She's totally soaked. But why did she freak out like that?"

"Probably because she didn't want my drink dumped all over her."

"Prude."

"Hannah. Come on." He groans and closes his eyes. "It doesn't have to be like this. We can all just... be friends. You and I agreed that we'd move on from the affair. That it was over and we were both okay with it being over."

"You and me? We'll never be over," I tell him. When he doesn't respond, I continue. "You want us to be friends?

Friends don't sleep together. They don't text all hours of the night, and they certainly don't look at me the way you do," I say.

"But you're with Mitch." He stares at me like he can't believe what I'm saying. "You two are together, and you seem happy."

Happy? No. I was happy with my boyfriend before Aimee took him from me.

"I'd be happier with you," I begin, but before I can say anything else, Mitch walks up.

He's holding a drink and a plate of nachos and looks utterly confused. "Where'd Aimee go?"

"For a dip," Dale tells him. "I, uh, I spilled my drink on her, and she's going to get clean."

Mitch glances down at the mess on her chair and towel, then hands Dale the napkins he's carrying. "I'll go see if she's okay."

Something blooms on his face—hope?—but it's gone again in an instant. I roll my eyes.

"No, she wants to be alone," Dale tells him, but Mitch doesn't listen. Instead, he turns from the two of us and hurries after Aimee.

Dale really needs to clean up this mess, but instead he sits still, his eyes locked on Mitch and Aimee.

She doesn't slow down, but he catches up with her before she reaches the water. He puts his arm around her shoulders and slows her down.

Dale stiffens as Aimee turns to look at Mitch.

Interesting.

I think back to how willing Mitch had been to pretend to be my boyfriend. Not like he really had a choice. Even if I didn't have... leverage, I'm sure I could have come up with something to ensure Mitch stood by me.

Men are so willing to believe whatever they want to, aren't

they? All you have to do is lead them in the direction you want them to go.

"Dale," I say, but he still doesn't turn to look at me. I reach out and squeeze his shoulder, but his eyes are locked on Mitch and Aimee. I follow his gaze, and what I see is so surprising I gasp.

They're talking. It's hard to tell, with the sun in my eyes, but it looks like Aimee is happy about Mitch's arm being around her. That thought is like a punch to the gut.

He likes her. That much is obvious.

How far is he willing to go to save her?

TWENTY-FOUR

AIMEE

I know shrugging Mitch's arm away is the right thing to do, but part of me likes the thought that Dale might look up, might see his friend's arm around me, might feel a modicum of the pain he's made me feel.

So I don't move away from him. But I don't step any closer to him either. It's not like I'm encouraging him. I'm just not discouraging him.

"How'd you really get so sticky?" he asks, finally moving away from me. A breeze blows between us, and I shiver at the feeling of it on my wet skin. "Did Hannah do that?"

"Hannah? No," I say, even though I can't shake the feeling that she was somehow involved in Dale spilling his drink on me. "It was an accident. Dale just... spilled it."

He clucks his tongue. "Only on you though."

I nod, and he sighs.

"She's harmless," he tells me. "I know Hannah seems tough and likes it when people are a little afraid of her, but it's all bluster. Believe me."

"It doesn't seem like bluster.'

"I get that, but Hannah... she's loyal to a fault. If she's your friend, she's your friend for life. If she's against you..."

"She's against you forever."

"Something like that. I know she doesn't seem like a girl's girl, but she is deep down. You just have to give her a chance."

I feel my face burn. "Whatever, I was just going to go for a swim," I tell him, purposefully walking towards the water. He'll follow—I'm sure he will. And that's good because I want to learn more about him without him rambling on about how great Hannah is. He could be a good ally, but I have to poke around first and make sure he's willing to be on my side.

Just like I thought would happen, Mitch walks quickly to catch up, then joins me as I wade into the water. It's refreshing and cool. The sunlight glints off the surface like it's made of broken glass, and I shield my eyes with my hand as I look out.

From here, standing in it, the ocean seems never-ending. I know there is an end, just like I know there are boats and submarines, sharks and fish, but it feels like I could be swept out to sea, could float forever, could never be found.

And I guess I could. But I intend on walking away from this nightmare of a weekend in one piece. If something were to happen to me, I'm not going to go gently into the night.

"You said that Hannah's a girl's girl, but she hates me," I announce, turning slightly so I can see the expression on his face. "She's made it clear, so why would your girlfriend loathe me like she does?" It's a loaded question, one I'm not sure he'll answer truthfully, but I want to know what he knows and if he'll come clean with me.

I have to know if he's on my side, or if I'm all alone.

"Hannah..." he says, then pauses. I can't help the fact that my mind fills in the blank for him.

Hannah... hates everyone.

Hannah... is an idiot.

Hannah... is not my girlfriend.

I don't know if that last one is true, but it would explain the separate beds. Still, it creates a lot more questions.

Are they really dating? Because they said they were, and they act like it, but now... Now I'm not so sure.

Why are they here? What is Hannah's plan? This is what I really need to know.

"She's difficult to get to know. But once you know her, she's on your side for life."

"How long have you been dating?" That's not the question I'm asking, not really. What I'm asking Mitch is if he's going to lie to me, if he's going to go along with the crazy story that the two of them are a couple when it's painfully obvious to me that they might not be.

"Dating?" He's silent for a moment, then he scrubs his hand down his cheek and chin before sighing. "We're not. That was a lie."

I knew it. Rather than jumping up and fist-pumping the air like I want to, I take a deep breath. Then another. It's only when I think I've calmed down enough to not make a total idiot of myself that I allow myself to speak.

"Why would you two lie about something like that? You both made it seem pretty clear that you were together." My voice doesn't shake, and I'm proud of myself for that.

His eyes flick to me, then he looks back at the horizon. "Hannah's great at getting what she wants, but it was just a stupid lie. A joke. I'm sorry. You deserve better than that."

I nod. My throat is tight. I don't know Mitch, not really, but it's validating to hear from one of Dale's best friends that I deserve better than what I'm going through. Because I think he's talking about more than just Hannah lying to me and Dale spilling a drink on me. I'm pretty sure he's talking about the two of them cheating, even if he won't come right out and say it.

As to why they lied about the two of them dating? It has to be because she thought she could mess with me. The pregnancy test, the journal of bad poetry, the matching necklace? Not to mention being here at the same time we are.

Hannah is dangerous. Again, I think about leaving, but despite the fact that she's dangerous, I want to see this through. Dale broke my heart. I loved him, and he deserves to feel some of the pain I did.

"Did you know about Dale cheating on me?" The question is out of my mouth before I can stop it, before I even have time to think about it. It's out and hanging in the air between us, and Mitch's mouth falls open like he can't believe I'd ask something like that in the first place. "Did you know he had an affair?"

I don't mention Hannah. If Mitch knows about the affair, then I'm pretty sure he knows who it was with. But it's entirely possible that he's in the dark, and I want to see how he responds to my question.

"Dale told me you two had broken up," Mitch says. He works his fingers together, and I can't tell if it's because he's lying to me or because he's torn up about what he's saying.

"He said that?" My heart pounds harder at the new lie. I shouldn't be surprised, but it still hurts. "We never broke up. Never. He just... stepped out on me. And Hannah..."

"Hannah what?"

The words won't come. I physically can't make myself say them.

Mitch's face twists in pain. He inhales sharply and drops his hands to his side as he turns to look at me. Behind me, some kids have entered the ocean. They're screaming and carrying on, splashing each other and yelling.

It feels surreal, to be having such a terrible, life-changing conversation with someone I barely know while the rest of the world is not only moving on, but enjoying itself.

"You don't deserve this," he repeats, more to himself than to me. I get the feeling he's talking to himself, like he's working up to saying something big to me, and I bite my tongue. My natural inclination is to keep talking, to try to get people to see things from my point of view, but I stay quiet.

"You're a better person than her," he finally says.

This is unexpected. Never once did I think that Mitch, of all people, would suddenly be on my side.

I swallow hard and try to sound innocent when I speak. "Who?"

He doesn't skip a beat. "Hannah. I can't believe she was the other woman. You're better than that. You deserve someone who treats you like a princess."

"I've never wanted to be a princess. They're too often in distress." Which is, I realize, exactly what I am.

"A queen then. Dale is not that guy."

When I speak, my voice is still small. "I thought he was. I really did, Mitch. I just wanted a real happy ending."

"I know. And you'll get one."

Again he turns in on himself, obviously thinking through something. I'm so tempted to ask him what's going through his mind, but I don't want to interrupt him. Sometimes, when people are close to figuring something out or making a decision, you want to leave them to it. Want to let them work it out on their own.

Finally, he speaks again. "I want to help you." Each word is loaded with conviction.

Excitement rises in me, but I fight to keep it off my face. "Help me do what? Find my phone? Because it's missing. Get out of here? I'd love nothing more than to be home right now." The words spill from my lips. I wonder how my girls are doing getting me moved out of the apartment. I should be with them, nursing a pint of Ben & Jerry's, sobbing over Elle Woods and Warner Huntington III until she learns that she's worth so much more than the value a man assigns her.

And I will be. Soon. After I get my revenge.

Mitch clears his throat, yanking me out of my thoughts. "Do

you remember meeting me a few months ago at that party Dale took you to?"

I frown, thinking, then shake my head.

"Well, I remember you. Not surprised you don't remember me. You didn't know then that Dale was going to be who he is, but I couldn't take my eyes off you." He pauses. "That doesn't matter now because I'm on your side, and I'm going to help you make sure Dale gets what he deserves. Will you let me?"

I don't have to think twice about my response.

Shock floods me, but I fight to keep it from my voice. "Hell yes."

TWENTY-FIVE

Then

The fresh air outside is bracing as I push through the crowd and onto the front porch. Even admitting this makes me feel like a terrible person, but part of me wants to go back inside, find Josh, discover if what Jess was saying about him is true.

But I can't do that without knowing where Steph is.

What if she's hurt? What if Connor did something to her, and she's crying and afraid to come back into the party?

If he did something to her, if she's hurt... I'll never forgive myself.

I push the thought of Josh out of my mind. With it, I get rid of Jess's face, of how she insinuated that she'd slept with my boyfriend. That's something I'm going to have to deal with eventually, but right now is not the time.

"Steph!" I scream her name into the cool night air.

There are some people out smoking on the lawn, and they turn to look at me, their eyebrows cocked in question.

"Hey, have you seen Steph?" I glance from one to the other, hoping that I'm going to recognize one of them. Just as panic has almost reached a screaming point in my mind, my eyes snag on the last guy. "Daniel. You have pre-calc with us."

He takes a drag on his cigarette, then tosses the butt to the ground. "Yeah?"

"Did you see Steph come out here?"

"She was with some dude," he says. "They went out to the woods."

"The woods?" My heart sinks. The woods bordering this huge piece of property are thick and almost impenetrable, except for the path Josh's folks cut into them that leads to a swimming hole.

"Yeah, but they weren't gone too long before that guy came back." Daniel takes a step closer to me, the expression on his face difficult to read. "Do you know him? I've never seen him before, and Steph..."

He doesn't have to finish his sentence.

"She didn't come back with him, did she?"

He shakes his head.

I don't wait to hear what else he's going to say before I take off towards the woods. I'm in heels and a miniskirt, so it's not like I'm prepared to go for a hike, but I don't have a choice.

Not when something bad might happen to Steph.

I hit the woods at a run. "Steph!" When I call her, it doesn't echo back to me. The woods swallow her name.

Even though there's a full moon, the trees around me are so thick that it's almost impossible to see the path again. I fumble my phone out of my pocket and call Steph, but there's no answer. I don't bother leaving a message and instead turn on the flashlight, cursing the fact that I forgot to charge my phone before coming here.

The little battery symbol pops up on my screen, letting me know that I'm on borrowed time, but I ignore it.

I race into the woods as quickly as possible, but because I have to watch each step, I'm sure I'm not going as fast as I think.

Every root, every rock, every pile of leaves holds a trap that could trip me, break my heel, or break my ankle.

I have to be careful.

But I also have to be fast.

"Steph!" It's creepy calling her name, but even worse when I don't. No animals move, probably all driven to be still and quiet by the way I'm crashing down the path. I don't know what would be better—hearing them in the woods and knowing I'm not alone, or the silence that tells me they're watching me.

The path splits, and I slide to a stop. As I do, I roll my right foot, and my heel pops off. I swear, then yank both shoes off and drop them on the ground. It's only when my flashlight is pointed straight down that I see the skid in the dirt.

I didn't do that.

Some of the fallen leaves have been brushed to the side. Now, I'm no tracker, but I'd bet my boots this is the way Connor came with Steph. Without giving it another thought, I tear down the path to the right.

I thought I'd be at the swimming hole by now, but maybe you have to take the fork to the left to reach it.

If he didn't take her to the swimming hole, where did he take her?

I'm still running as fast as possible; my feet are getting torn up by little sticks, but I don't stop. I don't slow down.

My plan is to keep running until I find Steph, then drag her out of here, get back in the Jeep, and leave. Forget Josh. Forget Jess. And whatever Connor did to Steph, we'll get through that together, but first I have to find her.

My body has other plans, however. As much as I'd like to keep running, there's a stitch in my side that I can no longer ignore. I stop, panting, and press my hand hard into my right side.

I'm not athletic. I don't jump around in a teeny skirt during football games, I'm not on the track team, and I've never been a good swimmer. I maintain my figure through minimal meals, not maximum effort, and that's catching up with me right now.

I pant, trying to hold my breath for as long as possible between inhales and exhales, and I feel my heart start to slow down. It's a relief, and I straighten back up. There. I feel a bit better, but even if it comes back, I have to keep fighting, have to find Steph.

When I start moving again, I'm walking, but at least I'm moving forward. I have my phone's flashlight angled down and in front of me, but suddenly I freeze.

Is the light growing dimmer? Without thinking about what I'm doing, I turn the screen back on to check my battery life. There's a flash of light as the screen clicks on, then the entire thing goes dark.

"Crap," I mutter, then mash the buttons on the side of my phone like that will cause it to turn back on. "No, no, no, come on, I need you!" I smack it against my thigh, but it remains dead.

Tears burn my eyes. I sniffle as I push the phone back into my pocket and slowly turn in a circle. It only takes my eyes a moment to adjust to how dark it is, but even though I'm now used to the dark, I can still just barely make out the shapes of the trees around me.

It's more of an awareness that the trees are there than me actually being able to pick out individual ones. Continuing down the path when I can't see a thing is stupid. No way will I be able to find Steph if she's not right on the path. And what if I get close to the water and slip?

A shiver races up my spine. Was it this chilly up by the house? I rub my hands up and down my arms and try not to cry, but a tear works its way down my cheek.

Angry, I brush it away.

"Steph?" While I was calling her with my whole chest just a few minutes ago, her name now comes out in more of whisper. I want her to hear me, but I don't think I'm brave enough to call her as loud as I need to.

"Steph." A little louder this time. I sniffle hard and wipe my nose on the back of my arm. "Steph, please, I don't know where you are, or what you're doing, but if you could just come out, we can head back to the house and get out of here."

There's a crash in the woods behind me, and I whip around. My eyes are as wide as they'll go, like that's going to let in more light, but I still can barely see anything.

Another crash.

I sink to the ground, crouching in an effort to make myself as small as possible. Could it be a bear? We have bears here in the mountains. Normally they don't cause a problem, but what if there's a cub? What if I get in between the mom and the cub?

Terror makes my muscles hurt. I inch over to the side of the trail, my hands out in front of me. The first touch of bark makes me recoil in fear, but then I push forward, feeling my way around the tree.

I have to get off the trail.

I have to hide.

A bear could mess me up, and nobody would know what happened to me until it was too late.

Another crash, this one closer, and I bite my lower lip and press my cheek against the rough bark. The pain grounds me, keeps me from crying out.

At least until a flashlight sweeps over me.

TWENTY-SIX

HANNAH

Dale's torn up over Aimee walking off with Mitch, but that's the least of his worries. He just doesn't know it yet.

He should be grateful to me for getting rid of her. If he knew what she was really like, he wouldn't want to share a bed with her. I'm so ready for this to all be over, for me to finally put the two of them in my past.

Not that there will be very much of Aimee to leave in the rearview. Not when I'm finished with her.

We're sitting where Aimee left us, but he's moved over to put some space between the two of us. I can tell he's thinking. He does this thing where he tightens his jaw periodically when he's trying to work through a problem he's facing.

Tighten.

Relax.

Tighten.

Relax.

Like a jaw workout will kick his brain into high gear and help him decide what he needs to do.

"Dale, I think we should talk." I wait a moment for him to turn and look at me, but when he doesn't, I speak again. "I'm serious. You and I have a history, and I want to make sure we have a future."

Barf. I want to make it very, very clear to him that I'm sticking around for the long run, even though that couldn't be further from the truth. I'm counting down the hours until this is over, but as long as he feels some of the pain he put me through, it will be worth it.

He doesn't respond. Abruptly, he stands, his eyes still locked on Aimee.

"What are you doing?"

Without speaking, he spins in the other direction and stalks away from me. He's left his towel, his empty glass... his phone.

"Where are you going?" I call after him but keep one eye on his phone. "Are you getting another drink? I want a rum and Coke. Dale. Dale!"

In response, he raises his hand but still doesn't turn around. *Jerk.*

When he gets to the bar, I reach over and grab his phone. All the times that we've been together, all the long workouts at the box, and he's consistently been careful not to leave his phone sitting around where I might pick it up.

When I tap on the screen, I'm not surprised to find that it's locked. I consider trying various combinations to see if I can guess his PIN, but what do I think this is? A thriller novel? That never happens in real life.

Instead, I open his camera and take a few selfies, making sure that my tits look as good as possible in all of them. There's no way to know if Aimee will open his camera roll and see them, but a girl can hope.

With a sigh, I put his phone back down on his towel and turn to see what he's doing. He's still at the bar, and I grin to myself when I see him turn around, two glasses in his hands.

That's what I need. Just a little something-something to take the edge off. Keep me feeling loose. The more I try to control what's happening, the greater the chance that I screw up and let this all fall apart.

I need to take a deep breath. Take a sip. Focus. Remember why I'm here. I've become so intent on torturing Aimee that I lost sight of my end goal. Not to put Aimee in prison, but to put her in the ground. The cops had their chance to lock her up, and they didn't do it, so it's my turn now.

When Dale sits next to me, he practically shoves the drink at me. Before I take it, I let my fingers trace along his.

"I appreciate you taking care of me." I take a sip of the drink and moan. When I look at him, he's closed his eyes. Remembering the last time I made that sound, maybe?

He clears his throat. "I didn't," he tells me, pointing over my shoulder. "He did."

I turn to look over my shoulder at the bartender. Even from this distance, I can tell how attractive he is. "Did he really? Well, that's sweet of him." Not a chance do I believe the bartender sent me a free drink. One, I've been a bartender before, and sending people free drinks only results in them wanting more in the future.

And for another thing, this place is crawling with hotties in bikinis. No smart bartender is going to send free drinks to someone hanging out with a member of the opposite sex. It's a waste of time.

When Dale speaks again, I drag my eyes away from the bar to give him my attention. "What did you say?"

His voice is lower when he repeats himself. "Where's Mitch?"

"Mitch?"

"Mitch. And Aimee. Where are they?"

I frown at him. "I don't know. Still in the ocean? Do I look like your fiancée's keeper?"

"You're infuriating, you know that? You don't have to be like this. We agreed we'd let things go back to how they were before... Everything. I want to make things work with Aimee."

It's probably too soon, but I reach out and trail my fingernails up his arm.

Swatting my hand away, he says, "I love Aimee. It would be great if you'd accept that and back off."

Yep, too soon.

"You didn't love Aimee very much when we were together."

He takes a deep breath. Closes his eyes.

"Just because you're here with her doesn't mean the two of us can't have a future."

"Like I told you. You and I are over. She has no idea that you're the woman I cheated with, and I want to keep it that way."

No. No way does she not know. Is he really that clueless or just desperate to think she is?

Dale might want to believe that Aimee is in the dark, but I don't think that's true. She's a lot smarter than he thinks.

He stares at me, but I don't immediately respond. When it's clear he's not going to keep talking, I finally speak.

"Dale—"

"No. Stop it, and tell me the truth. Did you take her cell phone?"

"Her cell phone? No. No, I did not." I do think back to when I saw it inside Mitch's suitcase though.

"It's missing. I thought you might have taken it."

"I don't have it in for her, if that's what you're worried about. Chances are good she probably set it down somewhere and doesn't remember where. We've all done that." I cross my arms as I wait for a rebuttal.

"No, not Aimee. She's more savvy than that."

I sigh. He's really head over heels for her, isn't he? Well, there's one thing I could say to him that would help him get over her really quickly, but I bite my tongue. *Not yet.* "Not savvy enough to keep you from falling into bed with me."

He glares at me. "Get over it, Hannah. What was going on between the two of us? It's over."

"You think you know her," I fire back. "But you've got your head in the sand about her, Dale. If you just listened to me—"

"Enough." The word comes out in a hiss. "Enough. Aimee is twice the woman you could ever be. I know you hate her because you want what she has, but you have to give it up. Give *me* up."

I laugh. I can't help it. It's so insane to me that Dale really thinks this is all about him. But of course he would. He doesn't know his fiancée like I do. If he did, just looking at her would chill his blood.

"You don't really think the only reason I hate her is because she's engaged to you, do you?" I move closer to him. I want all of his attention on me. He could turn and try to get away, but I want him focused. I want him to listen.

I want him to finally see Aimee for who she really is.

"Yes, I do. I think you're envious, and—"

"Let me stop you right there." I take a deep breath to steel myself for what I'm about to say. The bombshell I'm about to drop. "Just how well do you really think you know her?"

He doesn't answer, but that's fine.

When I tell him the truth about Aimee, about her past and who she is, he jerks back like I slapped him.

Good. I'd be surprised if I were about to marry a murderer too.

TWENTY-SEVEN

HANNAH

"You're full of it." He's breathing hard and has leaned back to put some space between the two of us. "A murderer? Aimee? Not a chance."

I don't immediately respond. The best thing for me to do right now is let what I told him sink in.

"Aimee wouldn't hurt a fly," he continues. "She's good. Kind. She saves lives. She cares for people at their worst. How dare you talk about her like this? You... you're pathetic, you know that?"

"I'm not talking about the Aimee you know. I'm talking about the younger Aimee. She's not who you think she is, Dale." My palms are sweating, and I move to wipe them on my shorts before I realize I'm in my bikini. Instead, I wipe them on the towel under me. "You have to trust me. Can you do that?"

"Can I trust you?" he hisses. "Give me a freaking break, Hannah. You're the reason I hurt Aimee so much in the first place. Why would I trust anything you're saying right now?"

Indignation blooms hot and fast in my chest. "*I'm* the reason you hurt Aimee? No way—you don't get to put the blame on me like that. If I remember correctly, which I do, it takes two to tango, and you were a most willing dance partner."

His cheeks are flushed. "You came onto me. Don't rewrite history." He runs a hand through his hair. "Knowing you, that's probably what you're doing when you run your mouth about Aimee. Are you just mad that I chose her? Is that why you're lying like this?"

"I'm not lying. She killed someone, Dale."

"She would have told me. You're just lashing out." He smirks and gives a little sigh like he couldn't be more pleased with himself for figuring out what's really going on.

It's so typically him—so typically *male*—that I have to fight to keep from rolling my eyes. "You don't believe me?" He shakes his head. "Fine. You don't have to believe me, but ask her."

Silence. I know he's thinking through what I just said and trying to decide if he should call me on my bluff, but he finally chuckles.

"You know what? I think I will. And she's going to tell me you're crazy." He was staying calm, but now his eyes are wide, and he's breathing hard. "You need to stop. I don't know what you think you're going to accomplish by turning me against her, but give it up."

"I only want you to know the truth about the woman you say you want to marry, because she did something terrible once before, and she'll do something terrible again."

And I'm going to kill her. But he doesn't need to know that.

"Well, guess what. I do know her. And I love her. And yes, Hannah, we had fun together, even though we shouldn't have. You and I have no future together. We never did! You were a mistake."

"A fun mistake," I point out.

He glares at me. "As I was saying, you and I don't have a future. Aimee and I do."

He slams his fist into his open hand to drive home the point, and I suddenly hate him. Not that hating him is decreasing my ire towards Aimee, but I suddenly see him for what he is.

A jerk. A loser. Someone willing to hurt the person they claim to love. Yes, Aimee deserves to be punished, but what about Dale? Why not him too?

"Fine. You don't want to listen to the truth? Be stubborn and stupid, Dale. I hope you two have a very long and happy life together."

Except it won't be, will it? Not happy.

And certainly not long.

TWENTY-EIGHT

AIMEE

Mitch wanting to help me get back at Dale isn't something I ever could have seen coming, but it's not a gift horse I'm going to look in the mouth.

Who better to bring a man to his knees than his friend?

"I think Hannah might have taken my phone," I say with a pout. The two of us have left the water and walked out of the line of sight of Dale and Hannah.

"Why do you think that?" When he frowns, a furrow appears between his brows. He's not an ugly guy, not by a long shot, but I really hope he's not looking to help me because he thinks I'm a prize to be won.

I'm not the prize, and I'm certainly not some damsel in distress waiting on my white knight to come swooping in to save me. I'm the knight, and I'll save myself.

"It's missing." I pause, unsure of how much of my hand to reveal to him. I don't know how much I can trust him, not yet, not when I'm not entirely sure of his loyalty to Dale.

I'll have to test it, that's all.

"If Hannah thought I was poking around in her room, she'd freak out on me, but I need to know if that's where my phone is.

If she took it, she would have hidden it in her stuff. I need it back." It kills me to drag this out and not tell him exactly why I want my phone, but I pause again, this time to chew my lower lip.

Men are all the same. They like to feel like providers. They like feeling in control, like the women in their lives need them.

Mitch's eyes flick to my mouth. "I can look for you. Is that what you'd like?" He sounds eager. "All you have to do is ask."

"Will you? Will you look for me?" I glance up at him from beneath my eyelashes and blink at him. "It would mean so much, especially when I'm not sure where it could be, or if Hannah is trying to do something to sabotage me. I mean, she slept with my fiancé, so who knows what else she's willing to do." My voice rises and cracks.

And the Emmy goes to... me. Obviously.

"I'll look for you." His eyes flick from side to side before he stares at me again. "If I find it—"

"I want it."

"I'm on it." He gives me a nod, then reaches out and takes my hand. I let him hold it before giving him a squeeze and pulling my hand back. I feel bad about using him like this, but I don't think I have a choice.

"Thank you," I whisper. "I'm going back to where we were all lying out. If Dale thought we were working together..." I let my voice trail off.

"He won't." Mitch rolls his shoulders back, and I have to fight to keep from rolling my eyes. "I promise you, he won't have any idea what the two of us are up to. You're not alone anymore, okay?"

"I'm glad." I take a step away from him before he gets the wrong idea and tries to take my hand again. "Just... be careful, okay? I don't want Hannah to catch on to what we're doing."

"She'll never see me coming," he promises, and I feel hope rise in me. I'm terrified to trust him, but what choice do I have right now? I have to trust him, even though I'm worried that he's not as trustworthy as I hope.

I feel eyes on me as I walk back over to where Hannah and Dale sit. "Hey," I say, dropping down onto the lounge chair next to him.

"Where'd you go?" There's accusation in his voice, an edge that wasn't there before. I stiffen, then force myself to let it roll off.

"Just went for a little walk with Mitch after we came out of the sea."

Dale looks past me. "Where did he go?"

"He said something about hitting up a vending machine," I say, but as soon as the words are out of my mouth, I know I've screwed up.

"Mitch doesn't believe in vending machines," Hannah says, sitting up and lifting her sunglasses so she can look at me. "He says they're cancer boxes."

I shrug to hide the fact that I messed up. "I misheard him then."

"Hmm." She yawns and stretches before hopping off her chair.

"Where are you going?" Dale asks.

"The room. I want to find my boyfriend." She grins at him, then offers me a smile. "Seeing the two of you lovebirds hanging out together makes me want to be with my man."

My man. Right.

"Oh, don't go." I'm on my feet before I realize what I'm doing. I don't want to run the risk of her catching Mitch going through her things while he looks for my phone.

"Let her go, Aimee," Dale says. There's a warning in his voice, and I turn to him in surprise. "She can leave if she wants to."

What did I miss? Something happened while I was talking to Mitch, but I don't know what. I nod, then sit back down.

Hannah wiggles her fingers at us in a wave, then looks at Dale one more time. "Think about what I told you." She sashays off.

My heart sinks. I watch her walk away before turning to my fiancé. "What did she tell you?" I don't want to know, but I have to find out what lies she's been telling him. Lies—or, even worse, the truth.

"Nothing, Aimee. Just drop it," Dale says, but fear grips me. He won't meet my eyes.

TWENTY-NINE

HANNAH

Dale might not believe me that his fiancée is a murderer, but that doesn't mean I'm backing off. Right now, though, I have bigger problems to worry about.

Like whether or not Aimee found anything else when she went poking around in my bag. Thank goodness I'd already used the positive pregnancy test on her because her finding it first would have really ruined the surprise.

But for her to find my pearl necklace and then take it? Yeah, that pisses me off.

I unlock our room door and let myself in, then close it behind me. Mitch's suitcase is closed and zipped, and I don't hesitate to walk over and unzip it. When I flip it open, I can't help but roll my eyes at what a pit it is inside.

At least he won't be able to tell that I dug through his crap. It was clear from the moment my eyes fell on my suitcase that Aimee had been through it, but Mitch's isn't nearly as organized as mine. He'll never know.

Still, I take my time so I don't miss any hidden pockets. After dumping all of his things onto his bed, I put the suitcase back down and run my hands along the inside of it, looking for any zippers.

I find one right away, and a flush of excitement bursts in me as I carefully unzip it. Inside: condoms.

"Oh, come on. You didn't think you were going to meet someone..." My voice trails off as I consider what I was about to say. Is it possible the condoms are from another trip?

Or did he bring them for someone specific?

"Aimee?" I whisper her name as I stare at the small foil packets. A quick check of the expiration date printed on them reveals it's four years out. That means they have to be fairly new.

No way was Mitch hoping to hook up with Aimee, right?

I zip the condoms back up in their pocket and resume my search. Without knowing what I'm looking for, it feels like I'm searching in the dark, but on the off-chance there's something here, I want to know about it.

Aimee's phone. Condoms.

Something is going on with Mitch, and I don't like it. I can handle Aimee, I can control Dale, but what if Mitch goes rogue?

That would be a problem.

When I'm finally satisfied that there isn't anything else for me to worry about in the suitcase, I pile all of his things back inside and zip it back up. Mitch won't notice if the suitcase isn't exactly where he left it, so I don't need to worry about it being perfect.

Then I turn my attention to mine.

When Mitch and I came back to the hotel room and startled Aimee in here, I only took time to quickly glance through my things. My jewelry box was thrown across the room, and my necklace was missing. But what else did she take? What else did she find?

There's no time to waste, so I dump my suitcase on the bed

and start digging through my clothes. Fear makes my movements jerky.

But did she find the small zippered pocket in the bottom of my suitcase? I hadn't even thought to check before—I was too fired up about my necklace going missing. Now, though, my hand shakes as I grab the zipper pull and slowly slide it to the right.

No way did she find this. If she had, she would have packed her bags and left immediately. Mitch hadn't wanted to drive to Florida, and I totally get it—Vermont to Florida is a long haul, and it would have been nicer to fly. As it was, we both skipped work yesterday so we could arrive at the same time as Aimee and Dale's flight.

But I really didn't have a choice about driving.

It wasn't easy getting my hands on an unregistered gun. Getting it on a plane would have been impossible.

THIRTY

I freeze, my cheek still pressed into the bark, my teeth sinking hard into my lower lip. When the light hits my face, I close my eyes—not because that will keep whoever has the flashlight from seeing me, but in a desperate bid to not see who's standing there.

It's too dark to make anyone out. It could be anyone.

It could be Connor.

"Hey, what are you doing back there?"

I know that voice. My eyes fly open. They burn with tears, and I rub them before I speak. "Daniel?"

"The one and only. Are you okay? Did I scare you?"

I nod and stand. When he reaches out and takes me by the elbow to help me back onto the path, I don't pull away from him.

"You're shivering." The light from the flashlight jerks as he holds it between his knees. There's movement and sound, then a jacket rests on my shoulders. "You okay? We should head back to the house and get you checked out."

"I have to find Steph," I tell him. "I'm not going back to the house until I do."

I can't see his face, but when he speaks, it's clear he's not happy. "You haven't found her out here?"

"Obviously not," I snap, but then I feel bad. Daniel is trying to help. I'm tired and cold and scared, but at least he's here, and snapping at him isn't going to inspire him to continue to stick around. "I'm sorry, I'm just..." I gesture uselessly around me.

"You lost your shoes," he tells me, shining the light on my feet. "I saw them back there—can you walk?"

"I'm fine." I glance down at my feet and can see blood on my right arch. I don't feel it though, not when I'm so stressed out. "Please, I appreciate you coming after me, but I can't go back, at least not until I know that Steph is okay. And my phone died, so I'm lost out here."

"Let me send a text to my friends to let me know if she shows up." He yanks out his phone and taps on the screen, then pushes it back in his pocket. "You sure she came this way?"

"I saw some markings on the ground," I explain. "So I thought this was a good way to go, and if she's not here, I was gonna backtrack and take the other path."

"Sounds good. Let's go." He moves out of my way, and I join him. Together we hurry down the path, him sweeping the flashlight from side to side so we won't miss any sign of Steph. With him at my side, I feel safer, and I call her louder than I did before, even going so far as to cup my hands around my mouth as I scream.

"Steph!" No matter how loudly I call her, however, my voice still disappears into the woods, and she doesn't respond. Just before I turn to him to tell him that maybe we came the wrong way, I hear water.

"You hear that?" he asks and picks up the pace.

I hurry to keep up with him. He's not running, but he is

close to jogging, and I fight against the stitch in my side so I don't lose him.

Running water could be a river. A waterfall. I don't know how the swimming hole sits on the property. Josh told me that it's spring-fed, but the water still has to go somewhere after it leaves the hole.

I pick up the pace.

It's not so cold out that I'm worried about Steph getting hypothermia if she ended up in the water, but I am worried about her swimming if she fell in. She's not a great swimmer, and who is when they've been drinking? She and I are much more likely to be stretched out in our bathing suits while other people swim.

And if she fell in? In the dark?

My heart is in my throat.

I pump my arms to catch up with Daniel. He's so much faster than me, but without warning, he skids to a stop. I stand next to him, still breathing hard, and reach out to grab his arm to steady myself.

"What is it?" I ask. Bent over like this, I'm relying on him to tell me what the problem is, but he doesn't immediately speak. "Daniel?" My bare feet hurt from sticks and small rocks cutting into them, but I ignore the pain and force myself to straighten up.

We're at a barbed-wire fence, which isn't that uncommon in the south. They're affordable and last for years, even when they're as rusted as this one. I've never been down this path, but the presence of the fence tells me that we must have reached the edge of Josh's parents' property.

"A fence," I finally say when Daniel doesn't speak. "So they couldn't have come this way. No way would Steph have gone over the fence; she knows the risk of tetanus."

"Look," Daniel says, but I ignore him and keep talking.

"We have to go back. They might have come this way originally, but it's pretty clear they turned around. We'll go back and see if they went down the other path." My mind and my mouth are both racing, but what else I was going to say disappears when Daniel moves the flashlight.

"The fence has been cut," he tells me. "Someone came through here with clippers and cut the fence." The clipped barbed wire has been rolled back, the sharp ends tucked around one of the half-rotten pieces of fence post.

"Doesn't mean it was Connor," I say, but as soon as the words are out of my mouth, I realize it doesn't matter if Connor cut the fence or not. What matters is the fact that he would have easily been able to get through the cut part of the fence.

"I think—"

"Steph wouldn't have come this way," I say, babbling even more now. "Trust me, she wouldn't have gone through that hole in the fence, no matter how cute she thought Connor was, no matter what he tried to promise her. She—"

I stop talking when my eyes land on the thing Daniel has obviously been trying to show me.

Blood. Splattered on the ground.

And it's fresh.

THIRTY-ONE

AIMEE

I force myself to take both of Dale's hands in mine and give them a squeeze.

I need to know what Hannah told him.

He takes a deep breath before speaking. "Hannah had some terrible things to say about you."

I'm sure she did.

"What did she say?"

"She's just being paranoid or pushing buttons or something. She said..." His voice trails off, and he shakes his head. "It's so stupid, I don't know why I'm even bringing it up."

"Dale. What did she say?"

"That you killed someone. Years ago."

The floor feels like it drops out from under me. My skin feels cold. "What?"

"I know, it's insane. I told her she was crazy for even suggesting something like that. Why she'd say that, I don't know."

I do.

"Because she likes you," I whisper. It's a Hail Mary, and I know it, but maybe—

"I don't know. Maybe." He sighs and runs his hand through his hair. "You didn't... you didn't kill anyone, did you?"

My heart is beating so hard I feel like it will come out of my chest. "No. No, I didn't." I lock eyes with him to get him to listen to me. "She's lying. She's—"

"I didn't believe her." He cuts me off, desperation in his voice. "Trust me, Aimee, I didn't believe her. I just had to ask. I had to know."

"Sure. Right." My stomach aches. *I'm losing control.*

I was stupid, thinking I was in charge. Keeping Hannah close so I could punish her and Dale at the same time had felt like such a great idea, only now it's blowing up in my face.

If she was willing to tell him that I'm a murderer, what else is she willing to do? My mind races as I think about what to do next. I want to get out of here, but I don't know how to make that happen.

I have to get Hannah out of my way. Get her before she gets me.

"Maybe I need to have some one-on-one time with her," I tell him, even though that's literally the last thing I want to do. "We can have a chat, just us girls."

"Are you sure?" He eyeballs me, and I'm suddenly grateful that he's never once been able to tell when I'm lying to him.

"Yeah, I think it's the only option."

"To salvage the trip. And my time at the box."

I force myself to nod. "Right. Exactly."

"Really? I don't want you to do something you're not comfortable with, but—"

"I want to find out why she'd say something like that about me. I want to get to the bottom of this."

"I'll be there when you talk to her."

"No way." I speak too quickly, and he arches an eyebrow at me. "I'm sorry, but no. I think this is best handled between the two of us without you there."

He's quiet but finally nods. "Okay. If you think that's best."

"I do." I force myself to smile at him.

Hannah's dangerous. She's already showed me that she knows things about my past—or she thinks she does. Looping Dale in by telling him I'm a murderer? It makes me seethe.

I have to be careful, but I also have to find out the truth. Find out who she really is.

But I also need to be careful and try to figure out how I'm going to make it out of this in one piece. Protect myself.

Four of us came on this trip. I only want three of us to make it back home.

I'll do whatever it takes to ensure Hannah's the one who doesn't make it.

THIRTY-TWO

AIMEE

I want to get out of here, but without my phone, I'm stuck. Maybe Mitch found it and will give it to me later, but fleeing isn't going to stop Hannah from coming for me.

I have to protect myself. I have to get her before she gets me.

In the hotel, I insert my keycard and wait until I hear it unlock before pushing the door open.

"What's your plan now?" Dale heads straight for the mini fridge and pulls out a beer. I'm about to remind him that everything in the fridge costs at least four times what it's worth, but I catch myself. Who cares if he's charged a ridiculous amount for a beer? I already cracked open the wine.

"I actually thought I'd see if Hannah wanted to hit up the boardwalk with me. Do a little window shopping."

His eyes widen. The bottle is to his lips, but he drops it so he can speak. "Seriously?"

"Yeah, I think it's better to do something while we talk than be stuck in a room together. It'll keep the tension down." I swallow hard.

"Are you sure about that? Even after what she said?" He

takes a long pull of his beer, but his eyes don't shift from my face. "I'm coming with you."

"Nope. You're not coming." I'm already grabbing my purse and checking inside for my cash. It's there, along with Chap-Stick and a few extra hair ties, but my phone hasn't magically reappeared. But there, at the bottom, in an old painkiller bottle? Yeah, I'm gonna need that soon enough.

I clear my throat. "Hey, I don't have any money. Do you have cash? Or can I borrow your credit card?" I already know he won't let me borrow his card—he's anal about not letting anyone else use it—but it's worth a shot.

"I've got some cash." He flips open his wallet and hands me some bills.

"Thanks. I appreciate it," I say as I pocket the money.

"Come on, Aimes. I know you think this is the right idea, but—"

"It is." I level my gaze at him, trying my best to look more confident than I feel. "She can't go spreading rumors about me. We need to have a chat and clear the air. What, you think I want her insane lies about me getting out when we get back home to Vermont? No way. She and I have to figure out how to co-exist without killing each other."

Except for, you know, the fact that I want to kill her. Suddenly, punishing Dale isn't even on my radar. He deserves it, but I'm way more worried about handling Hannah. I have to stop her.

He takes another drink. Dale and I have been together long enough that I can tell he's frantic.

"Fine. You do that. It's just that I thought you and I could—"

"Why don't you and Mitch?" I smile sweetly at him. "Whatever it was you were thinking about doing with me, why don't you do it with him?"

"A couple's massage?" he asks dryly, and I have to fight the laughter.

As I stare at him, his grip tightening on his bottle, his mouth pressing into a thin line, my heart breaks. I hate that the two of us ended up like this. I've never loved anyone the way I loved Dale. That's what makes the betrayal even more painful.

"I'm sure you can reschedule," I say, my voice gentle. "I'm going next door to see if Hannah will talk to me."

The smile he gives me is small.

Taking a deep breath, I turn to hurry back out into the hall. Before I do, however, a glint of silver catches my eye.

I pause, then drop to my knees and grab it from under his bed.

"A condom wrapper?" I ask, standing and holding it up for him to see. Anger flares in me. "Why is there a condom wrapper in here?"

His face pales. "The cleaning crew must have dropped it."

I stare at him. "The cleaning crew? Really?" Rage burns through me, and I force myself to take a deep breath to calm down. "You sure you didn't use it?"

"Use it? With who?"

I'm silent as I stare at him. He has to connect the dots, and I want to see his face when he does. Every muscle in my body is tense.

"I swear to you," Dale protests, "I don't know where that came from. What, you think I snuck up here and banged someone while you were on the beach with Mitch?" He's breathing hard, gearing up to turn this around on me.

"It wouldn't exactly be the first time, would it?"

"Great." He throws his hands into the air. "Well, since you're so worried about my extracurricular activities, let's talk about yours. You didn't seem too worried about Mitch putting his arm around you."

Oh, he did see it.

"He's your friend. You think he was making a move on me? Why, because the only time you talk to women is when you want to get in their pants?"

"That wrapper isn't mine." He closes the gap between us, snatches it from my hand, and tosses it to the floor. "But maybe it was yours."

"No way." I step back from him. I swear I can feel heat radiating off him, and it's making me sick. "I'm not doing this with you." Without giving him a chance to respond, I turn and race out the door, making sure to slam it behind me. In the hall, I lean against the wall and take a few deep breaths to compose myself.

Was the condom Dale's? Or did Hannah plant it in our room to stir the pot?

Does it matter at this point?

I straighten my shoulders and march the short distance to Hannah and Mitch's door. I could have used the internal door between our rooms, but I needed a moment to myself. Outside it, I take a deep breath and compose myself before knocking.

What would my friends say if they knew what I was doing?

I can imagine, but there's one thing they don't understand: the only way to get rid of her is to first get closer to her. I don't want to spend time with her, but I do want to punish her for what she and Dale did to me. Sure, I could try to ignore her and stay away from her this entire trip, but then what?

I go back to Vermont knowing full well that she never suffered for what she did to me? No way.

Taking a deep breath, I raise my hand to knock. But before I do, I hear a low voice from inside the door. The person is angry. It has to be Mitch, but I still lean forward and press my ear against the door, straining to hear what's being said. If Hannah and Mitch are getting in a fight, I want to know about it. They could be arguing about me, about her taking my phone, about this trip.

But I can't make out the words.

I knock.

The voice inside pauses, then I hear Hannah.

"Just a minute!"

Nervous, I step back and wipe my hands on my shorts. I'm dying to talk to Mitch alone, but it looks like that will have to wait for another time. When the door swings open, I plaster a smile on my face.

Hannah holds on to the door, keeping me from being able to see past her.

"Aimee. What a surprise." Her smile matches mine.

"I need to talk to you. Alone."

She pauses, looks me up and down. "Sounds great," she finally says, but her voice is tight. She pats her pockets like she's feeling for her wallet or phone before giving a satisfied nod.

I step back for her as she joins me in the hall. She closes the door, then jiggles the handle to make sure it's locked.

"You don't need to tell Mitch the plan?" I ask as we start walking down the hall.

"He's not in there." She glances at me, her face inscrutable.

I keep my face calm even as my mind starts to race. Mitch told me he'd come look for my phone in Hannah's things. If he didn't do that, then where is he?

And, more importantly, who was Hannah talking to?

Dale.

It had to have been Dale.

THIRTY-THREE

AIMEE

"What kind of stuff did you have in mind to go shopping for?" Hannah takes down her ponytail, then twists it back up, wrapping the elastic around an extra time to tie it into a bun. Everything she does looks effortless, and I can easily see why Dale was so smitten with her.

On the surface, the two of us seem nothing alike. Once you dig down beneath the surface, however... yeah, still nothing alike.

"Souvenirs for my friends," I tell her, glancing to the right and to the left to decide which way to go first. Just down the street from the hotel are overpriced gift shops—and bars. Good. I'll need to get her to drink something before we go back to the hotel.

"Like crappy plastic junk? That tracks." She wrinkles her button nose, and I have to fight the urge to smack her. "What about something cooler?"

"Okay." I turn to face her, crossing my arms as I do. "Like what? You obviously have something in mind, so spill."

"Bikinis." Her answer is immediate. She whips away from

me before I have a chance to respond and leads the way down the sidewalk.

I roll my eyes but follow her. "Bikinis sound great."

"You know," she says, slowing down so the two of us are walking side by side, "I'm really surprised you asked me to come shopping with you. I thought you hated me."

"Hated you?" I feign surprise the best I can. "Is it because you dropped a condom wrapper in our room?"

"What are you talking about?"

"A condom wrapper. In our room. It was under Dale's bed—"

"Then that sounds like a Dale problem." She tilts her head to the side a bit as she looks at me. "You really think I did that? Why?"

"To cause problems. Like you did with the pregnancy test."

"Oh, lighten up, would you? The pregnancy test was just a joke." She pauses, chewing her lower lip. "I was trying to mess with you, that's all. Get over it."

"Because you think I'm a murderer?"

There. It's out in the open—the fact that she said such a terrible thing to Dale, and he told me about it. She had to know that he'd turn right around and tell me, right?

She stares at me. "Dale came clean with you."

"He always does."

A smile plays on the corners of her mouth. "Always?" She spins away from me and stalks off towards a store.

I feel unsteady around her, like she's one step ahead of me.

I have to be careful.

"Yeah," I say, hurrying to catch up with her. "Just like he told me you're not from Vermont. Anyone can tell with that accent."

A stutter in her step, but she catches herself quickly. Without breaking her stride, she glances at me, then turns to look ahead of us again. "Pretty sure I don't have an accent."

"Oh, but you do. You're from Appalachia. Southern Appalachia, if I had to guess. North Carolina?"

"Yes, I'm from North Carolina. Very good, Sherlock."

My heart beats faster. "So when you told Dale—"

"Bikinis," she announces, then dives into looking through the first rack.

If I had my phone, I could look some things up. I could look into her past, do some research on Facebook, maybe find out more about her than she knows about me, because it's pretty clear she's going to make it difficult for me to learn much about her.

I really, really need my phone.

Or... *a* phone. It doesn't have to be mine; it just has to be someone's, and even though Dale didn't want to let me use his phone earlier, I have no doubt I can either sneak it from him to look Hannah up, or I can ask Mitch.

Mitch.

Mitch, the guy who told me he was going to his room to look for my phone. He told me a lot of things on the beach, and now I'm beginning to wonder who, if anyone, I can trust on this trip.

"You know what?" I ask, causing Hannah to look up from the rack of bikinis. "Here I was, thinking you had some master plan. You act like you knew me before this weekend. But no, you're just throwing things at the wall to try to break up my engagement."

"No master plan here," she tells me, but her eyes are locked on me, and I don't like the expression on her face. "Just trying to enjoy the weekend with my boyfriend."

Boyfriend. Right.

"On my romantic retreat."

She shrugs.

"So the pregnancy test, the condom wrapper, the—"

"The condom wasn't me," she tells me, but I know in my

heart she's lying. "But telling Dale that you're a murderer? Yeah, I did that."

The ground drops out from under me, and I grab the rack of clothes for support.

She eyeballs me. "You don't like that, do you? Let's get some hair of the dog." She's next to me in a flash and loops her arm through mine before I can stop her. "Come on—let's go to the bar. There's nothing like a little drinking to get to know another person, don't you think? We can talk all about your past and why I told Dale the truth about you."

This is exactly what I need to have happen.

I think about what's stashed in my purse and force myself to walk with her. "Hannah, I—"

"You had no idea I was such a great friend, am I right? You're probably wondering why Dale kept me away from you for so long when it's clear the two of us are meant to be best friends. Sure, we had a bit of a rough start, but I'm always in the mood to help a charity case."

Best friends? Yeah, maybe in an alternate universe. "I—"

"First round is on me." She gives me a mischievous grin and pulls a wad of cash from her pocket. "Heck, if you're lucky, I might pay for all of our rounds. Why not?"

Reaching into my purse, I find the Tylenol bottle.

This is my chance.

I have to get rid of her.

THIRTY-FOUR

Then

The adrenaline I feel is enough to power me forward through the fence and down the path. I run, Daniel right behind me, his flashlight bouncing and bobbing as the two of us tear through the woods.

"Steph!" My throat is raw as I scream her name, but I don't wait before calling her again. "Steph! Where are you?"

"Wait." Daniel grabs my arm, practically yanking me off my feet. Angry, I whip around to yell at him, to remind him that every second counts and that we need to find Steph *now*, but just before I can, I realize what I'm hearing.

The sound of the water has changed from far-off to so close it's like I'm standing under the spray of a waterfall. It's pounding, relentless, the type of noise that makes it impossible to think. It's in my head, in my bones, and I'm surprised I didn't realize how loud it was getting until Daniel said something.

I turn to him, my mouth falling open. When I lean closer to speak to him, he tilts his head so I can talk directly into his ear.

"If she's here, how will we find her?"

He doesn't immediately respond, and fear eats at me.

"Daniel, how will—"

"We just have to look." He sounds confident, and I draw on that since all I feel is terrified. If he's confident, that means he's not scared. And I need someone right now to tell me that things are going to be okay.

"Right. Okay. We'll look." Without thinking, I grab the flashlight and shine it around us. We're close to a waterfall, which is why the sound is so loud. Now that I'm standing still and paying attention, I can feel the spray on my face. It's chilly, and I shiver, grateful for the jacket he gave me.

"Come on." He takes me by the hand, and I let him. It's strange, holding someone else's hand, but when he pulls me towards the waterfall, I follow. Josh would be pissed if he saw me with Daniel, but Josh isn't here, is he?

Thinking about my boyfriend makes me think about Jess, then my brain loops to Connor, and I freeze.

"Down here by the rocks," Daniel says. He tugs on my hand, leading me closer to the water. "What if she slipped on them and fell? We need to find her and get her out of here."

I shake my head to clear it and force myself to follow him. One step, then another, then we're standing by huge rocks that are right at the edge of the water. Above us, the waterfall crashes fifteen, twenty feet into the pool at our feet. The water flows to the right, foaming and splashing up against rocks.

They're wet, some with moss growing on them. I know they're going to be slick, but I still move to step onto one. Maybe I can see better. Maybe I'll be able to crane my neck and see further down the river, but Daniel stops me, pulling me back next to him.

"You'll fall!" He yells to make himself heard. "Don't you dare get on one of those rocks!"

I nod, my mouth dry. Fear keeps me pinned up next to his

side. The dark pressing down around us keeps me only able to see what he's shining the flashlight on in that moment.

Nothing. I thought maybe a shoe, a bit of her clothing, maybe even Steph down here by the water, crouched and scared, waiting for someone to find her, but there's nothing.

"I don't see her!" I turn away from the light and lean up to speak directly into Daniel's ear. "She's not here! We must have missed her out on the path, or maybe that wasn't her blood."

I have to cling to that hope, that the blood we found at the fence is from some poor animal, not Steph. The alternative is far too terrible for me to allow myself to consider. I can't do it.

Daniel says my name, but I don't turn to see what he's looking at.

"We should go," I say, but he shakes his head. Puts his hand on my lower back.

Turns me.

That's when I see it.

No, not it.

Her.

Steph.

THIRTY-FIVE

HANNAH

There's no way I'll ever be able to get Aimee to admit to being a murderer, but I'm hoping that she'll slip up. I've been so careful following her, watching her. But I would still love confirmation from her.

She won't admit it outright, but she could say the wrong thing. Let some little detail drop. When I first found out who she is, I only wanted to punish her. I wanted to turn her in to the cops and have her locked up for the rest of her life. But they dropped the ball once, and I'm not letting that happen again.

"This is happening," I mutter, my heart pounding with excitement. I'm sitting at the bar, waiting on the bartender to make our drinks, and I turn and look across the room to her. She's at the high-top table where I left her, her chin resting on her hand, staring out at the street.

It's hot, and sweat breaks out on my forehead. There are tons of guys milling around, and some of them turn to look at me as I carry our drinks across the bar, but I'm not paying them any attention.

I don't give a crap about any men here, and Aimee is so locked on me that she's not noticing what's going on around us.

That's why it was easy to slip the condom wrapper into her room. My entire plan hinges on getting her off-balance enough so I can kill her, so she's finally punished for what she did when we were younger. Aimee may look perfect on the outside. People might think she's kind and wonderful, but that's only because they don't know the truth. She's evil, and she deserves what's coming to her.

"Jäger," I announce, carrying the shots back to the table and pushing one across to her. "Bottoms up."

She frowns and stares at the murky liquid. "I don't know if I can take it as a shot."

"But you can kill someone?" I down mine and shiver at the sensation. No way do I want to get drunk, but I have to drink a little to encourage Aimee to do the same.

She stares at me before taking her shot. "I didn't."

"You did." I plant my hands on the table and stare at her. "Getting away with murder for a decade is pretty impressive, I'll give you that, but it's time to fess up."

She shakes her head. "You don't know what you're talking about. You weren't even there!"

I take a deep breath. She's combative. I need her to let her guard down.

"I was," I say, but she's already shaking her head.

"No. You weren't. I remember everything about that night. I —" She stops herself and lifts her chin a little, her jaw tight.

"And you think I don't? You think I don't relive every second of that night?" I stare at her. She's so self-centered, so sure that she's right. I hate her. "You ruined so many lives that night."

"You don't understand anything." She stands, stopping dead in her tracks when I reach out and grab her arm.

"We're not finished." I dig into my pocket and pull out some cash. "Get another round and bring some water too."

There's a flash of something on her face. *Excitement?* But

just as quickly it's gone. She takes my money and hurries up to the bar. I watch her go, then pull my phone from my pocket and fire off a text to Mitch.

I'm out with Aimee. It's happening tonight.

Mitch's response makes my phone vibrate in my hand.

I think we need to talk about it.

I force myself to take a deep breath.
My thumbs fly across the screen.

Talk about what? I thought you supported me.

I send the text and slam my phone down on the table. Before I can take a deep breath to calm myself, however, it buzzes again.

You don't have to go through with the plan. Things can change.

"Things can change," I mutter angrily.

He'd agreed with me that Aimee deserved to be punished for what she did when she was younger. Sure, he may not have completely agreed with all of the ways I was going about it, but I don't care about that. Now, what? He has a crush and thinks that cancels out everything she did?

I was the one willing to sleep with Dale just to hurt Aimee. I certainly didn't ask Mitch to get involved in that. And look at this trip! He wants to act like we're doing the wrong thing now? Now that I paid for this trip, that I bought the gas and paid for the hotel? He knows I don't have the cash for extravagant trips, and he does, but did he offer to foot the bill?

No, he did not.

All he has to do is sit back and let me handle things. I wanted him here as a buffer, just in case things went south, but they're not going to. I could have done this by myself, I'm sure of it. The fact that he's getting cold feet pisses me off.

My stomach twists, the Jäger suddenly sloshing around as I take shallow breaths to try to calm down. When my mind races like this, it makes it really difficult for me to think straight. Still, while I don't want to be afraid of my plan falling apart, there's a voice in the back of my head that tells me it might.

And that if it does, it's all because of Mitch. Not my planning.

But Mitch. Backing out. Wussing out. Because he's... *in love* —no, I don't want to let that thought take root, don't want to give it any gravity, but I know there's a terrible possibility that that's what's going on, that that's why he wants to change the plan, that he loves Aimee or *thinks* he loves Aimee, and is willing to throw me under the bus, to screw me over, to—

"You okay? You look kinda green." Aimee gives me a tight smile as she sets the glasses down on the table. Before she has a chance to slip into her seat across from me, I grab the water and down it.

It's cool and somehow seems to settle the alcohol in my stomach. It's only when I drain every last drop and put the empty glass back on the table with a thunk that I grab the other drink she brought. I've had half of it when I look up and notice Aimee staring at me.

And she's smiling.

THIRTY-SIX

AIMEE

I guess the roofie I put in Hannah's drink is working even faster than I would have thought possible. She's leaning hard on me. I have one arm wrapped around her waist, the other angled out from my body as a counterweight so she doesn't make me trip.

"That drink was insane," she slurs.

"Yep."

"It felt like five drinks."

"I bet."

"Almost like someone put something in it."

I freeze. No way can she possibly know for sure that I spiked her drink. I was really careful and dropped the roofie in right before I brought the drink back to the table. She'd have to have super powers to somehow know the truth.

But then again...

She didn't drink the entire thing, did she? She had half of it and then declared that she was done. And, after that, vomited on my shoes and legs.

So maybe she's not as drugged as I'd like her to be, but it's clear she doesn't feel great. She'll perk up faster than I want her to since she threw up, but at least she'll be out for a little while.

This is my chance to get rid of her.

In the hotel elevator, I lean her against the wall and mash the button for our floor. My back is cramped from the way she was leaning on me, and I stretch it out. Hannah's blessedly silent for once, her eyes closed as we ascend.

On our floor, I help her to her room. I make sure she's inside. Then I close the door and enter my room.

Dale's head snaps up when he hears the door opening. "Aimes!" He looks like a puppy who's been waiting all day for its owner to get back from work. "How was it? Did you two talk about what she said?"

I arch an eyebrow at him. "You mean her calling me a murderer?"

He runs his hand through his hair. "Yeah, I thought that's why you went."

"She said it was all a joke. Like the pregnancy test." I think fast and hope I'm right. "And the condom wrapper. Then she got drunk and puked on my shoes, so I put her to bed in her room." I point down at my bare feet. "I had to throw my shoes away since they now smell like nasty Jäger."

"Oh. Yikes." He shifts position, and I wonder if he's trying to keep from rushing into the other room to check on his mistress.

"Yeah, I'd leave her alone. Let her rest." *Fingers crossed she doesn't wake up.* If she does, I have a plan on how to deal with her, but maybe she'll choke on her vomit; maybe she'll just stop breathing. A girl can hope. If not... she's incapacitated, and I can finally finish her off.

"Oh, for sure. She doesn't want people staring at her while she's sick." A pause. "Other than that, you okay?"

"Fine. I'm fine. Mitch wasn't there when I dropped Hannah off. Any idea where he is?"

"None, but I'm sure he's around here somewhere."

Frustration shoots through me. For someone who acted like he wants to be really helpful, Mitch sure disappeared quickly.

I turn my back on Dale and toss my purse on the bed. Without thinking about what I'm doing, I strip. It's only when I feel his gaze on me that I whip back around, my shirt held up to my chest.

"Are we... is this happening?" He sounds excited, and my stomach rolls.

No way. "There's vomit splattered on my shins. Do you really think something is happening?" When he shakes his head, I continue. "Good. I'm going to shower."

I feel on display as I walk to the bathroom. Once inside, I close the door and lean against it with a sigh. It feels really good to stand still for a moment, so I do just that, then reach into the shower and turn the water on as hot as it will go.

I want to burn the memory of Hannah's vomit from my skin. It was one of the most disgusting things I've ever had happen to me. She'd gone kind of green looking, then thrown up before I even knew what she was doing.

The sound of it splattering against the bar's floor isn't one I'm going to forget anytime soon. Thank goodness the staff there leaped right into action to clean it up.

I reach out and let the hot water hit my fingers. Scalding. Just the way I like it.

I put one leg into the shower, letting out a soft sigh of pleasure as the water hits me, then—

The necklace.

It's still in my shorts pocket.

Quick as a flash, I grab a fluffy white towel and wrap it around me. Normally I would trust Dale to be around my things without worrying about him snooping, but that was before.

Before the affair. Before the lies.

Before Hannah.

Panic eats at me, and I yank open the bathroom door. Steam billows out around me, and I step into our main room, my head on a swivel.

"Aimee!" Dale jumps back from my suitcase. For a moment, the two of us stand still, staring at each other, neither one of us wanting to make the first move. "I thought you were going to shower."

"I didn't want to leave my clothes in a pile on the floor." I speak slowly, but my mind is racing as I try to figure out a way out of this mess. "While the water heats up, I thought I'd pick them up really quickly."

My eyes fall on the tank top in his hands.

"I was just going to fold them," he says. "Don't you worry about it."

"It's not a problem." In just a few steps, I've crossed the room to him. I yank the tank top from him and wad it into a ball before chucking it into my open suitcase. "I'll take care of it."

He holds up his hands. "Suit yourself."

It isn't until he's walked over to check his phone on his bed that I dip my hand into my shorts pocket.

No necklace.

Frustration heats my cheeks. The other pocket then. It has to be here. I know I didn't drop it anywhere.

But if it's not here, then it has to be...

No. If Dale found Hannah's necklace in my shorts, there's no way he'd be able to keep it to himself. He'd say something to me—I know he would. *Right?*

But it's not in the other pocket.

I drop to my knees to look under the bed. Maybe it fell out of my pocket when I was stripping. Hurried, I yank the bed skirt up to look, but there's nothing under the bed. Nothing around my suitcase.

The necklace isn't here.

I eyeball Dale. His back is to me, his head tilted forward a bit like he's looking at something on his phone. He's being awfully quiet for someone who might have found his lover's necklace in his fiancée's pocket, but I can't rule out the possibility that he did.

Quietly, I get up and walk over to him. It's not like I'm going to poke around in his pockets and try to pick them, but I need to find that stupid necklace.

"Whatcha looking at?" I ask, peering over his shoulder at the same time I put my hands on his hips. This is what happy couples do, right? It's difficult to remember where to put my hands on his body, how to touch him without wanting to yank my hands back like they've been burned.

But he doesn't lean back into my touch like I expected he would. Instead, he stiffens, turning a bit so I can't see his phone's screen. He's too slow, though, because I see the picture he took.

Hannah in a bikini pouting at the camera. Her boobs are on full display, and I'm so filled with disgust that I drop my hands from his hips.

"Nothing." He clicks the screen off and slides the phone into his pocket as he turns to look at me. "Just an email."

Right.

"Well, I'm going to shower. The water's perfect."

He pauses. "Want company?"

"Don't bother. Looks like you have your hands full with your phone," I call back to him. A wave of anger hits. Without another glance, I hurry into the bathroom and close the door. The towel falls to the floor, but I don't bother to pick it up.

A moment later, I'm under the water, letting it pound my face, my shoulders, my back. I turn under it, hissing between my teeth at the heat. It hurts, and I'd never admit that to Dale, but the pain feels good.

It feels so good, in fact, that I almost don't hear Dale scream.

THIRTY-SEVEN

AIMEE

Dale calling me makes me turn the shower off and hop out. I yank the towel from the floor and wrap it around my body before running into the hotel room.

He's not in here, but my eyes fall on the open door to Mitch and Hannah's room. I hesitate.

Is she dead? Did my roofie do more than just knock her out? Was it that easy to protect myself?

If that's as dirty as I have to get my hands, I'm going to be really happy.

Excitement shoots through me as I rush through the connecting door into the other room. Dale's on the floor next to Hannah. She's sitting up, but only because he has his arm around her shoulders. There's vomit down her shirt, on her legs, and spreading around her on the floor.

"Aimee, do something!" Panic crosses his face, but I don't move.

Yeah, I'm a nurse, but come on. Helping her is not on my to-do list.

"Can you at least get me a wet washcloth?"

I snap to attention and hurry to the bathroom. Room service

must have been in here because there's a stack of clean towels. I grab a washcloth and run it under warm water before taking it back to the bedroom. Without being asked, I crouch next to Hannah, making sure my feet are in dry spots, and wipe her face clean.

"What do you think happened to her? Was she this drunk when you brought her back to the hotel?" Dale takes her by the chin and turns her head so she's looking at him, but Hannah doesn't seem to notice.

She's breathing.

Disappointment washes over me.

"No, she wasn't this bad at all," I tell him, and that's true. I knew I had limited time to get her back to the room, but I managed before she started to feel the full effects of the roofie. Kinda.

"Do we call the doctor? Or Mitch! He could help. Where is he?" His voice is tight, and my mind races.

"I think she'll be fine now that she's thrown up," I tell him, and, unfortunately, I'm probably right. The fact that she puked so much probably means that most of the drug will be out of her system, right?

I'd brought one single roofie with me on the trip so I could get Dale out of the way if he wanted us to be... together. I thought having a night to myself while he snoozed in the other bed would be the perfect way to ensure I was able to enjoy the trip as much as possible. But then the opportunity presented itself for me to give it to Hannah so I could get her out of my way, and I couldn't pass it up.

Stupid. It was stupid. I acted impulsively, without thinking about how it would affect me. She scares me; that's the problem. I'm afraid of her and what she might know and was willing to drug her. I just... I don't know what to do, how to get out of here, how to get help. I could use the phone at the front desk, but I don't have my friends' numbers memorized. A wave of panic rushes through me when I realize I might have backed myself into a corner.

"I'll go get help," I say, handing him the washcloth. "Unless you want to be the one to clean this all up."

He glances at the vomit on the floor and shakes his head. "But what about her? Shouldn't someone help her clean up?"

I mean, I've seen Hannah naked, and while she looks great, doing it again isn't on the top of my to-do list. Even Dale, who would normally love to catch a glimpse of her naked again, looks stressed.

"Mitch will have to do it," I tell him. "They're dating, so I'm sure he'd be comfortable taking care of that." Does Dale know that Mitch and Hannah aren't really dating? I stare at him, looking for any sign that he knows the truth.

"I'll call him." He shifts position to pull his phone from his pocket and thumbs it on. "He has to hurry back. We can't take care of this on our own."

"No way." Even though they're clean, I wipe my hands on my towel. It smells in here. If nothing else, I'm sure Hannah and Mitch will want to get a new room so they don't have to sleep with the smell of vomit in the air.

I allow myself a small smile.

"He's not picking up." Dale tosses his phone onto the closest bed. "Will you...?"

"I'll put on some clothes, go down to the front desk, and then I'll go looking for Mitch." As I speak, I realize I probably sound too excited about getting out of here. "You just stay with her, okay? Make sure she doesn't throw up any more and choke on it."

"She can do that?" He sounds horrified.

"Did you never watch *Breaking Bad*?"

He just stares at me.

"Just... hang tight. Help is on the way," I tell him, then hurry back into our room. I close the door behind me, shutting off the smell of vomit, the sight of Dale taking care of Hannah, the absolute mess of the room. It feels good to leave that all behind me, and I close my eyes and relax for a moment.

But just a moment. I don't want Dale following me in here, telling me that he's changed his mind, that he'll be the one to get help. Quickly, I change, then brush my hair and pull it back into a bun. After sliding my feet into a pair of flip-flops, I lean back through the door and call to Dale.

"I'm going down to the front desk to talk to them about sending a cleaning crew for the room. And I'll keep an eye out for Mitch." I pause, then consider what I'm about to say next. "How about I get your phone from you so I can answer it if he calls back?"

Silence.

Without giving him time to argue, I sweep into the room, hurry to the bed, and grab his phone. Hannah's is next to it— one of them must have tossed it on the bed. I hesitate only a moment before grabbing it as well. It's locked, and I glance over my shoulder at Hannah.

Could I use her finger to unlock it? Not with Dale sitting right there. I hate to do it, but I toss it back on the bed.

Dale, on the other hand... I know his password, not because he told me, but because this isn't the first time I've gotten into his phone. One time of him being sloppy keying in his password while I watched over his shoulder was all it took for me to remember it.

"I might need that," he says, but I shake my head.

"Trust me, Dale, I've got this totally under control." I throw him a grin and leave as I came, making sure to close the door so their room is cut off from ours. Out in the hall, I turn on Dale's phone and type in his password.

Sure, I'll get Hannah help, but I'm not in a rush. I kinda like the idea of Dale sitting with her, the two of them in a puddle of cold vomit. They deserve it. I'll head downstairs towards the front desk, but I have a detour in mind.

I want to check his phone. Make sure I'm not missing anything before I get rid of her.

Hannah coming on this trip was a surprise, and I haven't handled it well. She's had the upper hand this entire time. I have to get my head screwed on straight again.

The roofie took her down a notch, but she's going to bounce back.

I can't let that happen.

THIRTY-EIGHT

Then

Her eyes are so wide, and she's sitting so still, that I know she's dead.

It's my biggest fear come to life, and there's not a thing I can do about it. She's dead, and it's all because of Connor.

Anger flares in me, and even though I want to run and scream, all that happens is I start to cry. Huge sobs rip through me, but Daniel doesn't move.

"She's alive!" he screams at me, the cords in his neck standing out. "Don't just stand there! I need your help!"

She's alive.

Those two words are what make me start moving. I follow Daniel, listening to his instructions on where to put my feet, where to be careful, and in a moment I'm crouched by Steph's side.

My feet sink into the mud. It's freezing here at the edge of the water. When Daniel shines the flashlight over Steph, I can see that she's soaked. Water has wicked up into her clothing. She's shivering but manages a small smile when I sit next to her.

"I'm okay." The waterfall is so loud that it feels like she's whispering in my ear.

I hug her.

"We're getting you out of here!" I look up at Daniel. He's still shining the flashlight around, obviously looking for the right path to get her out. Did she fall down here? The two of us had to pick our way down to the water. It's not like the path leads straight down here.

So maybe she fell, or lost her balance, or slipped—

Or was pushed.

My mind latches on to that thought, and I try to ignore it, but it's not going anywhere. Connor could have pushed her, and that's why she's down here. That's why he came back to the party all satisfied, acting like the best of the night was ahead of him.

I snap back to my senses when Daniel hollers my name. He's behind Steph, the flashlight resting on a rock so its beam is pointed at the three of us, and is bending over her, ready to lift her.

"You have to catch her if she falls!" He waits until I confirm, then starts to lift. His hands are under her armpits, and he raises her quickly, giving her enough time to step forward. I meet her and immediately wrap my arm around her waist.

Water soaks my shirt.

"Got her?" Daniel asks. His mouth is right by my ear, and I shiver at the warmth of his words.

Instead of speaking, I nod. Yes, Steph is standing, but she's heavier than I thought, and her leaning on me threatens to knock me off-balance. I shift position, and my ankle strikes a rock. By now, though, my foot is so numb from the cold water and mud that I barely feel the pain.

Steph's trying to help—I know she is. She leans on me, breathing heavily but not saying a word as I try to help her navigate back up through the slick rocks. Behind us, the waterfall rages. Daniel must have picked up the flashlight because the light bobs ahead of us, sometimes illuminating the rocks at our feet, other times arching further out.

"You've got this," I tell her. I don't know if she can hear me over the roar of the water, but I keep up a running commentary. "Watch your step—the rocks are slippery. I'm glad you still have your shoes, but you might have to kick them off. Heels aren't going to do you any good when you're sinking into the mud. We're almost to the top, Steph, and then we'll be able to get you some help."

She doesn't respond. I don't know how long it takes. Ten minutes? Twenty? But by the time we reach level ground and are far enough away from the waterfall to speak, we're both exhausted.

I do my best to lower her carefully to the ground, but she collapses with a groan.

In an instant, Daniel is next to her. He presses his fingers against the side of her neck, obviously checking her pulse, then shines his flashlight in her eyes.

"All good?" I ask. I'm nervous, and I twist my hands together. The burst of adrenaline that helped drive me up the steep ground with Steph has worn off, and I feel a crash coming on.

"She's okay. I don't know what that guy did to her, but..." His voice trails off. When he speaks again, it's stronger. "We need to get her back to the house and probably call an ambulance." He pulls his phone from his pocket and taps on the screen.

I watch, my stomach sinking, as he turns in a slow circle, his phone held above his head. He stares up at it, reaching up to tap the screen from time to time. Finally, he lowers it, shoves it in his pocket, and shakes his head.

"No service?"

All the hope I was feeling—that someone could come to us,

that a doctor on a four-wheeler would show up, that Steph would get away from the water and magically feel well enough to walk on her own—they all disappear.

"I can leave you two here and bring help," Daniel begins, but I'm already shaking my head.

"No, I'm sorry. I can't be left alone in the dark." I glance down at Steph. She's sitting with her knees pulled up to her chest, and I feel a stab of frustration. If I were braver or stronger, I wouldn't stop Daniel from going for help.

But I can't do this on my own. I need him here with me.

"You can take the flashlight, and I'll stay here with her?" He offers the option like he already knows I'm going to turn him down.

I shake my head, hating myself as I do. I just... can't. What if I run into a bear? There are things in these woods, packs of coyotes and bears and mountain lions, all of them ready and willing to take me down.

And there's Connor. Don't forget about him.

I haven't, and maybe that's the real reason I can't go. I can't stay. I can't go.

"Then we have to take her with us. When we stop to rest, I'll check my phone for service. No big deal." Daniel's voice is tight. The flashlight is pointed at the ground between us, so I can't see his face, but I can imagine his expression.

He sounds worried.

No. *Terrified.*

"Okay. Sounds good." I lick my lips, then bend to Steph. "Up you go," I say, trying to make my voice sound happier than I feel. "Daniel and I are going to get you out of here. No big deal."

"No big deal." She doesn't so much speak the words as breathe them out, and that terrifies me.

We have to hurry. We're already losing her.

THIRTY-NINE

HANNAH

I feel like I'm dying.

My head pounds. My stomach twists like I'm going to throw up again, but there's nothing in my stomach for me to empty.

I'm exhausted.

But even though I feel terrible, even though my body hurts and I want to go to bed and sleep it off, there's one emotion that keeps me going.

Hatred.

Aimee did this to me. She ruins everything, just like she ruined my life so many years ago. I feel like crap, but thank goodness I threw up, or I wouldn't be able to think at all. And while I was thinking she was clueless, what did she do?

Drug me.

What a bitch.

I'll rest for now. Bide my time. Let Dale take care of me, at least for now. I'm safe here with him.

"Hannah." Dale shifts position next to me, and I force myself to turn and look at him. My eyes are only half-open. "You're going to be fine."

The fact that he still cares about me after everything is almost laughable, but before I can respond, he keeps talking.

"We'll get you home, but you need to know what happens next." He takes a deep breath. "I'm going to the police."

The what?

"I know you've been stalking Aimee. I know you used me to get closer to her. You're crazy, you know that? I won't let you hurt her."

My mouth is dry. I can't respond.

"I looked through your phone while you were passed out. Used your fingerprint to unlock it. I don't know what your plan is, but you're never going to bother her again."

My mind races. Dale wants to stop me from getting the one thing I want more than anything.

I won't let him.

FORTY

AIMEE

What I can't wrap my mind around is how Hannah could possibly know what happened when I still lived in North Carolina. I might not be perfect, but I'm pretty dang good at covering my tracks. It's been ten years. Nobody knows the whole truth. Not a single person. And the only person who could is dead.

Hannah said she was there, but I don't believe her. No way was she really there. *I* was there. I've read the police reports. She has to be lying.

I'm in the lobby on the first floor, and I pause, trying to decide where to go. The ceiling soars, and the front desk is decorated with ornate carvings. Large, off-white marble tiles under my feet keep the room cool, and huge ceiling fans spin lazily above my head. There's a crowd of people here, and while I could probably disappear into it and not be noticed, I want somewhere more private, somewhere—

Is that Mitch?

I shrink back against the wall, Dale's phone clutched to my chest. Mitch is on the other side of the lobby. He looks left, then right, then suddenly pushes through a door. It closes quietly behind him, and I pause, then walk to it to see where he went.

The stairs. Curiosity eats at me, but I don't know if I'll have another opportunity alone with Dale's phone to poke around in it. Even though I want to follow Mitch to see what he's doing, I turn away from the stairs and look for a place I can use to do my research. When my eyes land on a small sign pointing down a hall, I follow it to a shared office space.

There are a few people typing away on laptops when I let myself in the door, but none of them look up at me, so I hurry across the room to the cubby in the back corner and unlock Dale's phone before opening a private browser.

Even knowing my search history won't be visible to Dale, it feels dangerous to google myself. I guess the police could find out what I was looking for, but first they'd have to take Dale's phone and get a subpoena and use whatever technology they have to dig into his private browser history. They'd have to know I was looking for something, have to decide there was enough of a reason to see what I was looking for and...

I shake my head to shut up my worries.

When you spend enough time running from something, it makes sense that you're always scared. That you feel the fear of something evil grasping at your throat. I thought I'd put my past behind me, thought I'd built this future, where I was a good person who helped others. I'd made this life that would prevent anyone from ever wondering who I really was. Dale was supposed to be a part of that, a happy ending. Finally moving on for good. But Hannah knows more than she's letting on.

And that simply can't be allowed to continue.

I type in my name and tap enter.

No news reports in the past decade.

No armchair sleuth has been digging up what happened so many years ago and talking about me on a podcast. There are no new Reddit posts detailing that night. Still, nightmares can come true—that's something I've learned the hard way, and no way am I going to assume that my tracks are completely covered until I know for sure that they are.

My hands are sweaty, and I wipe them on my shorts. It suddenly feels like someone is watching me, and I sit up straighter to peek around my cubby. Everyone is intent on their own screen, and nobody is looking at me.

Still, I hunch forward, rolling my shoulders as if that's going to offer me protection from anyone trying to see what I'm searching for. It's been... years since I searched for that night.

My right hand pats out a rhythm on my thigh, and I take a deep breath, letting it out in one loud *whoosh* before forcing myself to type out another name. I can't back down now, can't weenie out.

Stephanie Olive Smith.

SOS.

Everyone made fun of those initials, as if a baby has any say in what they're named, until finally...

Well, it all stopped, didn't it? After that night, nobody had anything to say about those initials.

The cell phone's screen goes dark, and I tap it to wake it back up. My mind races as I try to think through what I need to do next.

No way did Hannah figure out anything about my past via Google. If she really knows the truth about what happened when I was younger, then she had to have been telling the truth about having a firsthand account of it. It's the only thing that makes sense.

As much as I hate to admit it, there's no other way for her to know what she does. Or... what she thinks she does.

If she learned about my past from an online source, then the police would also know what she does, and there's no way I'd be here right now. They'd be questioning me, trying to figure out what they missed that night. I'm sure of it.

I close my eyes and focus back to that night, even though it's the one night of my life I want to forget, but my mind keeps coming back to Hannah. She followed me out of North Carolina, to Vermont, and now down to Florida.

I need to look up Hannah. She's the key to all of this, even though I don't want to admit it. For the longest time, I thought she was just some woman who decided to sleep with my fiancé, but she's more than that.

She doesn't just want Dale. It's always been about me. I've never asked her last name, and Dale has never mentioned it either. But then icy dread climbs my spine. *Hannah.* I know who she is.

Her last name was buried deep in my memories, and I don't want to be right, but I have to know.

Hannah Ellis, Etowah, North Carolina.

I don't want to hit enter and bring up the search results. I'm terrified of having what I already suspect confirmed, but I don't have a choice. Not when I'm this afraid of the woman I left with my fiancé.

I hit enter.

The first result that pulls up is an obituary.

FORTY-ONE

HANNAH

A knock on the door makes me stir. My head feels like it's in a vise. Just thinking about moving makes my stomach lurch, although there isn't anything in there for me to throw up.

Aimee. She did this.

"She sure took long enough getting help. You'd think she went out for a beer or something," Dale mutters from where he's sitting next to me, then he lightly pats my cheek. "Hey, Hannah, we need to get you cleaned up. How are you?"

I mumble a few random words and let my chin drop to my chest.

Thank goodness I only had half of my drink.

Still, the effects hit me, just not as bad as they would have had I finished the entire drink. Puking was out of my control, but I do feel a bit better with the liquid out of my stomach. It was embarrassing throwing up at the bar, and scary when I got back to the room and was sick again.

But I'll admit it... I liked throwing up on Aimee. She deserved it.

Dale stands up. "That better be the cleaning crew to take

care of... this." He swallows hard, and I have a very good feeling he's doing his best not to throw up as well.

"Water," I croak. "Water, Dale."

"Hang on." He lets the cleaning crew in first. From under half-lidded eyes, I make out two women wearing surgical masks. I'm not going to judge, not when this place looks bad and smells worse.

"Now let me get you some water." He hurries to the bathroom, and I hear him run the faucet. Beside me, the women drag a huge mop and bucket into the room. I plant my hands on the floor and make a valiant effort to scootch out of their way.

The room spins, and I stop, closing my eyes and breathing slowly.

Dale is back by my side, holding the cup to my mouth. "There, just a little at a time. You're doing great."

I take three small sips, then let out a soft sigh. "Tylenol."

"Stay here. I'm going to see if Aimee has some," he says. When he stands, he leaves the cup on the floor by me.

"What in the world?" Dale says, and I turn to look at him. He's standing at the door that separates our two rooms, twisting the handle back and forth. "It's locked," he tells me over his shoulder.

Aimee locked it before she left. I almost want to laugh at the ridiculousness of it all, how she's almost one step ahead of me at all times.

At least she's making this weekend exciting.

"Aimee?" Dale calls her name and bangs on the door, but there's no answer.

She's not there, Dale. She locked you out.

"Aimee!" He calls her name louder, and the two cleaning women stop working as he does. They're staring at him, probably wondering what he's doing, wondering if he's even supposed to have access to that other room.

With a sigh, Dale bonks his forehead against the door. After a moment, he takes a deep breath and squats back down next to me. "Hey, I need to find Aimee."

Behind him, the two women are packing up their mops. The room now smells like bleach instead of vomit.

It's an improvement.

"Then go." I flap my hand at him.

The younger woman picks up a trash bag full of dirty rags. "Is there anything else you need from the two of us?"

Dale sighs. "Nothing, thanks."

They let themselves out, and he walks back into the bathroom.

"I don't want to leave you alone, but I don't know Aimee's number, so I can't call her from your phone." He smacks his thigh. "You did this by getting too drunk."

"But I wasn't," I tell him. "I only had one drink."

He stares at me. Even without him saying a word, I know what he's thinking. The vomit. The way I'm acting. One drink? Not a chance.

"You must have forgotten," he begins, but I cut him off.

"Really? You're gonna patronize me right now?" I groan as I reach for him, making him help me stand up. My head swims, and I take my time as I shuffle into the bathroom. Once there, I flick on the light, then plant both hands on the counter for support. I force my chin up and open my eyes, blinking in the brightness. Nobody looks good in hotel bathroom light. "I look terrible," I mutter, then turn to look at him. "I swear to you, I didn't have that much to drink."

"Hannah—"

"Honestly, Dale, shut up. All I know is that I went out drinking with your fiancée—who invited me, by the way—and then I ended up like this." I gesture angrily at the vomit on my shirt before catching myself on the sink again. "Don't even try to tell me she didn't have something to do with it."

"Aimee wouldn't."

"You're sure about that? I already told you that you don't know her nearly as well as you think you do, so is this really a hill you want to die on right now? Or did you not believe me that she's a murderer?"

"You've got to stop. I know you're obsessed with me—don't you remember what I said? You were stalking her. Following her. Give it up."

Frustration bubbles below his words. He squeezes his hands into fists and glares at me, but I'm not going to back down. Not now. Not any longer.

"I wasn't stalking her because I wanted you! I was watching her to get closer to her so I could confront her about what she did. That's all."

He pauses, frowning, then gives his head a little shake. "You can't prove she did anything. If she was a murderer—which she isn't—why isn't she in prison?"

Because I never told the police what I know. Instead of saying that, though, I ignore him and change tactics. "She drugged me today," I begin.

"No, she didn't."

"Yes, she did." My voice is loud. I'd love to turn to him and drive my point home, but I can't let go of the bathroom counter. "But what I'm talking about goes way back before that, to when we both lived in North Carolina."

"For crying out loud," he says, throwing his hands up in the air. "You two were teens when you lived in North Carolina. No way can you hold anything she did over her head. I'm sure you did stupid crap all the time. Just admit it, Hannah—you're envious of Aimee and the fact that I chose her. Get over yourself."

"Have you talked to her about what I told you? Or googled her?"

His eyebrows crash together. "Have I talked to my fiancée about the fact that you're claiming she's a murderer? I mentioned it, but, weirdly enough, we haven't gone into detail. Because it's insane. You have no proof of anything and are trying to hurt her, or me, or both of us. I thought we could stay friends, but now I'm through with your games."

"Will you listen to me?" My patience is gone. He's pushed and pushed, and I'm well past the point of breaking, which is why I shout the words. I know I should calm down, that you catch more flies with honey than with vinegar, but Dale just isn't getting it, and I don't know how to make him see that I'm telling the truth. He's so blinded by his love for Aimee that he refuses to acknowledge the fact that she killed someone.

She. Killed. Someone.

I take a deep breath and try to calm down. "I'm not pissed off over a small teenage slight. You really think I'm that petty to hold something small over someone's head for a decade? I'm not! I'm—"

"Going to be arrested for stalking as soon as we get back to Vermont." His words hit me like an arrow. "Do you understand?"

My throat closes. *He wouldn't, would he?* I stare at him, trying to read his mind, but all I see in his eyes is resolve, and it hits me: he's really going to turn me in. I can't go to jail, not when I've worked so hard to get to this point.

"I promise you, Hannah, I'm going to make you regret ever coming near me or Aimee. You might think that you're clever enough to get away with this, but I have proof you've been stalking us. I'll do whatever I can to hurt you."

My stomach drops, but I don't want him to see how affected I am. "You have no idea who you're about to marry—"

The hotel room door slams open before I can finish speaking. I turn slowly so I don't throw up, my heart hammering, and my eyes land on who interrupted me. It's Mitch; his eyes widen before they narrow.

"What happened to you?" he asks.

"She got sick," Dale begins, but I cut him off.

"Aimee drugged me." Three words are more than enough to catch his attention, but there's something else I don't say.

And I don't care what you think of her, what feelings you might have for her, I'm going to kill her.

But I have to protect myself: I'm taking Dale out first.

FORTY-TWO

Then

Steph's breathing terrifies me.

It's shallow and fast, like a trapped bird. She's still walking —or at least putting one foot in front of the other—but her left foot is dragging now, like she doesn't have enough energy to actually lift it to clear the ground.

She ditched the shoes shortly after we started walking. Or, rather, she collapsed to the ground, and I pulled them off. Tossed them to the side. Promised her we'd be back for them, but there's no way I'm ever walking down this path again. I'll buy her all the shoes she wants if we make it out of here in one piece.

Every step is painful. My feet are swollen, puffy, and I'm pretty sure there's a thorn in my right heel. It's a sharp pain, like a hot poker jabbed into my skin, and I hiss in a breath when I hit it just right.

Daniel offered to stop and take a look at my feet for me, but if I stop moving, I don't think I'll be able to start again.

When I set out looking for Steph, I had no idea how much

of an incline I was on. Down, down, down to the river I walked, and now it's all uphill, loose dirt and stones scattering under our feet, making me lose my balance from time to time.

But we only drop Steph once.

Daniel on her left, me on her right, the three of us like some grotesque creature with a flashlight bobbing ahead of us, but even that light is growing dim.

I haven't mentioned it. Neither has Daniel. But we both know it to be true.

"We're close," he gasps out, and I nod but don't respond. My body is exhausted. My feet hurt more than ever before. It feels like every single one of my joints is coming out of place, like I'm literally falling apart with every step I take, but I don't have the luxury to sit down and rest.

Steph needs a doctor. No, she needs the hospital, and I'm the reason she's at the party and needs help in the first place. No way am I going to be the reason something even worse happens to her.

"It hurts."

Those are the first words Steph has said since we started helping her back to the house, and I freeze when I realize what she said.

"What hurts?" I ask.

Daniel notices that I'm no longer walking with him, and he slows to a stop. We're angled across the path, the three of us, the flashlight so dim it's almost a joke now, but even though I know we need to get moving, the only thing I can do is stand here and wait to see if she has anything else to say.

"Everything," she gasps out.

Resolve settles on me, and I start walking again. "Come on, Daniel," I say. My energy was flagging, but it's back with a vengeance now, and I have to slow down for him to catch up with me.

Closer and closer we get to the house, and I can finally hear sounds from the party. Music and laughter, someone slamming a car door. It feels wrong, like we're venturing out of the woods after being lost for days, for weeks, and I hold on to that noise and use it to drive me even further.

"We're almost there, Steph," I say. My fingers dig into her side, and she'll probably have bruises thanks to how hard I'm squeezing her to keep her on her feet, but does that really matter when the alternative is her being left behind?

Her dying?

The flashlight goes out.

Something shifts in the woods to my left.

I jerk my head to the side, my eyes straining against the dark, but there's no way I can see what's in there, what's moving around, what might be watching.

"Just keep going," I mutter to myself. My voice is soft enough that I'm sure Steph and Daniel can't hear. "You got this. You got her into this situation, and you're going to be the one to get her out."

That admission of guilt, that I'm the reason Steph was... hurt, grips my heart and squeezes. If I hadn't been so focused on being with Josh, if I hadn't focused all of my energy on him and not on my sister, then would we be in this situation?

Probably not, because I would have seen the darkness in Connor's eyes. I would have done whatever it took to get rid of him, to make sure he wasn't given the opportunity to get anywhere near her.

But I didn't do that, did I?

A sob escapes my mouth. It's so dark I can't make out the expression on Daniel's face, but I feel him turn to look at me. No way am I saying anything. No way am I admitting that I'm the reason this is happening.

That's a guilt I'm going to have to deal with on my own. I don't want to excise it in public, hold it up in front of others, let Daniel look at it, examine it, comment on it.

It's my guilt to deal with, and mine alone.

That thought—that I did this, and I'll have to be the one to deal with it—is on repeat when we stumble out of the woods. My numb toes catch on a fallen branch, and I pitch forward but somehow let go of Steph before I fall all the way to the ground.

Daniel catches her.

I slam into the cold, unforgiving ground. My heart pounds, my palms hurt from where I caught myself. But there, ahead of us: light. A house. Cars. People.

Connor.

"We'll call the cops," Daniel says after I push myself back up to stand. "They can be here in, what? Twenty minutes? Half an hour?"

"No way." I think about Connor's cold, dark eyes. I think about the way he looked at Steph, how he lied to me about seeing her. No way am I letting him get anywhere near her again. I have to save her. Get her out of here. "Help me get her in my Jeep."

"Your Jeep?"

"I'm taking her to the hospital."

"No, we should call 911. They'll figure out what really happened and make sure she gets justice."

Steph's head rolls forward. It's a miracle she hasn't passed out on our walk, but I don't know how much longer she's going to be with us. It's not that she's a ton of help walking, but when she's fully dead weight, we're screwed.

"Daniel, please." I hate begging. Hate relying on someone else to help me out, but I don't have a choice in the matter right now. "Just help me get her to my Jeep. I'll get her the help she needs. The cops will probably be called to the hospital anyway."

At least, I think they will. They always are in the various cop shows I watch.

"She'll get justice," I continue, but I don't need to argue with him anymore.

Either I've worn him down, or he's relieved to be free of us. No doubt he wants to go back to the party, pretend this didn't happen. Or, because he's scared, he'll go home, remove himself from whatever else might happen tonight.

I don't care what he does as long as he helps me get Steph in the Jeep.

We half-carry, half-walk her to the Jeep. My keys are deep in my pocket, and Daniel has to hold Steph so I can yank them out and unlock the doors.

We get her in and buckled, then I slam her door and slide into the driver's seat. My bare foot finds the pedal, and I make it down the driveway and onto the main road when Steph starts moaning.

FORTY-THREE

AIMEE

My footsteps echo in the empty stairwell as I make my way up to the third floor. As soon as I finished my light stalking on Dale's phone, I beelined here to see what Mitch was up to. I keep thinking that I hear someone behind me, but each time I turn around, I'm the only one in here.

It doesn't help that I keep thinking Hannah is creeping up on me. Now that I know the truth about who she is, I know she's more dangerous than I thought.

I was right—I have to kill her. It's the only way to keep her quiet.

But first I need to find Mitch.

He was sneaking around; he had to be. But why? What does he know?

By the time I reach the third floor, I'm winded, but not because I flew up the stairs. Nerves eat at me, and I pause, pressing my forehead against the door for a moment while I think.

There's no way anyone will ever be able to tell that I roofied Hannah—I'm sure of it. Even if she tries to claim that I drugged her, I'll stick to my story that she had a lot to drink and that's why she got sick.

And as for Dale and Mitch? Hopefully Dale will want to spend time with Hannah and continue to make sure that she's okay. We leave tomorrow afternoon, so I have about twenty-four hours until I'm on the plane, my earbuds in, flying towards my freedom.

All I wanted was to get away from Dale. I wanted my friends to move me out. Then the plan changed when we arrived and Hannah had the guts to show up. I thought, while we were here, that I could get revenge on Dale for how he hurt me, but killing Hannah is the only way to save myself.

Mitch is the wild card. I thought that letting him think I might want a relationship with him would be smart—that having someone on my side was a good idea—but he seems to have gone off-book.

And that scares me. I really thought I'd be in control this weekend. When it was just Dale and me, I was certain we'd fly down here, he'd drink too much and pass out—with or without the help of the roofie I brought—and then we'd fly home to my freedom.

"Come on and think," I mutter to myself. "Hannah knows who you are."

Kinda. Not quite.

"And she's obviously unhinged."

Understatement of the year.

My heart starts to beat faster, and I turn, sliding my back down the door until I'm sitting on the floor. I pull Dale's phone from my pocket and unlock it, but of course he doesn't have any of my friends' numbers saved.

Could I contact them on social media? Let them know how badly I need their help?

It's an idea, and as far as ideas that I've had recently go, it's not a terrible one. I'm about to hop into his Instagram to message Laurel when the phone starts to ring.

It's Mitch.

His name pops up in huge letters, bold and accusing, and I exhale hard and run my hand through my hair. I have so many questions and am unsure of what to do right now. There's a possibility that he's calling Dale because he wants to tell him something without Hannah or me knowing what's being discussed.

And, of course, there's the possibility that he knows I have Dale's phone and they're looking for me. That's the best-case scenario, I guess.

Without letting myself think about it any longer, I slide my thumb across the screen to answer the call.

"Mitch?"

"Aimee. Where are you?"

I pause. I have no good reason not to answer the phone, especially if Dale told him that I have it and they're looking for me.

"I'm in the lobby," I lie.

Mitch pauses. He's silent long enough that I pull the phone away from my ear to look at it and make sure I didn't lose him.

"The lobby?" he finally asks.

"Yep." I force myself to smile so I sound as calm and natural as possible. I'm unbothered, in the lobby, not crouched in the stairwell like a crazy person. "Just was looking for you, but you must have made your way back up to the rooms."

"It doesn't sound like you're in the lobby."

I freeze. "Yeah, well, I am. Give me a few minutes and I'll come upstairs."

"No, you wait there. I'll come to you."

Goosebumps break out on my arms. Without thinking, I hurry to my feet and take a step away from the door. Chances are good he'll take the elevator, right? If he's coming to the lobby to find me, I'll just have to hurry, but I can beat him downstairs.

"I'm on my way," I say. My voice is strained. *Why is he so insistent on coming to me?* "Just give me a minute, okay. I have to make it to the—"

The door behind me flies open. At the same time, the hairs on the back of my neck stand straight up, and I freeze, my heart hammering away in my chest.

"You weren't in the lobby," Mitch says, and I force myself to turn and look at him. "I could tell you were lying to me. Want to know how?"

I don't answer.

"There weren't any other sounds. Just your voice, and it sounded like it was echoing."

The door closes behind him. The landing we're on is about five feet deep, six feet wide, but I suddenly feel uncomfortably close to him.

"I was looking for you." I slide Dale's phone back in my pocket and lift my chin, ready to do my best to take control of the situation. "You told me you were going to look for my phone in Hannah's things, but then you disappeared. I didn't have a choice but to come looking for you."

He stares at me, his eyes locked on my face. They're such a dark brown that it's impossible for me to get a read on what he might be thinking.

"Well, you found me."

I shrug and force another smile. "Shall we go back to the rooms and see how Hannah is feeling? She was in a pretty bad way when I left her."

Without giving him a chance to respond, I start walking, fully intending to brush past him and hurry out the door into the hall.

Do I think that Mitch would really hurt me? Well, that thought never crossed my mind before. But now? No way do I want to be left in the stairwell with him when it's impossible for me to tell what he's thinking.

"Wait one second." He moves faster than I was prepared for and stands between me and the door, his arms crossed, his eyes still latched on to mine.

"Everything okay?" A trickle of sweat works its way down my back, but I don't move.

"You and I have a few things to talk about before we join the others. I think it's time you came clean with me, don't you?"

FORTY-FOUR

HANNAH

Dale watches me for a moment like he's going to say something, then hurries out the door, even though Mitch is long gone down the hall.

I groan before staggering to my feet. Aimee is dangerous. The last thing I want is for her to come back to the room and catch me off guard in this state. She drugged me.

I never should have gone with her to get a drink, but I thought I had it under control. I thought I had *her* under control, but it was stupid of me not to realize that she was up to something when she invited me out. Her slipping me a roofie is probably the least-damaging thing she could have done to me, but I'm still kicking myself for putting myself in a position where she could hurt me.

But what am I going to do about Dale?

Aimee deserves to die for what she did, obviously. But Dale has suddenly become more of a pressing matter if I want to not only punish Aimee, but also stay out of prison.

That thought drives me to my suitcase. I have to check on something.

The cascade of clothing onto my bed when I dump out my

suitcase is actually pretty, but I don't spend time digging through the pile for something to wear. If the trio gets back to the room while I'm still in the shower, that's fine.

I'll just lock the bathroom door to keep them out.

But if they come back and interrupt me while I'm getting something from my suitcase, then I'll really be in trouble.

My hands shake as I unzip the hidden pocket, but even before I dip my hand inside, I feel sick to my stomach. The gun I brought isn't huge. It's just a little pocket pistol, designed to be deadly while also perfectly fitting in your purse. No way does it pack the kind of punch Dirty Harry would want, but I don't need to cause a scene.

I just need to be able to stop someone in their tracks.

But the pistol isn't there.

"No way," I mutter. My head throbs, and I'm exhausted, but I can't stop looking for the weapon. Stepping back from the bed and my suitcase, I close my eyes and count to ten. It's been a long day, and it's entirely possible that I simply missed the gun.

This time, when I put my hand into the pocket to search for the gun, I go slower. It's rather small, and maybe there's a chance it slid out of the way a bit. Tucked itself into the far corner of the pocket.

But it's still not there.

Screw being patient and calm. My movements turn frenzied, jerky. I unzip every single one of the side and hidden pockets in my suitcase and start looking through each one. After I've made sure the gun isn't in a pocket, I zip it closed and move on to the next one.

No gun.

No gun.

No gun.

There's a gasping sound in the room, and it takes me a minute to realize it's coming from me. I'm panting as I continue my search. When I don't find it, I scream, balling my hands into fists and slamming them into the mattress.

"Calm down," I mutter as I turn my attention to the pile of clothes. The gun has to be in there. If it isn't...

My brain shuts off, not letting me finish that thought.

I have to do this methodically, even though I don't know how much longer I have until Mitch comes back. It kills me to move slowly but I carefully pick up each piece of clothing, separating it from the pile, then put it in the suitcase.

Not that I think the gun could be hiding in my thong, but I don't have a choice in the matter. I have to go slow. I have to be careful.

I have to find my gun.

Bikinis. Tank tops. Shorts. I way overpacked for this trip, but I couldn't help myself. I'm just a girl who loves clothes, but by the time I finish digging through the pile, I'm kicking myself for going overboard.

The gun isn't here.

Crossing my arms, I perch on the edge of my bed. Could it be that Mitch took it? He took Aimee's phone, and I have no idea what his plan was for that. Did he want to cut her off from contacting her friends? It wasn't something we'd ever talked about and should have been my first sign that he was going rogue.

Whatever happened, and wherever the gun is, I don't have much longer to look.

Hurrying now, I drop to my knees and check under both beds.

No gun.

The nightstands then. Maybe Mitch took it and stashed it in one of the drawers. Maybe he—

No gun.

I eyeball his suitcase. *No way.* He might be cocky, and he

might be stupid enough to steal Aimee's phone and leave it lying around, but a gun?

If he's the one who took it, chances are really good he has it on him. It's small enough that in a man's deep shorts pocket, you'd never notice it was there. That was its appeal, but right now that's also the problem.

"Think!" I slap myself on the cheek. Hard. The sting is bright and painful, but it offers some clarity.

Mitch... He stole Aimee's phone, and I wasn't going to get involved in that because it worked in my favor, but now I'm wondering what his plan is.

I thought he was on my side. That was what we'd discussed —that he was coming with me to support me.

But what if I was wrong? What if I'm not the only one here with ulterior motives? Sure, it was weird that he took Aimee's phone, but people do weird things. I wrote it off because I was too focused on my task at hand.

And now I'm wondering if I really screwed up.

Goosebumps break out on my arms, and I double-check both doors to make sure the deadbolts are engaged. Only then do I lock myself in the bathroom.

I lather up and rinse without letting the shower heat up all the way. The water is freezing, but I barely notice how uncomfortable it is.

As I shower, my mind races.

I trusted my brother. What kind of game is he playing?

FORTY-FIVE

AIMEE

My mind races as I try to work through what's going on.

There's more to Mitch than meets the eye, and I have to admit... that's concerning.

"What do you think I need to come clean with you about?" I force myself to speak, even though my mouth feels dry, my tongue swollen.

"Hannah hates you," he begins, and I can't keep myself from barking out a laugh.

"Yeah, you think?" I take a deep breath to try to calm down. When he burst through the door, I thought for sure that he knew something, that he suspected me, but I think he's stabbing in the dark trying to get information.

As long as Hannah doesn't tell him what she knows—what she *thinks* she knows—

"She said you're a murderer."

There it is.

"She's willing to say or do anything to take my fiancé, and that includes ruining my life." I stare him in the eyes, hoping he'll listen, that he'll believe me.

But then the door slams open, and Dale's there. His eyes

flick between the two of us, worry clearly written across his face. "You two okay?"

"We're great. I was just coming back upstairs to get some ice for a glass of water," I lie. When I walk past Mitch, I don't look up at him. My shoulder brushes Dale's, but he stops me, his hand closing around my arm.

"You have my phone?"

I fight to keep from rolling my eyes. So much for using his social media to reach out to my friends. I slip it into his pocket and keep walking.

"I'll see you in the room," I say. "Just gonna get that ice." I gesture to the door and hurry inside the ice room. Behind me, Dale and Mitch start down the hall.

There's a small bag dispenser by the ice machine, and I rip one free before flapping it open, then using the supplied scoop to fill the bag.

Quietly, so I don't disturb anyone on the floor, I close the door to the ice room and walk back out into the hall. Mitch and Dale are only a few rooms down from me, which surprises me. I thought they'd be back to the rooms by now, but as I watch, Mitch stops walking and braces his hand on the wall.

They look serious.

I walk towards them but stop in my tracks when Dale speaks.

"You alright?" He sounds concerned.

"I'm good. You?" Mitch's voice is quieter than Dale's, but I can still make out every word he says.

"I'm fine." There's an undercurrent of anger in Dale's words.

"Is Hannah okay?"

"Okay? Who knows. But she is crazy. She was stalking Aimee; she was—"

I want to know more. I want to know what Dale is going to

say, but someone opens the door right next to me, and both men turn towards me.

"Is everything okay?" I ask, hurrying to the two of them. The ice hangs at my side. "You two look serious."

"We're fine." Dale rubs his hand across his forehead. "I think I'm just tired and a bit hungover."

"Makes sense. We've had a rough weekend." I pause, but neither of them speak up. "I'm headed to the room to get some water. You guys can check on Hannah. Hopefully she's showered by now. And maybe feels better."

Or maybe she's dead. I wouldn't mind dead.

I hate that I'm thinking that way about her, but it's true. Her being dead would make my life a hundred times easier.

"Sounds good." Mitch starts to walk down the hall with me, but Dale doesn't move. "Dale, you coming?"

"Yeah, of course." Dale gives his head a shake, which is always what he does when he's distracted and trying not to think about something. I've seen him do it over and over again, and it tells me how in his own head he is right now.

Before I can turn away from him, however, he grabs my hand.

I barely register the feeling of his skin on mine—I'm too busy thinking about Hannah.

I found the obit I was looking for online, which means I know exactly who she is.

No wonder she hates me.

She thinks I killed her boyfriend.

FORTY-SIX

Then

"This is my fault!" I slam my hand onto the steering wheel, then immediately regret it. The pain that shoots through my skinned palm makes me whimper, and I press my hand against my thigh to try to dull the pain.

It doesn't work, and now that my body realizes that I'm safe and can hurt without being in a lot of danger, all of the pain from that walk kicks in.

My feet ache. I stubbed my toes at least a dozen times, maybe more. I have scratches up and down both shins from when I tripped with Steph. My palms burn, my core is sore, my...

I glance over at my sister. Her head is turned away from me, resting on the window. I don't remember if she was like that when we put her in the car, then I realize she couldn't have been, not with the door open. She must have slipped and leaned against it and now is resting there.

"Steph?" Fear grips my heart, and I reach over to touch her shoulder. "Steph, you alive?"

She doesn't respond, but she does shift position a bit. I'm going to tell myself that she's moving to let me know that she's okay, not because of the curve we're going around.

I put my hand back on the wheel and squeeze it hard while I try to think.

If my phone weren't dead, I'd call Josh or Daniel and let them know that I screwed up, that I need their help, but it's dead, and I think I dropped it on the trail.

Mom and Dad will lose it when they find out what happened.

"No!" I scream, then swear, then pound the steering wheel once again.

I have to take her to the hospital. No way can we sneak back into the house without being caught, without being interrogated. I'm dead meat after tonight, but at least Steph will be okay.

My bare foot presses harder on the gas.

Jeeps aren't made for zooming around curvy mountain roads, but that's exactly what I'm asking mine to do. I need to be safe, but I need to hurry.

I need to get to the hospital as fast as possible.

At the same time, I need to slow down and drive safer.

My mind feels like it's splintering.

It's dark here, still so dark, my headlights like a surgeon's scalpels cutting through the night. Faster and faster I drive, my palms now slick with sweat, the salt burning my open cuts, but I don't slow down.

There's a hairpin curve, and I slow down, tapping the brake just enough to get around it. We end up in the left lane, but nobody's coming. I'd see their headlights if they were.

I guess that if there were ever a time to drive like mad, to ignore driving safety, this is it.

"Hang on, Steph," I say, then reach back out to squeeze her arm. She's going to beat herself up over this. I have to let her know that everything's going to be okay. "I'm gonna get you some help, okay? You're going to be just fine. I don't know what happened out there with you and Connor, but I promise you that it wasn't your fault. I don't need to know what happened to know that you didn't screw up."

When I stop talking, my brain starts working through all of the possible scenarios of what could have happened between the two of them.

She's clothed, so I don't think he... No, I really don't think he did that.

But no way did she end up in the mud and water by herself. I don't think she slipped, not careful Steph who knows how to be safe around waterfalls.

He had to have pushed her. Or tossed her.

My stomach twists.

"Just a few more minutes and we'll be at the hospital. I'll get to a phone. I'll make sure that everything is okay, that it's all taken care of." I'm rambling, but filling the car with random thoughts is much better than being alone with them.

"And then you'll get checked out. The doctor will make sure that you're okay. We're not going back to the party tonight" —*Josh is probably with Jess right now*—"but that doesn't matter. It'll be you and me, and we'll have a great rest of the summer before it's time for us to—for me to go to college.

Another sharp turn. No headlights coming, so I don't slow down as much as I should.

"And I'll visit you, and you'll visit me, and we can talk about tonight, but it won't ever be this big defining event, you know what I mean? It'll be this thing that happened, this crazy thing that we overcame this summer, and yeah, you and I will probably have some new scars from it, but scars are cool."

Another curve.

I press down harder on the gas, shooting out of the curve like a bullet. We're close to the hospital now—we only need to drive a few more minutes. Ahead of us, down the mountain, the town's lights twinkle like Christmas.

"Just hang on," I whisper. "Please, Steph, I'm so sorry. I did this to you, and it's my fault, and I don't know how I can ever forgive myself or live without you, so I just need you to hang on a bit longer. You'll be okay. We'll be okay."

Tears stream down my face, but I don't wipe them away. I'm too focused on the road ahead, at the way it spools out in front of us to realize that some of the lights I thought were from the town are actually from a car.

I swerve into the left lane to take the curve.

FORTY-SEVEN

AIMEE

Dale is different.

I picked up on it immediately, and while I don't know what's changed with him, it's clear something has happened.

A mindshift change?

Did he make a decision about something?

The way he linked his fingers through mine, like I belonged to him, like I was some prize he could claim, used to be something I appreciated about him. Who wouldn't want to walk around on the arm of a man who looks like him? But since I found out about his affair, I haven't wanted him to hold me like that.

Not that I had a choice on the way back to the hotel room. His fingers were tight around mine like he wasn't fooling around. And now that we're standing outside the door waiting for Mitch to unlock it, he lets go of my hand and loops his arm around my waist, pulling me close to him.

Mitch notices—I know he does. I see the way he glances at the two of us out the corner of his eye like he's not quite sure what he's seeing. He's not happy with how lovey-dovey Dale is being right now.

And I'm not either.

"Who's going to help Hannah shower if she's still dirty?" I ask in an attempt to lighten the mood.

In response, Dale's fingers sink into my hip.

"That's the job of a boyfriend," he says, his words directed at Mitch.

Dale doesn't know that they're not dating.

"You mean the boyfriend who was hunting down your fiancée when nobody knew where she was?" Mitch responds dryly.

"I bet she's fine," I say, right as Mitch pushes the door open.

I'm expecting Hannah to be on the floor, the smell of vomit to still be overwhelming, but the cleaning crew must have worked their butts off to make this place smell the way it does. It's not... clean exactly. I swear I can still smell the sweet scent of her puke, but it's a lot better than it was when I left her in here with Dale.

"Hannah?" Mitch leads the way in, and I follow him, leaving Dale in the rear. "Hannah, you okay?"

"In the bathroom!" Her voice is sweet. Angelic. She's not at all passed out the way I thought she would be after I drugged her. She sounds... perky.

Now what do I do?

"She sounds better than she did," Dale says, and I nod.

"I just got out of the shower. I'm still a little tired, but I think I got whatever made me sick out of my system, so you don't have to worry about me barfing on you." The bathroom door swings open without warning, and suddenly Hannah's right there, a small towel barely covering more than her bikini.

"Oh geez, what is this, some kind of party?" She brushes some damp hair back from her face. She's smiling, or trying to, but it's clear she's still exhausted and doesn't feel great. "Were you guys worried about me?" Her eyes land on all of us in turn but widen when she gets to Mitch. "You look sour. What's wrong?"

"I was trying to find Aimee. Nobody knew where she was." He glances at me, and although I see the movement, I don't turn to meet his eye.

"Well, she's here now. But you missed me being so sick." Hannah pushes between Dale and me to get to Mitch. Her hand flutters by his cheek, but she doesn't touch him. "I could have used you here to take care of me. I can't believe you chose Aimee over me."

My stomach sinks.

"I didn't choose her over you." Mitch cuts his eyes at me.

We're all silent.

"Well, let me get dressed," Hannah says.

I shouldn't be surprised that she yanks the towel from around her body and hands it to him, but I am. When I avert my eyes, Dale does the same. He even goes as far as to turn his head like he doesn't want even the memory of her naked body in his mind.

Mitch turns away from her but takes the towel.

"We'll leave you to it," I say. "When you're decent and feel better, we can all decide what the rest of the afternoon will bring."

"Oh, give me a second, Aimee. No need to be such a prude."

I don't wait to watch her flounce across the hotel room to her suitcase. Even without seeing what she's doing, I have no doubt in my mind she's going to make getting dressed as sexy as possible, and I'm not interested.

Dale follows me into the hall. He lets the door close behind him, then turns to me.

I clear my throat. "She's obviously feeling fine. What did you think of the little show in there?"

"Hannah?" He rolls his eyes. "She loves being the center of attention."

"That she does." I cross my arms and lean against the wall. Part of me wants to ask Dale what he thinks is going to happen now. He deserves to be punished, but that's not something I can worry about right now. I have to stop Hannah from hurting me.

"I think we should—" But whatever he was about to say is interrupted when the hotel door swings open.

Hannah stands there, her face free of makeup, her shorts so short I swear I can almost see everything, wearing a triumphant grin. Is this really the woman who was just vomiting all over herself? She looks amazing.

I really need to have a word with the guy who sold me the roofie. I paid for the real thing, but judging how she's acting right now, I'm pretty sure he took advantage of me. Drug dealers. Can't trust 'em.

"What's the plan?" Her eyes flick from me to Dale.

"We're going to take it easy," Dale says, and my stomach sinks.

I can't *take it easy*. That's not a luxury I have, not when Hannah has it out for me. If I hide in my room, I might be safe, but all I'll be doing is delaying the inevitable.

One of us won't make it home from this trip.

Dale's still talking. "I was thinking a massage. Maybe a nap." He comes to stand next to me, then loops his arm around my waist to pull me closer to him. "Aimee and I haven't gotten nearly enough alone time on this trip, and I want to be with her. Just the two of us. Besides, you probably need to rest." He squeezes my side.

"I was thinking shots," I say, stiffening and pulling away. "Dancing. Partying. No way do I want to be locked up in our room." My mind races as I think about how to stop Hannah. An idea hits me, and I think it might be my only shot at survival.

I have to get her drunk. Lead her to the ocean. That's my plan—to get her in the water.

Drunk people drown all the time. Usually it's a tragedy, but tonight it could be my deliverance.

Hannah's eyes light up. "I love it. That's what I want to do."

"You sure you can handle it?" I want to goad her a little so she's determined to come. "You rallied fast considering you were just barfing all over yourself."

"Well, I'm not any longer. Whatever hit me is over. Thank goodness I'm immune to being drugged."

"Hannah." Dale's voice is a warning that everyone ignores.

"Mitch?" I turn to him. "Thoughts? You feel up to dancing and partying?"

"I'm in." He winks at me, then turns to Dale. "You in?"

Dale's expression is dark. He takes a moment to compose himself, then drags his gaze away from Hannah. "Fine. I'm in."

"Great. Let me get my ChapStick, and I'll be ready to go. You guys wait for me." I don't make eye contact with Dale as I hurry past him to our room. When I press the keycard to the door and it beeps, I greedily push it open.

This time tomorrow I'll be home. And Hannah? She'll be dead too.

One more day and I'll be free of them. Free of him.

Literally nothing can stop me now.

Except for Hannah.

FORTY-EIGHT

AIMEE

To my surprise, Mitch follows me into my hotel room.

"Did you find my phone?" I refuse to let him see how shocked I am that he's in here with me, and I don't want him to feel like he can pick back up on the conversation we were having in the stairwell. Instead of letting him take control, I throw the question at him.

I'm annoyed with him. He knew I needed help, he offered to help me, and then he just disappeared.

And if I'm honest with myself, there's something about him disappearing and then showing back up out of nowhere that doesn't sit right with me. I need him to make it make sense.

"Hannah doesn't have it." He hovers by the door, almost like he's afraid to get too close to me. "I promise you, Aimee, I went through every inch of the room, and she doesn't have your phone. But don't worry—I can look out for you if you're honest with me."

"Honest with you?" I bark out a laugh. "Please. You told me you were on my side then completely disappeared."

He blinks but recovers quickly. It's clear he's surprised that

I'd call him out like that, but I'm done playing games. I want to end this.

"Everything's happening for a reason. I know we lied to you when we all first arrived, but I've got your back." When he smiles, he looks like the Cheshire Cat, all of his teeth on display. "Trust me."

I don't.

I don't trust anyone on this trip.

Instead of responding, I grab my ChapStick and shove it into my pocket. I'm uncomfortable, every inch of my skin tight, like I'm wearing a suit that's too small. I'm awkward and hyper-aware of all of my actions.

The question I have to answer is how far am I willing to go to save myself.

I make a decision. "You know what? I don't need your help. I've got this under control." I stand and walk past him without slowing down. Truth be told, willingly going out with this group feels like a bad idea. It's a dance, what the four of us are doing, and we all have our secrets.

But my secrets could end up with me in jail. Or worse.

Out in the hall, Dale leans against the wall. As soon as he sees me walk out the door, he steps towards me, and my gaze flicks to Hannah.

Messing with her by drugging her made me feel like I had the upper hand, but that obviously didn't work out for me. She just keeps surviving. Like a very blonde cockroach.

"I was starting to wonder what the two of you were getting up to in there," she says. "I thought Dale and I were going to have to go get the party started without you."

"Never." Mitch exudes confidence. "You know I'm always down to party." With that, he and Dale start down the hall, leaving me to walk with Hannah.

I try to catch up to the guys, but she stops me by grabbing my arm and looping hers through mine.

"Where's the fire?" She snaps her gum at me. "You took a while in your hotel room finding your ChapStick, and now you're in such a rush. Spill."

"Spill?" I keep my face as neutral as possible. "I don't know what you're talking about."

"Sure you do. I want you to tell me a secret. And then I'll tell you one too."

I scoff without meaning to. The thought of trusting this woman with anything is laughable. "Why in the world would I want to do that?"

"Because I already know your biggest one, and I bet you'd love to know mine." She stops walking and yanks me backwards so I'm facing her. When she speaks again, it's through gritted teeth, like she can't stand the fact that she has to communicate with me. "Do you not understand that? I. Know. Who. You. Are. You can pretend like you're not who you were back home in North Carolina, pretend like I don't know everything about you, but you can't hide who you are. You drugged me to keep it a secret, didn't you?"

I don't respond. I *can't* respond.

"Were you willing to kill me to keep your secret?"

Ice trickles down my spine, but she isn't finished.

"Because some people might say you deserve to die for what you did." She grins at me. "How does that feel?"

"I think you're full of it," I tell her, and I'm gratified when her eyes widen.

"Really?" She's leaned in so close now that I can feel her body heat.

"You're grasping at straws," I say. It's exactly what I'm doing, but she doesn't need to know that. "You're clueless."

"Oh, I'm not clueless. I want to make you pay for what you did. I wanted Dale, so I took him. But that wasn't enough, although I'm sure it hurt, didn't it, to know how easily someone else could take him?" She glances down at my engagement ring and smirks. "So eager to throw someone under the bus for what you did. Did you really think you'd get away with murder?" She pops her gum at me and glances down the hall at the waiting men. "Listen, there's one thing you can help me with that will wipe the slate clean—how does that sound?" Then she tells me something that I never, in my entire life, would have guessed would come out of her mouth.

I stare at her, trying to wrap my mind around what she just said.

FORTY-NINE

AIMEE

Hannah wants me to help her kill Dale.

That's what she whispered to me.

That's what she said would wipe my slate clean.

I can't wrap my mind around it, even as I stare at her as she gets us a round of shots. She leans over the bar, clearly flirting with the bartender. Neither Mitch nor Dale pays her any attention.

Doesn't mean a thing that they're not looking at her. My motto? Trust no one. Not even the man who acts like he wants to date me.

Scratch that: *especially* not the man who acts like he wants to date me.

"You good?" Dale asks, reaching over and lightly touching my arm. "I thought you wanted to drink and dance, but you're sitting there looking pretty sour."

I force myself to smile at him. "Drinking first," I tell him. "Then dancing." When I speak again, my voice is lower so it doesn't carry to Mitch. "Do you think Hannah should really be drinking after she was so sick?"

"She's fine. That's what happens when you work out and

take care of your body, Aimes. You get back to feeling better ASAP. Besides, you worry too much about other people." He takes my hand and lifts it to his mouth to give me a kiss. "Really, I just want you to have a good time. Who cares if they're having fun? You're what matters to me."

"Thanks." I pull my hand back and plant it in my lap while I wait for Hannah to return. She's sure taking her time, leaning over the bar and flirting harder with the bartender. When my eyes flick to Dale to see what he thinks, they snag on Mitch, who's staring at me.

I flush and look away.

But then Hannah's at the table. She sets the four glasses down in front of us, a triumphant grin on her face.

"Chocolate cake shots," she announces. "The bartender promised me they taste just like the real deal." She plops down into her seat next to Mitch and pushes a glass in front of each of us.

"Cheers," Dale says, taking his glass and holding it out in front of me to cheers him back. I have to force myself to do what he wants, but when I touch our glasses together, he smiles.

"Cheers," I say automatically. Just as automatically, I lift the shot glass and dump the liquid in a nearby plant. Before anyone else looks up, I put my empty glass down on the table.

Mitch stands up. "Next round is on me," he says. His eyes flick to me before he turns and smiles at Hannah.

"First round was on you too," she teases. "You just didn't know it."

We all laugh. Mine feels mechanical, but I don't think anyone can tell.

Mitch slaps his hand on the table and grins, then hurries off to the bar. I watch him go as Hannah speaks to Dale.

"What did I miss? You guys come up with a plan of where we're going after we take some shots?"

"I think we all need to talk, so let's go for a beach walk.

Maybe after we can go swimming," I pipe up, my heart pounding in my chest. This is the make-or-break moment. This night is hurtling forward, and I know for a fact there's only one acceptable conclusion it can come to. If I want out of this, I'm going to have to do what Hannah wants me to do.

"Definitely." Hannah grins and throws me a wink, but Dale doesn't notice. He's too busy watching Mitch get us more drinks at the bar. "Night swimming is my favorite."

I smile, trying to look as comfortable and in control as possible, even though my mind is spinning.

I came here to punish Dale, but not like that. Not how Hannah wants. Sure, he's a crap boyfriend, but that doesn't mean he deserves to die.

But what if killing him is the only way I get to live?

FIFTY

Then

Someone's honking.

The sound's loud and insistent, a constant, not the honking that you do when some idiot didn't use their turn signal, but the kind of honking that tells you someone really screwed up.

I open my eyes.

Why were my eyes closed?

My arms hang down by my head, and I stare at them, trying to make sense of why they'd be there, by my face, and not on the steering wheel.

The honking continues.

I turn to look at Steph. She's just like me, her arms by her head, but her hair is sticking straight up. It's comical, and I stifle a giggle.

Still, with the honking.

That sound is so constant that it's like a bug in my ear, and I finally realize what's going on.

My body hurts, but it did even before we got in the car. It

hurts worse now. I reach to my forehead, and my fingers come away red.

What's going on?

"Steph?" I turn back to her. Her eyes are open, but there's a cut on her forehead. It's dripping, but the blood isn't landing on her lap. It's hitting... the roof of the Jeep?

We're upside down.

That explains everything. The arms, the hair, the blood. The honking. Someone isn't honking at me—that wouldn't explain the sound filling this space so much. It's the Jeep, the Jeep is honking and the horn is probably screwed up, probably so damaged from... *the wreck* that it isn't working.

The wreck.

Those two words pinball around in my mind, and I try to push them out, but they're lodged in there now, and it all suddenly makes sense. There were headlights and a curve and...

"Steph!" I scream and reach over to her. When I grab her by the arm and give it a little shake, it wobbles and hangs just like it was before. "Steph! Are you okay?"

Her eyes are open, and she's staring, and I've seen enough movies—I'm a TV junkie, you know—to know that someone only does that when they're dead, and if that means Steph is dead, then that means I killed her.

Never mind how damaged her body was after whatever Connor did to her.

Never mind I was taking her to the hospital to make sure she got the care she needed.

Never mind any of it because if Steph is dead, then the only reasonable explanation is that *I killed her.*

I can't breathe. I have to get out of here.

Like a wild animal, I start jerking at my seatbelt, but it's locked in place, doing exactly what it was designed to do. I shriek, the sound splitting, but wailing doesn't undo my seatbelt.

Turning, I slam my open palm into the window.

"Help me!" I scream, ignoring the searing pain in my hand. "Help me! I'm alive! Help!"

Nothing. No movement outside. There's another car; I can see it—it's angled across the road, but at least it's still on the road. Its headlights shine out towards us, illuminating the field in front of us.

At least it was a field and not the woods because if we'd come to rest in the woods, then I have no doubt we'd be wrapped around a tree and Steph wouldn't be the only one dead. I'd be—

"Help me! I'm alive!" I scream again, trying my best to make myself heard over the sound of the horn. The sound is maddening. It never varies, never changes, just keeps on keeping on, and I can feel myself slowing going insane.

It's the horn making me crazy, not the fact that my sister's dead body is strung up next to me like we're in an abattoir.

"Please," I beg. "P-Please." Tears stream from my eyes, running in rivers across my forehead. "Please, I'm sorry. I didn't mean to—I was trying to help."

The horn is my only constant.

That and my tears. I can't stop crying. The entire time I'm crying, my hands run over the seatbelt, looking for some way to pull it away from my body, to release myself, then my fingers find the buckle.

I press it, but I'm not actually expecting it to work.

There's a moment where I've pressed the buckle and it's come loose and I'm still hanging upside down, then suddenly I'm falling. My head slams into the roof of the Jeep, and I cry out. Stars fill my vision, and I'm sure I'm going to pass out, but then they clear, and I blink hard, scrambling around so that I'm sitting.

Steph still hangs next to me. She sways gently from the movement of the Jeep, but I'm sure she isn't moving. Her body is.

Because that's all she is now, you know, a body, and you're the one who did that to her.

Another sob tears through me, and I bury my face in my hands. It hurts to cry, hurts like I never thought it could, but I deserve that pain, don't I? I'm the one who brought it on myself and on Steph. Besides, there's a saying about how pain proves that you're alive, and if that's the truth, I'm the most alive person to ever have existed.

I'm crying so hard that I almost don't hear the shifting next to me.

But there was something, some movement, and it lands just right in my ear, and I hold my breath, my face still buried in my hands.

I don't want to look.

I don't believe in ghosts, but if I did, this would be the perfect time for one to rear its ugly head, for it to show up and torment me, although I don't think it could do a better job than I'm doing right now.

I lift my head.

Steph's eyes are still open, but they're different somehow. Before they were blank, just her eyes, staring out at me, but mostly at nothing. Now, though, they're sharper—there's life to them.

"Steph!" I scream and rise up on my knees to get closer to her. "Steph, you're okay! I hoped you would be okay, but I thought you were gone." My hands flutter to her face. I cup her cheeks and brush her hair back. "I'm going to unbuckle you, okay? But I won't let you fall. I learned from last time."

The laugh that bubbles out of me doesn't sound like me.

"You're going to be okay, Steph."

The horn continues.

I position myself under her so that when I press the buckle and she falls, she'll land on me. I don't know how better to catch her. If there were someone else in here, we would support her head, protect it, make sure she didn't land on it, but it's just her and me and whoever still hasn't gotten out of the other car.

"I'm going to lower you down, okay? Just wait. You'll be fine."

My hand finds the buckle, but before I can press it, her mouth moves.

"Please."

"What?" I scoot over so that my ear is right by her lips. Her face is red. From pain or exertion or the fact that she's still upside down, I don't know, but I do know I need to help her, need to get her flipped around. "Say it again, Steph. What did you say?"

"Call 911."

My heart sinks. I can't, but she doesn't know that. If I tell her that I can't call for help, then she'll realize just how much trouble she's really in.

"There's no reason to call 911," I lie to her. "Not when you're going to be just fine."

FIFTY-ONE
HANNAH

It's my turn to buy the shots, but the last thing I want to do is pretend like I'm still drinking. I can't fake more shots, and I certainly can't stand being out with this trio any longer. You really think I would trust any beverage around Aimee ever again?

Never mind the fact that my head still pounds and I'm unsteady on my feet. I'd do anything to go back to the room and pass out, but I can't. Tonight is the only chance I have to save myself.

Ten years ago, Aimee ruined my life, and she's been allowed to walk around free without any consequences.

It isn't fair. It isn't right.

And while I don't want to allow it to continue, I have to get rid of Dale first if I'm going to save myself. He wasn't a key player in this until he threatened me. I'm sure if he went to the police with proof of me stalking Aimee, they'd dig deep into what I've been doing. They'd find out how long I've been following her, and I don't want to risk any repercussions.

He dug his own grave.

So here I am with Mitch, Dale, and Aimee. What's the

saying? Keep your friends close and your enemies closer? She thinks she's safe, that if she helps me punish Dale, that I won't hurt her.

Yeah, right. I hunted her for years. I can wait a bit longer to get my revenge, but it's inevitable, no matter what I tell her so she'll help me get rid of Dale.

"I have an idea!" I shout and slam my hand down on the table to get their attention. Nobody else in the bar looks up. Last night when we were here, we were in the back room, so it would be quiet and we'd be able to chat. Now, though, music and voices hum and throb around us. It's difficult to hear the person sitting across the table from you when everyone is shouting.

"What's your idea?" Aimee asks, and the way she says the words makes them sound like a dare. Dale reaches out and puts his hand on hers, trying to loop their fingers together, but she pulls her hand away.

"Not just swimming. Skinny. Dipping." I squeal, then cover my mouth with both hands like I can't quite believe what I just said. "Thoughts? Shall we vote?"

Do I really want to be naked around these three? No, I don't.

But if Mitch has my gun with him and he strips down first, I might have an opportunity to go through his clothes while he's in the water. It's not a great idea, but it's also not the worst I've ever had. Besides, it gets us out of the bar, away from prying eyes.

I have to find that gun. The problem is, anyone at this table could have taken it. Gun or no, swimming after drinking is a recipe for disaster.

People drown when they're goofing off in the ocean.

"Skinny-dipping?" Aimee takes a deep breath. "That sounds like a blast."

"That sounds dangerous," Dale interrupts. "We've been drinking, and—"

I roll my eyes at him, even though I agree. "Killjoy," I say, then turn back to Aimee. "You're really game?"

We stare at each other. She's searching my face for answers, for proof that I'm going to hold up my end of the deal.

"Of course I am. But I have to pee." Aimee pushes back from the table and stands up, her movement so abrupt that she knocks into the table with her hip. Without looking back at the three of us, she calls over her shoulder. "Don't wait for me to take more shots. I'm done drinking."

Dale's eyes lock on her as she winds her way between tables on the way to the bathroom.

"You need to give her a break. She's not who you think, okay? She's better." Mitch grabs me by the hand and yanks me towards him. "I know your plan, but give it up."

"What plan?" Dale asks, but I ignore him.

"We're just going swimming, I promise." I stare at Mitch. "Trust me." I can't loop Mitch in on my change of plans. Not here, not with Dale listening.

"Trust you." Mitch cocks an eyebrow. "Sure."

Dale stands and shoves back from the table. "I don't know what plan you're talking about, but you need to drop it. Aimee is great. I love her. Get over it."

And then he's gone, leaving me alone with my brother.

I whirl on him.

"What game are you playing?" It's the first time the two of us have had any time alone tonight, and I can't hold back my frustration. "You told me you'd come here and help me out. You'd support me. And what are you doing? Acting like you care about Aimee."

"She's not the terrible person you made her out to be. She's—"

"*A murderer*, Mitch. Or did you conveniently forget that? She killed my boyfriend. Your best friend, I might add. You weren't there that night." I stab my finger into his chest. "You have no idea what it was like to lose him. To see him dead and not be able to do anything to bring him back."

I'm breathing fast, too fast, and I try to slow down. It doesn't matter how many hours I've spent working with a therapist, every time I stop and think about the night I lost Brian, I can barely breathe.

It wasn't just the accident. It wasn't just losing him.

It was the lies.

And the fact that I couldn't go to the police about what happened.

I made a vow years ago that I would do whatever it took to get the justice he deserved, and here I am trying to do that, and the one person who promised to help me is dragging his feet.

"Are you on my side or not?" I snap the question at him, and when he hesitates, I feel myself getting pissed and change topics. "Did you take what was in my suitcase?"

"What are you talking about?"

I lean closer so there's no chance of anyone overhearing us. "My gun, idiot. Did you take my gun?"

"You can't kill her, okay? I'm not going to let—"

"You did! Idiot," I hiss. "What, did you seriously think this trip was going to end with the four of us holding hands and singing 'Kumbaya'?"

"She's not the evil person you made her out to be. She made a mistake."

My mouth falls open, and I lean back from him. "You fell for her."

He doesn't respond.

"You did." I close my eyes and rub my temples. "You're just as bad as those stupid housewives who fall for murderers in prison, you know that? You think she's going to suddenly have feelings for you? That you two will ride off into the sunset together? That she'll *care* for you?"

He doesn't answer, but he doesn't need to. I can see it written all over his face.

"I'm serious, Mitch. Whatever game you're playing, you need to stop. You trying to get her to feel bad for you? Do you really think that she'll suddenly decide to leave Dale for you? Please. You have to stop this stupid game you're playing." Once again, I lean closer to him. "I found her phone in your suitcase. What, you had to take it so you could feel close to her? You're pathetic, you know that?"

"You shouldn't have taken it from me."

"Shouldn't I? Remember why we're here, Mitch! To get revenge!"

"She didn't—"

"Dale is going to pick up on the fact that you're smitten with her or something. It's gross."

"I just think we need to—"

"No." I grab him by the shoulder and squeeze as hard as possible. To his credit, he doesn't flinch, even though I know my fake nails have to hurt as they dig into his skin. "You don't want to get your hands dirty? Fine. That's fine. What if I tell you I have no interest in hurting Aimee tonight—does that make things better?"

He stares at me.

"Does that make things better?"

"It does." He lifts his chin and looks down his nose at me, but then takes a deep breath and continues. "But I don't know if you can really stop. You're taking this too far, Hannah. Eventually you have to give it a rest. Brian wouldn't want you to—"

"Brian doesn't want anything, and it's because of her." Tears burn my eyes, but I don't let them fall. I'm angry. Scared. I'd love to tell Mitch that we're going to punish Dale too, but he's already a loose cannon. I can't trust him to not do something stupid. "I'm ending this, Mitch. Tonight. Back off."

FIFTY-TWO

AIMEE

The cold water I splash on my face is bracing, but it helps me focus.

It's hard for me to believe that Dale, Hannah, and Mitch didn't notice that I wasn't drinking. Every time they took a shot, I poured mine into a plant behind me.

What? You think I was going to take a single shot with them around? I have to keep my wits about me.

There's an energy in the air, almost like the night is alive, and I feel excitement course through me. I'm terrified of what's about to happen, and I'm not sure if I can go through with it. It's one thing to want to make Dale sorry for hurting me, another entirely to... kill him.

But it's worth it if Hannah will really back off. She promised she would, said that this would clear my name in her book, but...

But what if she was lying? Can I really trust her? No. I don't know if I can, but I don't know what other choice I have.

I smack my hand into the counter by the sink, surprising a woman coming into the bathroom.

"Cockroach," I say, and her face whitens.

She turns and hurries out of the bathroom, and I sigh, then run more water on my hands. After splashing water on my face again, I give myself one last glance in the mirror and follow her out of the bathroom.

It's not that I have much of a plan. If I had a gun, or my phone so I could contact my friends, or *something*, that would help, but it's just me and my wits.

And the hope that Dale had enough to drink that he'll be sloppy. He'll make mistakes. We'll go skinny-dipping and he'll drown, or maybe Hannah will have to hold his head under the water...

I just have to make sure he gets in the right position. Hannah will take care of Dale. And then if I have the opportunity to take her out? I should because the more I think about it, the less I believe her that killing Dale will wipe my slate clean.

She's a liar, and I believe she lied to me about that too.

Taking a deep breath, I push open the bathroom door and walk down the hall, but I don't make it very far before running into Dale. He's turning the corner to the bathroom just as I'm turning it to sneak out the front door. I want to take a moment to myself, but before I realize what's happening, his arms are around me, and he's pulling me into a hug.

"Glad I caught you on the way back to the table," he says, the scent of alcohol on his breath washing over me.

I force myself to smile. "I was actually going to get some fresh air," I tell him. As I speak, I plant my hand on his chest and lean back from him. The loud music, the heat from his body, his strong cologne... all of my senses are on overdrive, and I need to put some space between us.

The itchy feeling that I'm coming out of my skin intensifies.

"I'll come with you! It will be nice to get outside."

He turns, looping his arm around my waist and snuggling me close. I'm pressed up against his side as we walk through the bar. Even though I know we're going to walk right past our table, I keep my eyes locked ahead.

"Hey, wait up!" That's Hannah, and in a moment, she's at my side, grinning at me.

Mitch doesn't call to us, but I feel him fall into step behind the three of us. With Dale and Hannah on either side of me and Mitch behind me, I can't help but feel like I'm under arrest.

But then we're outside, and I can finally take a deep breath of fresh air. Without thinking about what I'm doing, I push away from Dale and walk a few feet from the three of them. It doesn't matter that someone out here is smoking, and it smells like someone else just barfed on the sidewalk.

The sky is big and open, and I no longer feel like I'm choking.

"Just where are you going?" Hannah appears next to me. "We have a plan."

"I just want to stretch my legs." I just need a moment to get my head on straight. It's one thing to daydream about killing someone, another to actually take steps to do it.

"You better not be going back to your room. It's so early! We were going to go skinny-dipping. Don't you remember our conversation?" She grins at me, and I have to steel myself to keep from moving away from her.

"Hannah." That's Mitch, his voice low with frustration, but neither of us turn to look at him.

She's dangerous, and I need to be careful.

"Just give me two minutes. I don't feel good," I lie, but she's already shaking her head.

"You feel fine! And come on, look at me. I rallied, and if I can come back from how terrible I was feeling, why can't you?"

"I'm just tired."

"Tired, shmired. Let's go." She loops her arm through mine and jerks me close. "You owe me if you want this to end."

I do owe her.

She narrows her eyes at me, clearly waiting for a response, waiting to hear what I'm going to say to her, but my tongue is dry, stuck to the roof of my mouth.

I swallow hard. We're still walking, but I can't seem to slow my feet.

"Listen: someone isn't going to make it home from this trip. We can make sure it's Dale if you work with me. Otherwise, it's you."

FIFTY-THREE

HANNAH

Aimee's toe catches on a crack in the sidewalk, and she tips into me.

"Whoa there," I say, pulling her closer. "Bit of a lightweight, are we?"

"I didn't drink."

"Really? Because you had just as many empty glasses in front of you as the rest of us did. So tell me again how you didn't drink—because all of us would swear that you did." I'm needling her.

"I was dumping the alcohol," she says, which is true. I caught her doing it with the first shot we ordered, but I wasn't about to say anything.

"So no liquid courage needed for our plan?"

She takes a deep breath and exhales slowly. I can almost see the cogs in her brain turning as she looks for a way out of this, but there isn't one.

"Are you sure it will wipe my slate clean?"

"Cross my heart."

"Why?"

"Why what?"

"You hate me. You've wanted to kill me for... for years. And suddenly you've changed your mind? It doesn't track."

"Plans change." No way do I want to get into it with her. If she knew the truth—that I only want to kill Dale to save myself —she'd turn on me. I know she would.

"I doubt that. You don't seem like the kind of girl to randomly change plans."

Frustration surges through my blood. "Just... trust me, okay? Dale isn't who you thought he was. He's not a good guy. You got a taste of that when he cheated on you, but he's worse."

She's silent, and I search her eyes for a sign that she's going to believe me. Finally, she nods, the movement abrupt. I exhale slowly in relief.

"I'll do whatever you tell me to do."

Relief washes over me. Her eyes bore into me, and I get the distinct feeling she's peeling back my layers, looking for any sign of who I am, of whether I'm telling the truth.

"Good. Believe me, you want to be on my team for this."

She has to believe that I'm on her side, and I think she does. She thinks she's safe.

She thinks that I won't still kill her.

I will.

But not quite yet.

I lean forward, my lips brushing her ears. "This is what we're going to do..."

FIFTY-FOUR

Then

"I'm going to go get help."

I lean over Steph and carefully brush some of her hair back from her face. Her eyes are wide open, but I'm not sure if she can see me. She blinks, slowly, and when she opens her eyes again, it looks like it takes a lot of effort.

"Don't leave me."

Her words are a whisper, so quiet I can barely hear them, but they're sharp enough to hurt. I feel them worm their way into my heart, twisting and stretching, and I swallow hard to fight the pain they cause me.

She's on the ground now—or the roof, rather. The sound of her body falling and hitting it like a slab of meat turned my stomach. I held it together, just barely, but now I have to get out of the Jeep.

The scent of our blood is thick. There's sweat. Fear. It's choking me. The smells blend together and slide down my throat, making it difficult for me to take even the smallest breath.

"I can't stay," I whisper back. "I have to get you help." I lied to her about not needing help. Our phones are gone. As much as I want to stay here with her and comfort her, I have to go if she's going to survive.

I drag my eyes away from her and look at the car I hit. It's smaller, like a Camry or an Accord, and the front of it is completely demolished.

My stomach twists.

One of its headlights still works, and it shines a beam into the dark, cutting through the gloom to illuminate the woods. I stare at the other headlight, which exploded on impact.

What if they're dead?

I need them to be alive. I need them to be okay.

More than that, I need their phone.

It hurts to stand, but I force myself to my feet, gritting my teeth as pain shoots through my right leg. A quick glance confirms my fear. A shard of glass juts out from my thigh. It shakes and wobbles as I walk, slowly working its way in or out of my flesh. Blood pours from the wound, and I reach down, my hand trembling, to touch it.

Do I pull it out?

There's a voice in the back of my head telling me to leave it, that pulling it out will only cause more problems. My hand shakes as my fingers touch the edge of the glass. Searing pain rips through my fingers as the pads of my fingers are sliced open.

I scream and suck them. Blood floods my mouth. I stand still, swallowing my own blood, trying to keep from passing out until I can move again. Each step to the car sends a wave of nausea over me, and I have to fight to stay on my feet.

When I reach the driver's door, I stop.

The window is shattered.

The handle is disfigured. I grab it anyway and jerk it out

from the car, trying to open it, but no matter how hard I yank it, the door doesn't budge.

It's then that I see it—how twisted the metal is, how the door has buckled in on itself. This thing isn't going anywhere, not without the Jaws of Life.

A guy slumps over the steering wheel. Even without lifting his head to get a better look at him, I think I know the truth.

"You okay?" My voice is small.

He's not okay. He'll never be okay again, and I'm the reason. I did this. I might not have killed Steph, but I killed this guy.

Turning, I vomit on the road. It's mostly beer, and my mouth burns as I wipe the back of my hand across my lips.

Focus. He might not have been alone.

I stumble around the front of the car, barely aware that what I'm doing is stupid, barely taking in the blood and spiderweb cracks on the windshield.

How many movies have I seen where a car accident turns into an inferno? All it takes is a bit of gas to catch and then this thing is going up like the Fourth of July.

I have to get away from it.

But I can't. Not until I know how many people I killed.

"Are you okay? Hello?" I bang on the passenger-side window. The internal lights are all off, and I can't see anything in the dark. "Hello!" My voice is raw, but I scream the word anyway.

Nothing. No sound. No movement.

I try the door. This one opens easily, but I shut it just as quickly. I'm going to throw up again.

"Oh no." Snot drips from my nose as I turn back to my Jeep. "No, no, no." I stare at my vehicle. It rolled once, twice... then came to rest like an overturned beetle. The windshield is shattered. The hood and roof have paint scraped off. Thanks to the one headlight from this car, I can see the damage.

And I can see Steph.

Her eyes are closed. Blood runs down her forehead. Without thinking, I reach up and wipe my nose on the back of my hand. When I pull it away, I'm surprised to see my skin is now red.

Bleeding. We're both bleeding. I remember now. I already knew this, but I'd forgotten. I'm okay. I'm walking around, and it hurts, and my feet already ache from our trip through the woods, but Steph is...

"Steph!" I call for her and hobble towards the Jeep. My foot catches on a bit of pavement, and I lurch forward, planting my hands on the front undercarriage of the Jeep to catch myself. It's hot and jagged from when it overturned.

"Steph! Look at me!"

When I bend over to look through the window, I can see she's not moving.

The sound of sirens in the distance distracts me, but only for a second.

"Steph!"

My knees give out. The sharp pain when I hit the pavement and bits of rocks embed in my skin makes me cry out. There's a vice around my head, and it's squeezing tighter and tighter, causing bits of dark to appear at the edges of my vision.

"No. Steph!" I fall forward onto my hands. The headlight cuts across my form, elongating my shadow. It looks like a beast, all long-limbed and hunched. The thought makes me shiver, and I shove it to the side as I start to crawl.

The glass shard bounces every time my thigh tightens. It sends waves of pain through me. They keep coming, coming, coming like a clock ticking, washing over me, drowning me.

I move my right leg forward, my thigh tightens, my vision goes blurry.

Without thinking, I reach down and touch the glass. If it cuts me again, I don't feel it. My hands and feet are numb; my head feels like it's full of cotton.

"Steph, you're going to be okay. You're going to be okay." She can't hear me. I don't know if she's still alive or if she died, but either way she can't hear me. She has no idea what I'm saying, but the words are my mantra, a prayer, something that will help me survive this.

Help her survive this.

I reach up and touch the tire tread. My arms are heavy, like sandbags, and my muscles shake as I grip the tire and try to pull myself up.

My feet skitter uselessly as I try to stand. Every time I think I've found purchase, I slip, until I fall forward.

My chin smacks into the pavement. The skin splits.

And I pass out.

FIFTY-FIVE

AIMEE

I can't believe what I agreed to do to save myself. Hannah gives me a nod, a smile playing on the corners of her mouth.

Will this really work? We kill Dale and she stops? No way is she going to back down. No, if I'm going to be free of her and keep the life I've worked so hard to build, I have to end her. It's my only option.

The guys have been slowly making their way closer to us. Taking a deep breath, I spin around to Mitch. She stopped me from yelling at him before, but it's showtime now.

I need to make it good.

"You," I say, staring at Mitch, "you acted like you were going to help me, but then you took my phone, didn't you? Hannah just told me!"

He immediately reacts. "I didn't! She's lying to you, Aimee. I promise you, I didn't take your phone."

"You didn't take it?" My mind races as I try to make things make sense, but then I whip around to look at Hannah. "You stole my phone, didn't you?"

"Oh, are we talking about stealing things?" Hannah's cheeks are red. "Because if you want to point fingers, Aimee, then why don't you explain to everyone what happened to my necklace? The one you stole from my suitcase?"

My skin feels too tight. I force myself to stay on track. "You slept with my fiancé," I say, enunciating each word like that will get my point across.

She rolls her eyes. "Old news."

Dale hasn't said a word. He seems to shrink away from the three of us, his hand sliding slowly into his pocket.

Because her necklace is in there.

Rage boils through me as I think about him stealing the necklace back but not having the guts to tell me he found it in my shorts pocket. He took it and hid it and now is holding it like he has to protect it.

This would be the perfect time for him to get his head on straight and help me out. But he's not going to.

"You have anything you want to add?" I ask him.

He swallows hard, his Adam's apple bobbing as he tries to buy himself some time. "I think we're all heated, and we've all been drinking, and it's time we—"

"She killed my boyfriend! You want us to forget any of this happened?" Hannah screams the words as she points at me. There's a young family with two small children walking down the sidewalk towards us, but they pump the brakes and hurry in the other direction.

I know she wanted us to cause a scene, but is this going too far? It feels too real.

A wave of dizziness hits me.

"You don't get it, do you?" Hannah's still going. She spins to Mitch, and her voice takes on a pleading tone. "She killed Brian. Do you hear me? She killed him! He was your best friend, and suddenly you're willing to turn your back on him because you think you have a crush on Aimee?"

If she hadn't told me that this was the plan, that we needed to look pitted against each other, I'd be terrified, but—wait, what did she say? My jaw drops open as my mind races.

Mitch and Brian were friends? He never once mentioned that. Can I trust anyone here? My throat feels like it's closing up, and I clench my hands into fists. "I didn't kill anyone!"

It's not a lie. It might come across like a lie, but it's not. I'm not the one who—

"Oh, stop lying. I was there! Have you seriously not been paying attention? How else would I have figured everything out?"

Her words freeze me in place.

My mind races as I think back to that night and how to address Hannah. "No," I whisper. "You weren't there. Nobody else was there. It was me and Steph and..."

"Brian. His name was Brian."

Everything is going from bad to worse. Why is she acting like this? I thought we had a plan.

"You've been lying to me. All of you have been lying to me." I take a step away from the three of them, then another.

"Aimee, wait." Dale reaches for me, but I step back. "Where are you going?"

I ignore him. "I promise you," I say slowly to Hannah. "I didn't kill your boyfriend. I swear on my life I didn't do anything to hurt him."

"See, but you're lying again. I was there, Aimee. I was in the car with him when you hit us. I wasn't supposed to be with him, but I'd snuck out to go to the party. I had to call a friend to come pick me up and never told anyone I was there. Do you know how hard that is? To look over at your dead boyfriend and not even be able to stay with him? But my parents would have killed me! I had to leave the accident." She pauses and takes a deep breath. "My parents never knew the truth. Nobody knows I was there. I was confused. *Disoriented.* I got out of the car and ran. But before I ran for it, I called 911. And then I saw you."

"No," I whisper.

"Yes. I saw you. And I saw your twin when she got out and walked around. She came over to our car, did you know that? She looked at Brian and knew he was dead, but she never looked for me. You killed him. You killed my boyfriend."

"I wasn't driving." Even to my ears, my words ring with desperation. I need to make her see that she's wrong about all of this, that I'm not the bad guy, that I didn't do what she's saying, but—

She barks out a laugh. "Yes, you were. The eyewitnesses at the party saw you get behind the wheel. Daniel said that he helped you put Steph in the passenger seat, that she was hurt and could barely walk." She eyeballs me. Pauses.

I know what she's thinking. If she was really there, then she'll be able to figure out the truth.

"Your twin was hurt," she repeats. "She could barely walk."

"Please," I whisper.

I've hidden this secret for a decade. I'm not ready for it to come out. I'll do anything to keep it from coming out, even if it means going through with Hannah's plan and sacrificing Dale.

And then what? I kill Hannah as well? No way will she stop, not when she knows I'm desperate to hide the truth. She wants me to kill Dale so she can kill me or have me locked up or *something*—

Hannah told me to go to the ocean, but I don't know if I can trust her.

I turn. Run.

FIFTY-SIX
STEPH

Then

Flashing lights play across my face and finally wake me up.

My neck aches from how I'm lying; my left wrist curls in. I try to move it, and a bright flash of pain shoots through me, causing me to cry out.

Broken.

Even without a professional telling me, I already know. My wrist is broken, and I whimper, cradling it to my body with my right hand. It's dark outside, but bright lights press back on it, surrounding me in a bubble of light.

I remember...

Flashes of the night come back to me. Aimee, looking cute as always. How many times had she tried talking me into wearing the same thing she did? She loved dressing the same and really driving home the point that we're twins, no matter how much I told her I hated it.

But I did it last night, just to show her how much I love her. She was thrilled, especially when I agreed to wear my hair the same as hers and flip my septum piercing up.

We look exactly the same!

She squealed the words and pulled me into a hug before I could move away.

Then: the party. The guy I walked off with. He said he had drugs, but then led me out into the woods, away from the noise and light and safety, and before I knew it, he was trying to...

Well, it doesn't matter what he tried, does it? He failed, but he still pushed me, still hit me, still threw me down by the water and left me there.

Aimee showed up. She helped me. She and someone else, but I don't remember who. And then we were in her Jeep, driving.

And now I'm here.

"Aimee?" My voice breaks as I call her. "Aimee?"

The window next to me is shattered. She left me and obviously had to crawl out that way. I turn, ready to follow her, but a scream rips from my lips as I twist.

I pass out.

It's not flashing lights that wake me up this time—it's beeping, people talking, and the sound of someone crying. When I open my eyes, I do it little by little, trying to let the smallest amount of light possible in so I don't blind myself.

My mouth is dry, and speaking hurts. "Mom?"

Movement to my right, then the lights dim as she leans over me.

"Oh thank goodness. You're okay." She sniffles and calls over her shoulder. "Ken! Get in here! She's okay!"

"Mom." My heart beats faster as I realize what's going on. I'm in the hospital. I'm alive. I hurt, every cell in my body seems to scream for relief, but I'm alive, and I'm okay, and—

My dad appears, interrupting my thoughts. His eyes are puffy and red, and he starts crying again when he reaches out to take my hand. I want to squeeze back, I really do, but I've never been in this much pain.

It's not just the accident. It's also what happened before.

"Darling, you're okay." That's my dad. He's never, not once in his life, called me darling. I hate pet names, and he knows it.

I frown.

Immediately, Mom reaches out and rubs between my eyebrows. "Shh, no, don't you worry about anything, okay? You're going to be just fine. I promise you, you're okay."

She's crying, tears dripping off her chin. With an angry jerk of her hand, she wipes them away.

"The police want to talk to her," my dad says. He's turned a bit to speak to Mom, but I hear him anyway. "As soon as she can."

"She can't yet." Mom stands up and faces him. "Look at her. She hasn't said anything; how in the world is she supposed to talk to the police about what happened?"

Dad glances at me, then lets go of my hand. I want to reach for him, to have him take my hand again, but I can't lift my arm.

"I'm not arguing with you." He pulls my mom into a hug. "I'm just telling you, considering the scene, they have questions."

"What happened?" I lick my lips, but my tongue is just as dry as they are. It feels like rubbing sandpaper over my skin. "Where's—"

They both whip around to look at me.

I freeze.

"What were you going to ask, darling?" Dad asks me. He sits down on the edge of my bed and takes my hand again.

I stare at him, the reality of what they're asking and what happened slowly dawning on me.

They don't know who I am.

"Your sister," Mom begins, but Dad sharply raises his hand to cut her off.

He reaches out and lightly brushes some hair back from my forehead.

I stare at him, then look over at Mom. There's so much hope in their faces, an eagerness to know not only the truth of what happened, but also which daughter is still alive.

Tears leak from my eyes as that thought hits me. She left me in the Jeep and went to get me help—I'm sure that's what happened, but after that? I have no idea. Was she so badly hurt that she died there, or did they bring her here?

I must take too long thinking about what happened and how I'm going to handle this because Mom leans over me. "Honey, I know this is hard, and it's a terrible thing to have to ask you. But—"

"Sara." My dad cuts her off.

"Aimee," I gasp out. My mind races, and I feel my stomach twist. I want my twin; I want—

For a moment, only the sound of the machines I'm hooked up to make any noise. It feels like the three of us are holding our breath, collectively waiting to see what's going to happen next. Nobody wants to be the one to break the silence.

"Aimee," my dad says slowly. There's relief on his face, but it's clear he's trying to keep his expression neutral until he knows the truth. "You're Aimee. Thank heaven you're okay."

I nod, the knowledge that he would rather my twin than me be alive crushing me. It hurts more than the pain I'm in, but I can't let them know that. "I'm Aimee."

The lie sits heavy in my mouth, coating it like lard, and I swallow hard to rid myself of the feeling. It stays, though, thick and cloying, and I'm so focused on how uncomfortable it is that I almost miss what happens next.

Almost.

Mom exhales. Her shoulders roll in, but not in defeat. I watch as her face changes from tight and worried to relaxed, as the lines in her forehead even out, as she closes her eyes.

She looks calm. Beatific. Relieved.

Happy. She's happy that Aimee is alive and Steph is dead.

And as for Dad? He does the same, then lightly cups my cheek. "Aimee." His voice breaks when he says the name. "Steph didn't make it after the accident. She had... she had a shard of glass in her thigh and another in her stomach. She bled out. They said it would have been painless, that she never would have known she was even dying. Honey, I'm so sorry, but she's gone."

I'm so sorry, but she's gone.

I'm so sorry, but she's not here.

I'm so sorry, but you're here.

I'm so sorry that you're here.

I can't breathe. The blankets on me are light, but they feel like they're crushing me. I try to sit up but struggle against them until Dad grabs me and pulls me to him. It's only when he hugs me, his arms tightening around me, that I realize I'm sobbing.

"Aimee, you're okay," he whispers, rubbing my back. "You're okay. I'm so sorry about Steph, I really am, but you're okay. I promise you."

I'm not okay.

I'm also not Aimee.

But I don't have a choice now, do I?

FIFTY-SEVEN

HANNAH

My heart pounds from racing up the stairs behind Aimee.

No, Steph. Not Aimee. Right?

Whoever she is, I'm not letting her out of my sight. She practically flies up the stairs. I don't know if she's going to follow through on what I told her we needed to do, and I wouldn't blame her if she didn't. She's already gone off course by coming here instead of going to the beach like we planned.

But that's probably my fault because I went off on her. All of the anger I've felt over her for years came pouring out of me, and she looked terrified. I told her it was coming, that we really had to play it up so the guys didn't expect what was about to happen, but I might have screwed up.

What if I pushed her too far?

Instead of beelining for her room, however, Aimee swerves at the last minute. *I can make this work.* I slam through the door onto the third-floor balcony after her, pushing her out of the way.

She steps back from the door, panting hard. Her eyes dart from side to side, but we're the only ones out here. Behind me, I hear the door open and close again.

It has to be Dale and Mitch. Perfect. She didn't run to the ocean like I wanted her to, but I can still finish this tonight. Dale needs to learn the truth about the woman he thought he loved. And as for Mitch?

I will get revenge for both of us and for the person we lost, even if it doesn't happen tonight.

"You're not Aimee," I say, advancing on her like a hunter. "You're Steph."

"I didn't kill anyone." She holds her hands up and takes a step back from me. "I promise you, I'm a victim in this just like you are."

"Everyone thought that Aimee survived the car accident, but that's not true." I feel like I'm back there that terrible night, crouched by the woods, watching. I saw one girl crawl out from the Jeep. I saw her walk over to our Camry and look in at Brian. Yes, she was hurt, but she was able to walk just fine.

And then I saw her walk back to the Jeep and collapse.

And die.

It being Steph who was walking around goes against everything that the eyewitnesses at the party said.

That Aimee, not Steph, was in the driver's seat.

That Aimee, not Steph, was the one who could walk and wasn't hurt when they got in the Jeep. Aimee killed my boyfriend, got out of her Jeep and walked around, then died.

The woman standing in front of me stole the life of her twin. She might not have been the one to actually hit our car and kill my boyfriend, but she was there when he died, and then she capitalized on her twin dying.

I turn, making sure that Dale is watching. That he's close.

Both he and Mitch are staring at us, but neither of them gets involved. It feels like everything around us has disappeared, and Aimee and I are the only two people left on this planet. She's my focus, my life's work, and now I find out that she's not even the one who killed Brian?

It's enraging. All of the years watching her, following her. Mitch was there with me the entire time, helping me track her and keep an eye on her. I glance at him and am not surprised to see that he's completely focused on her.

But I am surprised at the expression on his face. *He really cares for her.* That's something I'll have to deal with later, and I tear my gaze away from him and stare at the woman in front of me.

"You're insane," I whisper and take a step forward. "Did you struggle being Aimee? Was it hard suddenly not being a loser anymore? What was it like, going from being some druggie slut to a college-bound kid?"

"Stop it." Her hands clench into fists at her side. "You don't know anything about what happened!"

"I know exactly what happened," I tell her, but my mind is racing. For a decade, I've wanted to get her on her own and punish her for what she did to Brian. I wanted to kill her. And now, to find out that *she* isn't the one who killed my boyfriend?

It tears me up inside. It's so confusing, and I don't know what to do, but this realization changes nothing. I don't care that the police would say she's innocent since she wasn't the one driving. She's still a liar. She's still the reason Brian is dead.

She still deserves to be punished.

She takes a step back. "I didn't do anything."

My mind races. It's clear from the expression on her face that I'm right. The woman standing in front of me is the screw-up twin, the one everyone thought died in the accident, the one her parents didn't love as much as the other. I called it.

"Aimee died," I say slowly, feeling out the words as I go, "and you saw the perfect opportunity to be someone who didn't suck. Am I right?"

Her eyes shine with tears.

"Hannah." That's Dale, finally butting in right on cue.

"What are you going on about? First you try to tell me that Aimee killed someone, which is insane, and now you—"

"This woman isn't who she says she is!" I shout, pointing at Aimee, but I don't look away from her. Dale needs to think I'm totally focused on her.

"You told everyone that Steph drove that night," I continue. "That you were the passenger, but that's not possible, not with Steph being in such terrible condition after what happened to her." I pause, thinking. "After what happened to *you*, I mean. You could barely walk. No way would you have been able to drive. But you were more than happy to throw your old life away, weren't you? Did your parents suspect? Did they look the other way when you told them you were Aimee? I bet they were relieved, weren't they? The good twin survived. The useless one died. Or, at least, that's the lie you told them."

"Aimee? Is this true?" Dale steps next to me. A flash of excitement rips through me. *It's working.*

"She's full of it," Aimee says.

No, not Aimee. Steph.

Mitch clears his throat, but neither one of us look at him.

Dale needs to be closer to the railing. I can still make this work.

"Listen to me, Dale." She's using a calm voice like she's talking to a little kid or a mean dog and needs to keep them from flying off the handle. "Hannah has been trying to come between us for a long time now. You know it, I know it—"

"This has nothing to do with wanting Dale!" The words leave my mouth in a shriek. "This has to do with punishing you for killing Brian!"

She takes a step back from me.

"I loved him!" I follow her, closing the gap between us. "Do you understand what that's like? To love someone, to want to spend the rest of your life with them, then to lose them? You have no idea what that pain is like!"

Wind whips around us. It's getting dark out, heavy clouds gathering and blocking out what's left of the sun. The cool breeze against the back of my neck makes me shiver, but I keep screaming.

"You don't deserve to live after what you did to him! Do you understand that? You deserve to—"

Too far. I've pushed her too far. I didn't mean to keep screaming at her, but it felt good to let it all out, and now—

She rushes me, her arms outstretched, her mouth wide in terror. I can't move as she plants her hands on my shoulder and shoves.

Panic shoots up my spine.

What is she doing?

I take a step back, my feet moving automatically as I try to keep my balance.

How far behind me is the railing?

FIFTY-EIGHT

STEPH

Then

"Aimee, you're going to have to get out of the car eventually," my mom says.

Her voice jerks me from my thoughts. Every time I have a spare moment when I'm not actively doing something, my mind slips back to the night of the party.

The night I lost Aimee.

"Right," I finally say. I reach down to unbuckle, but she moves faster than me, pressing the button to release me. The seatbelt slithers across my chest and snaps into place, and I exhale hard.

"Hey. I know this is hard." My mom turns to me and lightly cups my cheek. "We can—"

"It's fine." I turn from her and get out of the car before slamming the door behind me. I know it's going to hurt her feelings that I acted like this with her, but I can't help it. I don't want her to look me in the eyes, not because I'm afraid she's going to pity me, but because I'm afraid she's going to be able to tell that I'm not Aimee.

Will she recognize the wrong daughter staring out at her if she slows down and takes the time to really pay attention? Or is she just so grateful that Aimee survived, so happy to know that it was the right daughter who walked away from the accident, that she wouldn't be able to tell the truth?

I don't know which would be worse.

If I keep her from really looking at me, keep her from getting too close, then I don't have to know how much it would disappoint her that I'm the one who survived.

The house is silent when I let myself in. My mom is still in the car, probably crying, but I can't force myself to turn back. It's the first time I've been home since the accident, and I walk slowly through the kitchen, trailing my fingers along the counters.

There are dirty dishes in the kitchen sink, and I force myself to try to remember if Mom ever left dishes for more than a few minutes before the accident. She's always been a bit of a clean freak, something Aimee picked up from her and I patently eschewed.

Now, though, there are breakfast dishes, the yolk dried on the plate, the coffee rings in the mugs dark and brown.

I shiver and turn away. What I really want to do is go upstairs and get in bed. Sure, I've been in bed all day for the past two days since the accident, but that's different. There's no quiet at the hospital, no moments of peace so you can think.

Besides, my mom hasn't left my side. She's fluttered around the bed like simply staying close to me will be enough to ensure nothing bad happens to me.

It's exhausting.

I leave the kitchen and walk around the living room. There, on the coffee table, is the book Aimee was reading before the party. It's a romcom, her favorite, and I tear up seeing it there. Behind me, in the kitchen, I hear the door to the garage open and close, but I don't turn to talk to my mom.

"Aimee," she calls, right as I walk to the bottom of the stairs, "do you want something to eat?"

I swallow hard. My stomach is a tight ball. I can't imagine putting anything in it right now. "I'm fine," I call back, then walk slowly up the stairs.

Aimee and I have shared a bedroom since we were babies. The first day we went to kindergarten, our parents spent the day setting up a second bedroom so they could separate us. In the end, we kept our shared room.

Even though it's been a decade, I still remember the shock on both of our faces when we got home. It felt like a betrayal, like someone was trying to remove a part of who I was.

Yes, I know Aimee was going to go to college and I was going to stay home, but that was to be our first time apart from each other. And now...

"Now I'll be alone." The words slip quietly from my lips but feel like an arrow to the heart.

I stumble forward into our room and stop, my eyes flicking around the space as I take it all in.

Two sides. Two different sisters.

Aimee's is pink. A pink comforter, pink corkboard covered with photos of her and her friends. Pink rug, pink fluffy pillow. There are stuffed animals on her bed from Josh and a neat closet full of heels and cute tops. Her bookshelf groans with novels, and she has a dozen journals stacked on her bedside table full of scribbled short stories.

Then there's my side. It's... not pink. Not bright and cheery. Not like something out of a Pottery Barn catalog. No photos of me and my friends because the people I hang out with aren't ones I'd bring home to meet my parents. No stuffed animals, and my closet explodes with combat boots, cargo pants, leather jackets. If you were to lift my mattress, you'd find my weed.

We couldn't be more different.

And I couldn't possibly miss her more than I do.

My mind reels as I walk to my bed and kick off the sneakers I have on. They're Aimee's. Of course they're Aimee's—my mom wouldn't bring me anything of mine at the hospital. My sister's clothes fit me like they were made for me, but they feel like I'm wearing a costume.

Without thinking, I flip back my navy blue comforter and slide under it. The sheets haven't been washed, and they smell like my shampoo. Tears stream down my face as I press into my pillow.

Who knows how long I stay here before I feel the foot of the bed shift. A moment later, Mom is rubbing my back, her hand moving in slow circles. I stiffen, then force myself to relax.

When was the last time she touched me like this? Like she really loved me and wanted to comfort me? It had to have been when I was a little kid and sick, because I don't remember her ever coming and sitting on my bed to talk to me.

Did she rub Aimee's back like this? I was out of the house as much as possible, drinking and doing drugs and skipping school and family dinners, so I would have missed it. The thought that my mom was loving on Aimee when I was out with people who didn't really care about me tears through me, and a sob escapes.

"I know you miss her," my mom says. "I do too."

No, you don't. You don't miss me. You don't even realize I'm right here in front of you.

I don't respond.

"I promise you, things will get better, okay? You'll go off to college soon. You'll live your life, and you'll heal."

Is that how she sees this? As something I can magically heal from?

I still don't respond. It's not that I don't know what to say, but rather that I don't trust myself to make a sound without screaming at her.

"Steph was trouble," my mom says, and her hand keeps moving in slow circles on my back. "She had her issues, and she's free from them now. I want you to remember something, Aimee."

A long pause, and I suddenly realize she's waiting for me to respond.

"What do you want me to remember?" My voice is muffled from the pillow but I don't roll over to look at her in fear she'll know the truth.

"You will get through this. Without her bad influence, without her dragging you down, things will be better in the long run."

I can't move. I can't breathe.

"Her funeral's tomorrow. And after that, we can put this nasty business behind us." She leans down and kisses the side of my head before standing and hurrying out the door.

I still don't move.

Even when I hear her walk down the hall. Even when I hear her go downstairs. I lie as still as possible, her words on repeat in my mind. I turn them over, look at them from different angles, try everything in my power to make them make sense.

We can put this nasty business behind us.

She's talking about Steph when she says that.

No, not just that. She's talking about *me*.

FIFTY-NINE

AIMEE

Hannah's falling.

Her eyes are wide, her arms outstretched as she reaches for help. I see the judgement in her eyes, that I went off book and she's not happy, but what was I supposed to do? Help her kill Dale and then let her kill me?

The expression on her face mirrors Aimee's right before she fell outside of the Jeep.

My breath catches in my throat.

"Hannah!"

Dale or Mitch? Mitch or Dale? I'm not sure which one of them called for her—their voice was caught by the wind and whipped away from us, much like she's going to be caught and whipped, only she's more substantial than a few letters screamed into the air and she'll fall, fall, fall.

Then land.

I wince at the thought.

Mitch pushes past me. I gasp and step to the side, swinging my arms out for balance. When I grab something, I grip it, not realizing at first that it's Dale.

"What did you do?" He hisses the words into my face and shakes me. When he does, his fingers dig harder into my flesh.

"You're hurting me!" I jerk away from him, but he doesn't let me go. "Dale! Let me go!"

"You could have killed her!" Dale's screaming now, apparently no longer worried about whether or not any passers-by hear him. He shakes me, and my head snaps back and forth. Stars burst on the outer corners of my vision. "Do you realize that? What were you thinking?"

She's right. Hannah was right about what we have to do.

This time, when I yank my arm away from him, his grip slips, and I'm able to step back. I'm breathing hard, my eyes locked on him, but I'm dying to know what's going on with Hannah.

Dale said I *could have killed her*. Not that I did, and I'm clinging to the hope that she's okay. I hate her and wouldn't mind looking over the railing to where her body lay, sprawled on the sidewalk, but that's not what's going to happen.

"She's fine," I say, even though I'm not entirely sure that's the truth. "Hannah is fine. You need to back off."

Dale's jaw is tight. The muscles in his cheek jump. He stares at me like he's never seen me before and can't quite believe what he's looking at. I keep his eye contact, then finally turn to look at Mitch and Hannah.

Mitch's back is to me; his arms are around Hannah. She's sobbing, the sound loud in the quiet of the evening, but then Mitch steps to the side, and I can see her.

Her face is pale under her fake tan. Tears well in her eyes as she stares at him. At the same time, Dale takes me by the arm, his hand closing around my bicep.

"We should go," he whispers, but I can't tear my eyes away from the others.

"You're a terrible brother," she says. "What, do you really think Aimee is going to fall for you? That she's going to decide that you two should ride off into the sunset together, that you'd be the perfect couple?" She laughs, then slams her open hand into his chest. "You're an idiot."

"Aimee, come on." Dale's mouth is so close to my ear that I feel his breath on my skin.

The smart thing would be to leave with him. Dale will protect me; I have a good feeling he will. Why else would he be trying to get me to leave the balcony with him?

I swallow hard, pushing down the mental image I have of him with Hannah on our kitchen table.

"I know the plan, but plans can change." There's power in Mitch's voice, and I glance over at him in surprise. "You don't get to run the show any longer, Hannah."

"Oh, please." Hannah reaches out and steadies herself on the railing. She's acting as tough as possible, but it's clear she still doesn't feel her best. "I'm the reason for all of this!" She sweeps her arm out to the side to encompass Dale and me. "I put this entire thing in motion, but only because of her."

She spins and points at me, and I swallow hard.

"She's not really Aimee." Hannah takes a step closer to me. *Closer to Dale.* Mitch moves with her, staying close to her like he's going to be forced to stop her from doing something stupid. Seeing the two of them approach, even though I don't think Mitch is going to hurt me, sends my fight-or-flight response into high gear.

"Give it up, Hannah." Dale sounds exasperated, and I'm surprised when he reaches out, putting his arm in front of me and pushing me gently back like that's going to protect me. "If Aimee is really Steph, then that's something we can worry about later." He cuts his eyes at me, and fear grows in my stomach. "The police can figure that one out."

"The police couldn't figure it out before!" Hannah's five feet from me, but she's close enough for me to feel the rage boiling off of her.

My knees feel like they're going to give out. I reach out and grab Dale's arm for support as I struggle to stay on my feet.

"Everyone thought that Steph died in the car accident." It's like she has blinders on, the way she's staring at me. "But it wasn't Steph who died. It was Aimee. You stole her life. Did you really think that nobody was ever going to find out?"

"Aimee?" Dale turns to me. "Tell her that you're who you say you are." A pause. "You are Aimee, right?"

Even Mitch looks confused. There's a furrow between his brows that wasn't there before, and he looks between Hannah and me like this is one puzzle that's simply too difficult for him to solve.

"I'm Aimee," I tell her. Desperation oozes from my voice, and I hate myself for it. I don't want to admit the truth, but I don't think I have a choice. "Now. I was Steph before. I didn't kill Brian, I swear to you. The real Aimee died, and I—"

"You took over your sister's life. And now you think you get to walk around pretending like everything is okay? It's not okay." She pauses, her chest rising and falling rapidly, then she screams and runs at me.

No, she's running at Mitch.

There's a moment where I'm sure that she's going to reach me, that she's going to attack me, and that my life as I know it is going to be over.

And then there's a gunshot.

SIXTY

HANNAH

Something hits me in the right shoulder, and I stumble, losing my momentum and twisting to the side. I fall to my knees, the pain of the hard balcony ricocheting through my legs.

"You can't hurt her!" Mitch stands over me. Even without turning around, I know he's got a gun pointed at me. He took it from my suitcase. He pretended like he didn't know what I was going on about.

And now he's going to kill me.

I should have looped him in on what Aimee and I talked about, but there wasn't time. And when I don't trust his loyalty, what was I to do?

My shoulder still hurts, but it's not the burning, searing pain I thought would come with being shot. Slowly, so he doesn't think I'm going to do something stupid, I reach up with my left hand and touch my right shoulder.

No blood.

No entry wound.

He didn't shoot me. He pushed me.

Fear and relief rush through me, and I slowly turn, my hands above my head so he can see that I'm not a threat.

The gun is only a few feet from my face. I chose a small one on purpose, but even though I know how tiny it is, it feels huge this close to me. I blink at it, then slowly raise my eyes to my brother.

"You're really going to shoot me in the face?" It's a miracle I keep my voice from shaking. "The police will know it was you. They'll lock you up, and you'll never see daylight again." I pause, my mind racing as I think. "Or Aimee. You'll never see her. She'll be gone from you forever."

His eyes flick to her before landing back on my face.

"They're probably already on their way, Mitch." That's Dale, using that stupid placating voice he sometimes slips into when he thinks it's going to help him get his way. "A gunshot? Someone will have reported it, and it won't matter that you shot into the air. You still discharged your weapon."

The gun wavers. Just a bit. Just enough for me to know that Mitch is listening to us. He's hearing us.

He's worried.

"Give me the gun," I say. When I stand up, I move as slowly as possible. My hand extends out in front of me, and I stare at it, willing him to put the gun in it. "We can make sure you don't get in trouble, okay? We'll make sure nobody knows you were the one with the gun. Just... give it to me."

"No!" Dale shouts, and Mitch's head snaps to the side so he can look at him. Frustration bubbles in me, and I think about reaching out and snatching the gun from him, but before I can move, he takes a step back.

The gun is still leveled at me.

"Don't give her the gun, Mitch," Dale says. "She wants to hurt Aimee. You know it. I know it. And Aimee is innocent in all of this."

"Innocent?" I turn to him but make sure I keep Mitch's gun in sight. "Innocent? She stole her dead sister's life. She lied. She pretended to be someone better than she could ever hope to be. She—"

"She survived." Dale steps forward and takes Aimee's hand. *Steph. Not Aimee.*

She lets him, but there's a moment where I see a look of disgust flash across her face. *Good.*

"Dale's right," Mitch says. "Steph or Aimee, I don't care. You did what you had to do to make it."

"Aimee," she whispers. "Please call me Aimee. My name—"

"Is Steph!" I scream. My skin suddenly feels too tight for my body. With every beat of my heart, my head pounds. I don't know what to do or say to get these people to understand what I know.

That this woman is a fraud. An imposter. That she deserves to be punished. That even though she wasn't the one driving the night Brian died, she's the reason they were in the car going so fast in the first place.

Her sister—the real Aimee—isn't here for me to punish. I told myself that I'd get revenge for Brian's death, that I'd make sure the person who killed him died as well, and even though my plans have to change a bit, I'm still going to hurt this woman.

Just not tonight.

Police sirens cut through the night. Mitch's gunshot called them to us, just like we knew it would. Time is running out.

I need that gun.

"Mitch," I say, turning to my brother. "Give me the gun. Your fingerprints are on it. The police are going to be all over you as soon as they arrive. You think they're going to give you a slap on the wrist just because you didn't shoot anyone?" I level my gaze at him, trying to make him see reason. "Once they know who you are, there's no way they'll look the other way. Not again."

He seems to freeze. His eyes dart to me before cutting back to Dale and Aimee. Poor idiot isn't sure what to do, and I have to take deep breaths to fight down the frustration and anger I feel at his inaction.

The sirens grow louder.

I don't have any time to waste.

"Give it to me!" Desperation drives me to lunge for him. I grab his wrist, but he's bigger than me, and stronger, and he jerks his hand back, the gun pointing up to the sky.

Out the corner of my eye I see Dale. He takes off like a sprinter from the blocks, his head down, leading with his shoulder, aimed right at the two of us.

Breath catches in my throat.

We're close to the railing. Too close?

Dale hits the two of us. My finger brushes the trigger, and I squeeze it. There's a click.

No gunshot.

We stumble back, the three of us intertwined, then the cold metal of the railing hits me. We've turned, twisted and rotated, and my back is to the railing when Dale rams into me again. He's off-balance, thrown to the side a bit, and I look up and lock eyes with Aimee.

She's breathing hard, terror written all across her face, but I don't have time to say anything.

I shouldn't have trusted her to help me punish Dale. I came here to hurt her and got distracted, and while I wish there were a way back, a way to undo what happened and try again, I think I'm out of time. Because this time, Dale catches me in the shoulder, and I feel myself lifting up, my toes no longer touching the ground, the cool night breeze grabbing at me like a greedy creature, helping lift me up, up, up.

And then down.

SIXTY-ONE

AIMEE

My mind can't accept what I'm seeing.

Three stories is a long way to fall, and when you land on pavement...

There's no forgiveness there. No bounce. Just blood. A pool of it. A cracked skull. Bits of brain.

My stomach rolls, and I step back from the railing. After a few deep breaths, I'm finally able to turn to the person standing next to me.

"Oh no," I breathe. "What did you do?"

SIXTY-TWO

STEPH

Then

There were times, when Aimee was still alive, that I would steal her clothing and wear it, but I really only did that to annoy her.

Now, though, I stand in front of the full-length mirror on her side of the room and smooth my hands over the dress I took from her closet. It's white, with small flowers all over it, and is her favorite one.

On my feet? Strappy espadrilles. I'm wearing some of her jewelry, the fine gold chains so light they almost feel non-existent. As much as I would have liked to wear something from my closet, to dress myself in the armor my clothing provides, no way could I have done that.

Not only would it have been a huge red flag to my parents and easily clued them in to the fact that I'm not Aimee, but my clothes are gone.

My closet sits open, a gaping mouth, with only a few shirts hanging in the middle. I'd gone out for a walk this morning to prepare myself for the funeral, and my mom had...

My mind whites out.

She erased me from the house.

There's a knock on the door, and I slowly turn around, already plastering a small smile on my face. I'm heartbroken, absolutely crushed over what happened, but nobody can know the truth of what's going on in my mind.

"Hey, Aimee, you about ready?" My dad stands in the door in a black suit. He looks... fine. Put together. In control.

I hate the fact that both of my parents don't seem bothered by the fact that they think I'm dead.

"I'm ready." Aimee and I were together for eighteen years. How often did I stare at her, drinking her in, wondering what it would be like to be considered the perfect child? How many hours of my life did I spend chatting with her, even when the two of us grew up and realized how very different we are from each other?

I'm not her by any stretch of the imagination, but nobody has to know that. They *can't* know that. When I walk towards my dad, I have to focus to keep from tripping. These shoes aren't ones I'd ever normally choose to wear, and each step feels awkward.

"You must still be sore from the accident, huh?" He loops his arm around my waist and pulls me closer to him. "You're walking like a baby deer."

"Still sore, yeah." I feel stiff standing this close to him. When was the last time either of our parents pulled me into a hug? They became standoffish with me after I got arrested for buying drugs from an undercover cop two years ago. Even before that, they didn't act like they really liked having me in the house.

But Aimee? They loved Aimee. Loved having her in the house. Loved hugging her apparently.

She wouldn't stiffen and pull away from him, even though that's exactly what I want to do. Instead, I force myself to relax, to breathe in his aftershave, to draw some support from his strength.

Is this what it's like to have your parents love you? To want to spend time with you?

The guilt I've been feeling over taking Aimee's life is slowly disappearing. I know I'm never going to be able to fully relax and enjoy the love they had for Aimee, but it feels good.

It feels better than knowing that I'm a huge disappointment, that much is for sure.

"I know this afternoon is going to be hard for you," he tells me. "But your mother and I will be with you every step of the way, okay? There's nothing you can do that will make us turn our backs on you."

My stomach twists.

"Thank you," I whisper, but he isn't finished.

"Just remember, after today, the rest of your life begins."

I can't answer him. There's literally nothing I can say that will assuage the guilt brewing in my stomach and keep him from knowing the truth. It doesn't matter that I don't know what to say because he squeezes me close one more time, then gestures for me to lead the way down the stairs.

I do, only stopping at the bottom when my mom steps in front of me. She's frowning, her eyes flicking up and down my body, and I feel a trail of ice work its way down my spine.

"Everything okay?" I don't know how I manage the words, but I do.

She frowns. "Yes, it's fine; it's just..."

"Just what," I ask, ignoring the voice in the back of my head screaming at me to shut up.

"You looked like Steph for a moment."

I grip the banister harder. "Well, we are twins." My voice cracks, but she doesn't seem to notice.

"Were," she corrects, and I blink at her. "You *were* twins, Aimee. You *had* a twin. You don't any longer." She takes a step back from me, a look of confusion still splashed on her face. Finally, she shakes her head and walks off to the kitchen.

"Everything okay, Aimee?" My dad's still behind me on the stairs, and his voice spurs me to action. I jerk and nod, hurrying down to the foyer.

"Fine," I lie. "Just going to wait on the porch until you two are ready to go."

Outside, the day is warming up, the sun shining right on the front porch swing, but I settle down into it anyway.

If I were in my black jeans and combat boots, I'd be roasting. But in Aimee's clothes, the sun feels good on my face, on my arms.

Slipping into my sister's skin isn't going to be easy. But it's going to make my life better.

Happy.

Worth living.

She'd understand—I know she would.

SIXTY-THREE

HANNAH

The police huddle around Dale's body. In just a moment they're going to look up and see our faces staring over the balcony at them. Mitch is the first to step back, and he turns, ready to run for the door, to hurry inside, to spill his guts about what happened.

But I'm in front of him before he makes it. Aimee's next to me, her eyes wide in shock, her mouth hanging open.

"Where are you going?" My voice is low, and I reach out and grab his arm. "You're in a rush, Mitch, but you and I need to get our stories straight."

"Get them straight?" His voice is high and pinched. "Get them *straight*? Dale is dead. He's dead, and you—" He turns to Aimee. "No, you," he says to her, stabbing his finger through the air at her. "They'll know you did something. You already were involved in the death of one person."

"I didn't mean—" she begins, but Mitch cuts her off.

"Don't finish that sentence. It doesn't matter. They'll be all over you," he says. "We have to figure out how to keep you safe." As he speaks, he slides his hand into his pocket, and I realize he's putting the gun in there. The cops will surely pat him down, right? What is he thinking?

"I'll protect her," I say, and even as the words leave my mouth, I can't believe I'm saying them.

Mitch keeps his gaze on me for a moment longer, and I know he's trying to read me and see if I'm lying. I tilt my chin up and don't look away until he does.

"We have to get inside and talk to the police," he says. As he speaks, he reaches out and takes Aimee's hand. I see the hesitation written on her face, but she relents and lets him link their fingers together.

I clear my throat. "We'll tell them that Dale was drinking. That it was an accident. That he fell before we could save him. It's all true."

"An accident," Aimee echoes, and Mitch nods encouragingly.

"Very good," I say. "Just an accident."

"We'll tell them that we came here together," Mitch says, obviously warming to the idea. "That the four of us are all friends and wanted to get out of town and spend time together. Accidents happen, and they happen fast. There's no reason why they wouldn't believe us."

"Of course," I say, but my mind is racing as I try to figure out how to take Aimee down without going down with her. That's the fine line I have to walk—to make sure that she's punished without letting the cops know that I was coming here to handle justice myself.

Can I do it?

Mitch squints at me. "You will go along with our story, right? There's no spinning the narrative to suit you, no room for you to come up with your own story. You stick with what we plan."

"I wouldn't," I lie.

"I tripped him." Aimee's confession is so sudden that the

two of us stop and turn to her. My mouth is already falling open as Mitch starts shaking his head.

"No, you didn't. The three of you were all wrapped up together. You didn't do anything wrong. You—"

"I tripped him on purpose." Her eyes dart to me. "You told me to."

Mitch turns so slowly to look at me that it feels like we're in a horror movie. "Hannah. Is this true?"

My spit sours in my mouth, but I nod.

"I told her that we could take him out together." I glance around, looking for any security cameras that might be up here, but I don't see any. Still, I don't feel myself relax. "I said—"

"That he deserved to die for hurting me," Aimee interrupts. "That any man who would cheat on someone didn't deserve to live. That if I helped you—" A sob rips out of her mouth, and she claps her hand over her lips.

"That if you helped her, what?" Mitch asks. "What, Aimee? What did she promise you?"

I speak up. "That I wouldn't punish her for killing Brian."

"So, what? Your freakout on the sidewalk down there was just for show?"

"Yes." *Until it became real.*

Mitch takes a step towards me, and I freeze. "She didn't kill Brian, and you need to get over that. I know you want revenge, but you can't have it. Not with her. Not without going through me."

Then I'll go through you.

I stare at him. "I'm not going to hurt her," I whisper. "I took pity on her. We were working together—she said it herself." He has to believe me if I'm going to have another chance to get to her later.

"You better not. If you don't tell the cops the story we agreed to, I'll tell them the truth."

Ice trickles down my spine.

"They wouldn't believe you," I say, but my words have no strength. As much as I want to think that the cops would side with me, if Mitch were to—

"I'll show them your texts. The research you've done. How many years have you been stalking Aimee? And then, if you continue to fight, I still have the gun. I'm hiding it, but I'll know where to find it. Did you buy it legally, or will we have to find some loser who gave it to you for a few hundred bucks cash? I don't care what I have to do, Hannah—I will take you down if you do anything to point suspicion at Aimee. Am I making myself clear?"

This can't be happening. Not Mitch, not my brother, not when I need him now more than ever.

He can't really be turning on me. Not for that bitch, Aimee.

Steph.

Aimee.

It doesn't matter who she is. I'll never let her walk away from this.

But I don't say that. Instead, I plaster a smile on my face and reach for Mitch's hand. "I'll do whatever you say," I lie. "You know best."

He might be able to protect Aimee now. He might think he has this under control. But I've waited a decade for revenge. I can wait another week, month, year. I can wait until Aimee thinks she's in the clear, that I've forgiven her, that nobody suspects her for what she did.

And then, I swear it, I'll kill her.

SIXTY-FOUR

AIMEE

I'm prepared for the good cop/bad cop shtick.

And the fact that they separate us.

And the offered cup of water.

It sits in front of me on the table, but I don't reach for it. Not that they won't be able to get my fingerprints if they take me to the police department, but I don't want to make anything easy for them.

And I certainly don't want them to figure out that I'm Steph, not Aimee. I wrack my brain, trying to remember if Aimee has ever been fingerprinted. I was, of course. That's what happens when you get arrested.

"Tell us again what happened." The woman sits across from me, leaning back in her chair, looking for all the world like she has nowhere else she'd rather be. I knew from the moment I saw her that she's a detective, but even though she introduced herself, I can't remember her name.

"We were all on the balcony," I begin, but she interrupts me.

"Please go ahead and give me the names of everyone you were with."

"Right. Sorry." I swallow hard. My mouth feels sandy and dry, but I don't reach for the water. "It was Dale, Mitch, Hannah, and me." She nods, and I continue. "The guys had been drinking, and Dale was goofing off by the railing."

When I pause, she pushes the cup of water towards me.

I shake my head and continue. "He... lost his balance. One moment, he was sitting on the railing laughing and carrying on, and the next, he'd fallen."

I don't have to fake the tears streaming down my face. My stomach twists and contorts, and I take little breaths to try to stay calm.

"Just like that?" She snaps her fingers, and I wince. "He fell that fast?"

"So fast," I whisper, nodding. "He was there, and then he was gone."

She doesn't respond. Instead, she cracks open a fresh bottle of water and takes a sip, then another, then she drains half of it.

My mouth feels like it's on fire watching her. I'd love to chug the water she gave me. Heck, I'd lunge across the table at her and yank the bottle out of her hands if I thought I could get away with it. I could drink it all and still be thirsty, but it would be a start.

"And the gunshot?" Her tone is casual, but the way she stares at me isn't. She's waiting for me to crack, to make a mistake, but I can't. Not if I'm going to walk away from this.

"We heard it too." I close my eyes like I'm thinking and only open them when I speak. "Part of me wonders if Dale heard it and got scared, if it surprised him and that's what caused him to go over the edge." I clamp my hands over my mouth after I say the words.

My heart hammers. I'm sweating. Every inch of my skin hurts like it's been stretched too tightly over my bones, but she can't tell how uncomfortable I am just by looking at me, right?

"You think the gunshot is what caused him to lose his

balance?" She cocks an eyebrow at me, and I immediately wonder if I screwed up. "Mitch didn't mention that as a possibility."

Of course he didn't—it wasn't part of the plan. But I'm willing to lay it on thicker if that means I walk away from this.

"It was just a thought. I know I certainly jumped when I heard it." A tear works its way down my cheek. It's only when I can tell that she's seen it that I wipe it away.

"Aimee, this isn't the first time you've been interviewed by the police, is it?" She plants her elbow on the table and rests her chin on her palm. "You were in a pretty bad accident in high school, right? Your twin died. And so did another teen."

I nod slowly. "That's right. My sister was driving and lost control of her Jeep."

"Right, right." She pauses a moment. "Strange how tragedy follows you, isn't it?"

I stiffen. This is the moment where it could all fall apart, but I refuse to let that happen. "I hardly think two accidents a decade apart means I'm being haunted by tragedy. What happened with Steph was terrible. And now I've lost Dale."

Tears stream freely down my cheeks. They come so quickly I don't have to worry about giving her time to see them.

I'm not heartbroken over losing Dale. Seeing his lifeless body on the pavement below us was terrible, yes. But he and I didn't have a future.

Dale treated me like crap. I should be happy he's dead, but instead I feel this hollow emptiness. It was going to be one thing to pawn my ring and break it off with him, but it's another entirely for him to be dead.

"Well, we'll be in touch." The detective stands so abruptly that the cup of water rocks back and forth. Without thinking, I reach out to steady it but yank my hand back at the last minute. No way am I touching that and giving her the perfect opportunity to get my fingerprints. She'd know in an instant that I'm not really Aimee.

She eyeballs me, and I force a smile to my face.

"Thank you. Am I free to go?"

"You sure are. Might want to get something to drink since you're so thirsty." She smiles at me, but it doesn't reach her eyes.

When I walk to the door, I feel her gaze on me. Slowly, I open the door and step out into the hall. As calmly and quietly as possible, I close the door behind me. The last thing I want is to move too fast or be too loud and give her a reason to call me back in.

I'm almost free.

Mitch turns at the sound of the door clicking into place. He groans when he sees me, then rubs his hand down his face. Before I can stop him or even react, he rushes to me and pulls me into a hug.

"You good?" His voice is quiet, but I still hear the words.

"Fine." I struggle a bit until he lets me go. "Was it okay when they talked to you?"

He nods. "Yeah, I have everything under control."

His words hang in the air, and a chill creeps through me. "Where's Hannah?"

"Hannah... she's still talking to the cops." He looks at a closed door further down the hall and shakes his head. After a moment, he reaches out and puts his hand on my shoulder like what he's about to share is something I should take seriously. "She should be done by now, but she told them she had something to share with them."

I suck in a huge breath. My mind races.

There's only one thing she'd want to tell them.

SIXTY-FIVE

HANNAH

Aimee's not waiting in the hall with Mitch when I'm done talking with the police, but he immediately hurries to me and puts his hands on my shoulders, so I'm looking right at him.

"What did you do?"

I fight a smile. This was my time to shine, to take Aimee down, to make her pay for Brian dying. No, she isn't the one who drove the night he died, and I can accept that. But I still want someone to be punished for what happened to him.

And since the real Aimee isn't alive, who better than her twin sister? After all, Steph decided that Aimee's life was worth stealing, so why not let her have all of it, the good and the bad?

"Hannah." Mitch gives me a little shake and looks like he's going to say something else, but then the door behind us opens, and the detective I was just speaking to walks out.

"Everything okay here?" She raises an eyebrow as she looks between the two of us. Mitch nods, then takes me by the hand and pulls me to stand next to him.

"We're just really shaken up," he tells the detective. Next to him, I nod and sniff. "Dale was such an amazing friend, and we're going to miss him."

The detective's face softens. "What you've been through is traumatic, and you're going to need time to heal. If you were local, I'd recommend a great counselor in the area who could help you work through what you just experienced. As it is, though, I do think you need to find someone when you go back home. Individual and couples therapy is a good idea." She pauses. "And that goes for Aimee as well. All three of you will need help, and there's no shame in that."

"Thank you." Mitch clears his throat. "We'll tell her. And get in some counseling ourselves."

She nods, and I get the feeling we're being dismissed, so before the two of them can talk more, I pull Mitch towards the elevators.

We're silent on the way to the third floor and don't speak until we're in our room, the door locked behind us. On a whim, I try the door that leads into Aimee's room, but it's locked.

"You didn't tell them the truth about the accident ten years ago," Mitch says, causing me to turn around and look at him. He's standing by the bed, his arms crossed, a genuine look of confusion on his face.

"I didn't." Without looking at him, I grab my bikini and shove it into my suitcase.

"Why not?"

"I didn't want to." I brush past him to the bathroom and start packing up my toiletries.

"Hannah." Mitch is next to me, and I didn't even see him move. He yanks my toothbrush from my hand and tosses it into the sink. It lands with a clatter, and I look up at him. "You know as well as I do that you never do anything without an ulterior motive. You screwed Dale just to get to his girlfriend! Do you really think I'm going to believe you that you just *didn't want to?*"

See? Right there. That's the problem with working with

family. They know you too well and aren't afraid to call you out when you're acting out of character.

"You have to trust me," I tell him.

"Yeah, but I don't. You, more than anyone I've ever met, are willing to do whatever it takes to get what you want. I thought you wanted revenge, Hannah. What is it that you're really trying to do? And what was the big thing you wanted to tell them?"

My heart hammers in my chest, but I keep my face as calm and placid as possible. Mitch is absolutely smitten with her, and that's the main reason I didn't tell the police what happened ten years ago.

Sure, they might have believed me. But what if they didn't? Mitch would know then, in no uncertain terms, where my loyalty lay. He knows that I was willing to destroy the woman he's grown to care about, even though that should have been clear from day one when I told him my plan to hurt her.

I don't want Mitch as my enemy. Not because we're blood, but because I'm afraid of what he would do if he thought that I'd screwed him over. He's not shown the best judgement in the past, and I don't want that ire directed at me.

The best outcome if I'd told the police the truth would have been for them to believe me, for them to fingerprint this woman, for them to find out the truth and... what? Not lock her up—she wasn't driving. But make her go back to being Steph? That's not enough of a punishment.

No, I'm back at square one, only this time I have a lot more information about this woman. I know who she really is. I know she's not a murderer. But even though she didn't kill Brian, she's not innocent.

And someone has to pay for his death.

"I told them that Dale hasn't been sober since he got to the hotel. That he's an alcoholic, and that's probably the main reason why he fell. I laid it on thick to protect us." I exhale hard. "And as for what I'm trying to do? I'm trying to forgive her." Tears well up in my eyes at the perfect time. "I know she's important to you, and she's not technically the one who killed Brian."

Mitch's face softens. "Thank you. You have no idea how good it is to hear you say that. She's... special. I think she and I really have a future together, and I don't want her to come between us." He takes my hand, and I have to fight to keep from jerking back. "You're my sister. I love you."

"But you also love her."

He smiles. "Yes."

"Then we'll make it work," I lie. I have no intention of making anything work with Aimee. All I want is to get back home, sleep in my own bed, let the two of them fall into a sense of false security. Sure, Aimee might move. She might try to hide, just like she did when she fled North Carolina, but I'm onto her now.

There's nowhere she can go that would be far enough away for her to stay safe.

"Thank you." Mitch looks so happy that I almost feel bad for lying to him. "You have no idea how much that means to me. She's... amazing."

Amazing. Right.

"She's something else," I agree, but he doesn't pick up on my tone. "I know we're leaving tomorrow, but she might want to head off early. This place is going to have bad memories for her, but you don't want her to leave without you knowing."

"You're absolutely right. I know this has got to be hard for you, and I know that learning she's innocent is difficult, but trust me, you two will grow to be close. I believe you will. It might take a while, but you'll have to be patient. It will be worth it."

Yes, I can be patient.
And it will definitely be worth it.
Just not in the way he thinks.

EPILOGUE

Most of the funeral crowd has left the bar, and I quietly make my way to the front door so I can step outside.

An after-funeral party at a bar might seem like an odd choice to a lot of people, but Dale loved to drink, and he had more friends than I thought coming out of the woodwork to celebrate him. It probably doesn't hurt that he died in a freak accident—I'm sure there were a handful of people here who only wanted to talk about him getting drunk and falling to his death in Florida.

Pushing through the door to step outside, I trade the smell of stale beer and a sticky floor for a soft breeze and the sun on my face. I'm in a black dress, one I grabbed off the rack at the store yesterday, and the sun feels nice on my bare arms.

How long do I need to stick around here? Do I need to wait until everyone leaves, or is it okay to be the grieving fiancée and head out early? Besides my best friends, nobody here knows that I was in the process of breaking things off with Dale.

And as for Laurel and Natalia? They've already left. I gave them a free pass to have a drink and head on out. No reason for them to have to hang out and pretend like they miss Dale when they know the truth about how he treated me.

The door opens behind me, and I step out of the way to let the person through, but instead of walking past me, Mitch steps to my side and loops his arm around my shoulders.

I stiffen. What is he doing? Doesn't he realize what people will think if they see the two of us standing like this? All I want to do is put this trip behind me. Just like the accident a decade ago, I want to move on, keep my head down, and avoid scrutiny.

But it's impossible with the way he's acting.

I've already considered moving. Sure, I like it here, but I can be happy anywhere. I proved that by moving from North Carolina to Vermont, and there's no reason I can't do it again. Somewhere out west this time. Maybe Oregon.

You may call it *hiding from my past*; I call it *securing my future*.

"Hi, Mitch," I say as I step to the side so his arm falls from my shoulders. "How are you holding up?"

"Fine."

We're standing next to each other, both staring out into the parking lot. I can barely hear the hum of the bar's jukebox through the closed door. Regret fills me. If I'd stayed inside, he might not have approached me.

Or maybe he was always going to approach me. He followed me to the beach. He confessed that he cared for me. He was... always around, wasn't he?

"We need to talk." He jerks his chin to the right where there's a picnic table under an oak tree. It's far enough away from the parking lot that we could sit there and not be overheard. "Come on."

He walks away from me without waiting for me to respond. For a moment, I consider ignoring him. I could run to my car, get in, drive away.

But he'd follow me. I know he would. It's best to get this over with.

A minute later, I'm sitting across from him. His back is to the parking lot, and I keep my eyes locked over his shoulder in case someone were to come too close. When he doesn't speak, I clear my throat. "What did you want to talk about?"

"Us."

That gets my attention, and I look at him. "Us? What do you mean? There is no *us*. There is you, and there is me, and we're going to go our separate ways after this. I never want to see you again." I'm really getting going now, and I lean forward, bracing my arms on the table. "I never want to hear from you, think about you, or remember what happened in Florida, do you understand me?"

His expression doesn't change. "Is that really how you feel?"

My jaw drops open. Is he not listening to me? Does he really think there's any other way for me to feel after everything I just went through?

"Yes. And now we're done here." I stand, but before I can step over the bench, his arm snaps out, and he grabs my right wrist. "Mitch," I say slowly, "let go of me."

"Not until we talk. Sit back down."

His fingers press hard into my skin. Not hard enough that I'm going to bruise, but he's strong, and it's clear he's not going to let me go.

I slowly lower myself back onto the bench, and he exhales, then nods.

"Good. Okay. You have to be reasonable about this, Aimes."

His use of Dale's nickname for me makes the hair on my arms stand up. "Reasonable about what?"

"Our future. Now, I know it's not technically the life you wanted, but—"

"We have no future."

"Will you listen?" He's still holding on to my wrist with one hand and smacks the table with the other. It makes a dull thunk, and I blink at him. "Just... listen, okay?"

I nod, but I'm really trying to figure out a way to get out of this.

"You and I have a future together. Hannah wants revenge—"

"I'm not the one who killed Brian."

"She doesn't care. She wants you to pay, and even though she didn't turn you in to the cops in Florida, that doesn't mean she's over what happened. She just wants to get you on her own terms."

Oregon is looking better and better. Or—Spain. Portugal. New Zealand.

"I'll leave," I hear myself saying, but he shakes his head.

"Not good enough. She's not going to stop."

"And you think that me being with you will stop her?" I yank my hand back, and his fingers slip free from my wrist. "You can't be serious. If she wants that badly to hurt me, then nothing will stop her from coming for me."

"She'll listen to me." His voice takes on a dark edge. "I can control her. But I want you to marry me."

I don't even realize I'm laughing until I'm standing and stepping over the bench. "You've lost the plot. Marry you? I don't even know you! No way am I going to—"

My words fail me as he retrieves the Manilla folder he had tucked under his arm. I didn't even see it there at first, but he pulls it out and opens it on the table between us.

Curiosity gets the better of me.

"What is this?" I don't sit down, but I do lean over the bench so I can get a better look at what he has. As soon as I realize what it is, my heart sinks. "Where did you get this? And how? Who gave it to you?"

"Enough money buys you anything." He has one hand on the file, so I can't lean down and jerk the papers away. "If you hadn't gone to juvie when you were younger, your fingerprints wouldn't be on file, but they are, and that means it's easy to prove you're really Steph."

Sweat trickles down my back. The sun felt so nice and warm before, but now I'm overheated and uncomfortable. Being faced with my lies was one thing when Hannah was flinging accusations at me without any proof. But now? I clear my throat. "What do you want?"

He continues without acknowledging that I asked a question. "How do you think your patients would feel knowing that you're not really Aimee Hill, nurse extraordinaire?"

"I don't think they'd care because I'm the one who went to nursing school."

"And the boards? Your fellow nurses? You really think that you'd be allowed to set foot in a hospital when all of this came out? Not a chance. They'd strip you of your license. You don't want that, do you?"

I stare at him. "You're blackmailing me."

"I'm saving you. As long as I keep my sister in line, you're fine."

I'm fine. Right.

"And what do you want in return?"

He grins, the smile spreading slowly across his face. The happier he looks, the more my stomach drops. "You."

"Me? No. No way." I shake my head but stop when he taps the papers.

"Everything you worked for can still be yours. Your career. The respect you have. You cleared your name by stealing your twin's and then built it into a new life. It would be horrible to watch it crumble."

I don't see a way out. Not yet.

"Okay." The word is out of my mouth before I realize I'm speaking.

"Yeah?" His eyebrows crash together. "This is a good decision, Steph. I mean, *Aimee*. Trust me—you'll be safe with me."

I force a smile. No way do I believe that to be true, not when he's willing to threaten me to keep me with him.

But that's fine. He can think I'll be safe with him.

But he won't be safe with me.

"Mrs. Aimee Ellis," he says, and the words make my stomach twist. They yank me back to the present, and I stare at him.

"No," I whisper, but he's not listening. He's still talking, and as he does, he gets a far-off expression on his face that terrifies me.

"—my wife," he says, more to himself than to me. "Nobody will question it. It's been long enough since my first wife died."

Wait. What?

A LETTER FROM EMILY

Dear reader,

I want to say a huge thank you for choosing to read *Uninvited*. If you did enjoy it, and want to keep up to date with all my latest releases, just sign up at the following link. Your email address will never be shared, and you can unsubscribe at any time.

www.bookouture.com/emily-shiner

If there's one question I get asked more than any other, it's *how did you come up with the idea for your book?*

And I get it. Authors are fascinating creatures, aren't we? (I mean that in a good way, not in a weird way. Mostly.) Unfortunately, most authors tend to be solitary beings, lured out of the writing cave only with promises of good reviews and snacks, so you may not get many opportunities to ask this question.

But in case you're interested about my inspiration for *Uninvited*, here you go.

Step one: I thought about a vacation with my husband.

Step two: And then I thought about what I would do if his ex-girlfriend showed up.

(Please note: this book is not autobiographical; my husband is a walking green flag and does not have a mistress or any ex who would dare pop up on our vacation. I like to think they stay away partly because I'm a thriller author and can think of dozens of ways to hide a body, but I'm sure it's mostly because we've been married sixteen years and everyone has moved on. I digress.)

But what if he did? And what if she was there not only because she wanted my husband (which would be understandable really), but because she knew my deepest, darkest secret?

Not that I have any, but you get the point. You see how the idea was created and how I poked at it, little by little, creating backstories for the characters and coming up with new deliciously twisted ways to torment them.

That's half the fun, isn't it? I love coming up with insane situations and figuring out how to get out of them. I bet everyone reading this has felt the joy of coming up with great rebuttals to an argument six hours later in the shower. That's all writing is, just making up amazing dialogue that you'd never think of when put on the spot and writing and rewriting scenes until they're perfect.

Or... as close to perfect as possible.

Now you have some backstory, and I hope you loved *Uninvited*! If you did, I would be very grateful if you could write a review. I'd love to hear what you think, and it makes such a difference helping new readers to discover one of my books for the first time.

I love hearing from my readers—you can get in touch through social media or my website.

Thanks,

Emily

KEEP IN TOUCH WITH EMILY

authoremilyshiner.com

 facebook.com/authoremilyshiner

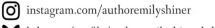 instagram.com/authoremilyshiner

bsky.app/profile/authoremilyshiner.bsky.social

ACKNOWLEDGMENTS

A huge thank you to everyone involved in bringing this book to life, especially the entire team at Bookouture! My pit crew consists of Kelsie Marsden, Donna Hillyer, and Laura Kincaid. They were there every step of the way as I wrote and rewrote *Uninvited* to take it from a seed of an idea to the novel you just read. They're amazing.

I snack a lot when writing and drink loads of tea, so a huge thank you goes to my husband, Bruce, for recognizing signs I'm getting hangry and moving quickly.

To my wonderful daughter, Claire, who reads all of my first drafts, thank you. I love your notes on every book and chatting with you about ideas. How did I get so lucky to have you as my daughter?

Authors need support, and it isn't just my immediate family who has my back, but also my parents, sister, and friends. Love y'all.

To every reader who has tagged me, commented on my posts, or told a friend about my books, thank you! Authors are nobody without their readers, and I have the best ones.

PUBLISHING TEAM

Turning a manuscript into a book requires the efforts of many people. The publishing team at Bookouture would like to acknowledge everyone who contributed to this publication.

Audio
Alba Proko
Melissa Tran
Sinead O'Connor

Commercial
Lauren Morrissette
Hannah Richmond
Imogen Allport

Cover design
Debbie Holmes

Data and analysis
Mark Alder
Mohamed Bussuri

Editorial
Kelsie Marsden
Nadia Michael

Copyeditor
Donna Hillyer

Proofreader
Laura Kincaid

Marketing
Alex Crow
Melanie Price
Occy Carr
Cíara Rosney
Martyna Młynarska

Operations and distribution
Marina Valles
Stephanie Straub
Joe Morris

Production
Hannah Snetsinger
Mandy Kullar
Ria Clare
Nadia Michael

Publicity
Kim Nash
Noelle Holten
Jess Readett
Sarah Hardy

Rights and contracts
Peta Nightingale
Richard King
Saidah Graham

RAISING READERS
Books Build Bright Futures

Dear Reader,

We'd love your attention for one more page to tell you about the crisis in children's reading, and what we can all do.

Studies have shown that reading for fun is the **single biggest predictor of a child's future life chances** – more than family circumstance, parents' educational background or income. It improves academic results, mental health, wealth, communication skills, ambition and happiness.

The number of children reading for fun is in rapid decline. Young people have a lot of competition for their time, and a worryingly high number do not have a single book at home.

Hachette works extensively with schools, libraries and literacy charities, but here are some ways we can all raise more readers:

- Reading to children for just 10 minutes a day makes a difference
- Don't give up if children aren't regular readers – there will be books for them!

- Visit bookshops and libraries to get recommendations
- Encourage them to listen to audiobooks
- Support school libraries
- Give books as gifts

There's a lot more information about how to encourage children to read on our websites: **www.RaisingReaders.co.uk** and **www.JoinRaisingReaders.com**.

Thank you for reading.

Made in United States
North Haven, CT
25 August 2025

72094456R00182